Free as a Bird

Lindsay Woodward

For Debs. I couldn't ask for a better friend.

ONE

Beth's parents were starting to irritate her now. They were fussing far too much. All Beth wanted was to be left alone so she could dwell on what had happened.

It was now June. She'd lost three months of her life. She couldn't remember a thing. And it got worse: not only had three months mysteriously disappeared from her life, but she'd woken up in that man's house. The scariest man on the planet. How could she be married to him? None of it made any sense.

'Do you think I should book an appointment with the doctor?' Beth asked. She was sitting in bed finishing off the chips that her dad had bought. She had nothing in the cupboards. It was like she didn't even live in her little studio flat anymore. All of her stuff had been at that awful man's house. Why would it be there?

'No!' her mother replied. 'Remember what he said.'

'Mr Bird?' Beth asked, horrified.

'No, Jim. They said they'd figure it all out. They'll get you a divorce and they'll find out what happened. Let's leave it to them.'

'How could you let me marry him?'

Her parents glanced at one another, then her mother

said, 'You seemed happy.'

'I think I need to go to the doctor.'

'No! Promise us you won't, Beth.'

'What? Why? I could have a brain tumour or something. Aren't you worried?'

'No, because it can't be anything like that. We know that for a fact.'

'How?' Beth snapped.

'Because Mr Bird couldn't remember anything either. You can't both have simultaneous illnesses. As they said, this is all some sort of practical joke or something. Let them look into it for you.'

Beth mulled over her parents' logic. They were right. There had to be more to it if Mr Bird also couldn't remember. Or apparently couldn't remember. That creepy man must have done something to her.

'We want you to come home with us,' her father said.

'No!' Beth replied, quite stubbornly.

'But-'

'No! I live in London now. I'll admit I am majorly freaked out by everything that's happened, but I refuse to let it ruin my life. I've lost three months, I'm not going to lose anymore.'

'It won't be forever. Just for a few weeks,' her mother added.

'What part of no don't you understand? I have a job. I have bills to pay. If I'm ever going to make it in this world then I have to persevere.'

Her father opened his mouth to argue again when his mobile rang. Her mother looked at who it was but neither of them said a word.

'Hello,' he answered walking out the front door.

'What's that about?' Beth asked.

'Coffee shop stuff. Nothing important. Shall I put some telly on?' Her mother stood up to find the remote. She flicked through the channels and decided on Eastenders. Beth couldn't focus on the telly, though. Her mind was consumed with what had happened. It was like some sort of living nightmare.

'Any news?' her mother asked when her dad finally returned.

'Everything's well in hand,' he replied. 'We're going to be kept fully up to speed on all related issues. Apparently we have nothing to worry about.'

'How can we not worry?'

'It's not our world, Ally. We have to trust them.'

'What are you talking about?' Beth asked, picking up on the cryptic nature of the conversation.

'Nothing for you to worry about,' her dad replied.

'As I said, work stuff,' her mom added. 'So you won't come home with us?'

Beth rolled her eyes. 'This is my home now, mom. I am home.'

Although Beth was eager to get to work the next morning and get her life back on track, she was also incredibly nervous about it. It was a beautifully warm Thursday morning but Beth felt a darkness hover over her. She said goodbye to her parents and she walked through Heaningford towards to the office of Bird Consultants.

She hadn't slept well. She felt so uncomfortable. The more she thought about it, the more she realised that Mr Bird had to be to blame for what had happened. He'd done something to her that had stolen months of her life. It was ridiculously unnerving.

As far as she could recall it was March. She couldn't get her head around the fact that it was now June. She was now twenty-six. She'd woken up on the floor of that horrid man's house without one single idea as to how she'd got there. She felt queasy just at the thought.

As far as her memories served her, she'd been working at Bird Consultants for about a week and she was about to start her training at The Rose pub. In reality, though, she'd been working at the office for months and she'd quit her bar job for reasons that no one could explain. Why would she do that? She'd barely started working there. What could have happened?

This was all Mr Bird's doing. It had to be. He'd tampered with her somehow. He was such a powerful man with great connections, he must have brainwashed her for his own selfish reasons. Nothing else made sense.

She sighed as the terror of it all circled round and round her head. At least she had chance to think now. As grateful as she was that her parents had been there when it all happened... Then she stopped. What if them being there was the reason she'd started to remember again? Maybe they'd helped her overcome the brainwashing? That made sense.

She had a lot to thank her parents for, but she also couldn't help but feel relief that they'd gone home now; back up to Stonheath. The three of them in her tiny studio flat was quite stifling and she didn't want the fuss. She loved them dearly, but the more they worried about her, the less she could process her thoughts. She needed time on her own to sort through things in her head. She was convinced that maybe, if she tried really hard, she could remember something.

It was no good, though. It wasn't as if she knew she couldn't remember anything, like there were blanks. It was actually as if time hadn't moved on at all. She could remember moving to London so clearly in her mind, like it had all happened just days ago. Her brain was convinced that it had all happened just days ago.

She had to stop thinking about it. It was sending her dizzy. She had a job to focus on and she had to try and get through the day. She had to try and get back to normal.

But what was normal? She'd clearly started to build a life for herself in London, but she had no recollection as to what it was like.

That bastard! How could Mr Bird do this to her? She thought back to when he'd woken up from the floor. No matter how confused he may have seemed, he must have been messing with her. The more she thought about it, the more she was convinced it had all be an act. He was evil. He'd clearly tricked her into marrying him, hypnotising her somehow for months, and then, when he'd got caught out, he'd just refused to even acknowledge it. Pure evil.

Her head was still spinning when Beth arrived at her destination. She stood at the end of the pathway that led up to the ten storey office block and she glared at it. She expected the usual prickly sensation to tingle her skin as she'd experienced on her first few days working there, but instead she just felt strangely at home.

That made sense, though. If she'd been coming to this building virtually every day for the past three months, it would feel like home. She had to remember that she couldn't remember, as nightmarish as that was.

Then Beth noted something else. She'd been vaguely conscious of a strange sensation inside of her all morning, but it was only now, when she'd properly stopped to consider her feelings, that she processed it.

She felt empowered. Physically so. It was if she was stronger and more alive than ever before; as if electricity was surging through her veins. It was amazing and unnerving both at the same time.

Not able to justify it in any other way, she told herself it must be adrenaline caused by her increasing indignation about Mr Bird's actions. That, and the added stress of going into a job that she could barely remember having.

Then her heart stopped. How could she not have thought of this before? Mr Bird would be there. He worked in the very building that stood before her. More than that: it was his business. He was in charge.

She took a deep breath and prayed to herself that she wouldn't have to see him. She was gifted with a moment of relief when she recalled that he spends most of his time in New York. In fact, if she was lucky, he could already be back on that plane. She felt her fingers cross, a knee-jerk reaction to her desperate hope that she'd never have to lay eyes on that horrid man again. Or at least not for a long time.

Knowing she couldn't put it off anymore, she walked on towards the glass doors and made her first step into the building. Trying to calm herself, she waved at Margaret, the receptionist, and headed on up to the ninth floor.

She got out of the lift, walked through the door to the main office, and made her way to her desk. She suddenly stopped in her tracks, though, when she saw that her computer was missing. Her desk was there, just as she'd remembered it, but it was completely empty.

Not knowing at all what to do, she turned to Trisha's office. Again, she stopped in her tracks when she saw Gayle sitting at Trisha's desk, typing away.

Michelle walked in, but she didn't say a single word to Beth. She threw her bag on the floor, turned her computer on and sat down, not acknowledging Beth at all. Beth was just left standing frozen, completely at a loss as to what to say or do. Had she been sacked? She suddenly felt sick.

'What can we do for you, milady?' Diane snarled as she approached from behind. Beth just stood agape, not sure how to respond. Diane turned her computer on and then glared back at Beth. 'Well?' she demanded in rather a harsh tone.

'Where's my computer?' Beth finally uttered.

Diane and Michelle both regarded Beth with confusion.

'Certainly not with us mere folk, that's for sure,' Diane said.

'What does that mean?' Beth asked.

'What are you doing down here, Mrs Bird?' Diane pushed.

'Mrs Bird?' Beth replied, astonished.

'Isn't that your name?'

'No. No, it's not.'

Diane paused at this. Then she hesitantly asked, 'What do you mean?'

'Where's my computer?' Beth sat down on her chair, utterly bewildered as to why everything seemed so unpleasant and difficult. 'What's going on?'

'What do you mean you're not Mrs Bird?'

'I haven't got a clue what's going on.' This was all too much for Beth. 'Last night I woke up in Mr Bird's house, with no idea as to how I got there, and then I find out that we're supposedly married. I don't remember anything. Not a single thing for months. I still thought it was March! I don't want to be married to him.'

'Oh Beth!' Diane's tone immediately softened. She rolled her chair around to be closer to Beth. 'You seemed so delighted to be his wife. I should have known. I should have.'

'You knew about it?' Beth asked.

'You were pretty stoked to be fair,' Michelle added, coming around to join the sympathy. 'You said he was the best man you'd ever met.'

'What?' Beth was utterly shocked by this. 'What has he done to me? You were so right, Diane. He is a man to be feared.'

'He must have been grooming you for something,' Diane deduced. 'Men of his type do.'

'Diane!' Michelle warned.

'You've heard the stories, Michelle. We all have. He could get a lot of money for a pretty girl like Beth. He's a dangerous man. We all know it.'

Beth's nausea went into overdrive. He clearly wanted something from her. Would he really have sold her on? Of course, she must have been drugged! That made far more sense than brainwashing. And it would explain how alien she felt in her own skin. The surging adrenaline that was racing through her must be the side effects of some drug.

'I'm so sorry, Beth. I wished we'd been there for you. We didn't know. You actually seemed really happy. We couldn't have known,' Diane explained.

'I don't blame you. None of this is your fault.' Beth

looked at her desk again. 'Where's my computer?'

Diane looked at Michelle before answering. Their hesitation worried Beth. 'It's upstairs.'

'Upstairs? What's it doing up there?'

'I don't know how to tell you this, Beth. When you married Mr Bird, you also got... promoted. You're now the Administration Director. Have been for weeks.'

'What?!' Beth squealed. She was now fearful of what shocking revelation was to come next.

Her outburst caught the attention of everyone on the floor, including Gayle, who came straight out of her office to see what was going on.

'Beth, are you okay?' she asked.

'I told you!' Diane jumped in, turning to Gayle. 'I knew it from the second I started working here. Mr Bird is a bad man. He tricked her. He duped her into marrying him, promoted her so he could keep an eye on her, and then he was going to pimp her out at his discretion. I knew it!'

'What are you talking about?' Gayle asked.

'I didn't want to marry Mr Bird,' Beth explained. 'I don't remember any of it. How come I've been promoted? I haven't got a clue what's going on. I mean, where's Trisha?'

Gayle looked at Beth with worry. Not in the same way as Diane and Michelle, though. She looked less sympathetic, more confused.

'Trisha left,' Gayle confirmed. 'You promoted me, I'm the Admin Manager now. You sit upstairs with Mr Bird as the Admin Director.'

'So I've been actively doing the role?'

'Yes. And you've been good at it.'

'So I'm the Administration Director?' Beth didn't know whether to jump for joy or throw up. She was a director of a company. She only remembered being junior admin; that was quite a step up. She didn't know what to make of any of it.

She turned back to her desk and tried to clear her

thoughts. 'Do I have to be upstairs?'

Gayle shrugged. 'You're the boss. It's not up to us.'

'So I could just get my computer back down here?'

'I don't see why not. But you'll have to speak to Mr Bird about it,' Gayle said.

'What?' A sickening feeling churned over in Beth's stomach again.

'He's your line manager now. You'll have to sort it out with him.'

'I don't want to see him. Don't make me see him!'

'I think you'll have to.'

'Be brave, Beth,' Diane said.

'What if he drugs me again?'

'He drugged you?' Gayle asked.

'Of course he did!' Diane replied.

Gayle put her hand on Beth's shoulder. 'It's going to be fine. I'm sure there's a logical explanation. Just go up to his office and talk to him. From everything you've told me, I think he really listens to you.'

'Why would he listen to me? He was tricking me.'

'We know the truth now, Beth. We've got your back,' Diane stated. 'If you seem to be acting oddly again, we'll know it and we'll protect you. If you have anything good to say about Mr Bird then I'm taking you home with me until you go cold turkey. Got it?'

'Is he definitely in the office today?' Beth asked with a small spark of hope that she could avoid him.

'Yes, I saw his car when I got here,' Gayle replied.

Beth took a deep breath as the reality that she'd have to see him again set in. At least she felt stronger for knowing her friends were there for her.

He wasn't in New York at that moment, but she reminded herself that he spent most of his time there and it wouldn't be long before he returned. Although he was now her line manager. How do you avoid your line manager?

She chose not to process her new found promotion for

the time being. There was a lot to get her head around and it was making her dizzy. One thing at a time, and her first priority was to ensure that she was working at a distance from Mr Bird. That meant moving her computer as quickly as possible.

She took a deep breath and stood up. 'Wish me luck,' she whispered.

'If you're not back in half an hour, Gayle will come looking for you,' Diane asserted as Gayle just rolled her eyes.

TWO

Beth's heart was pounding as she stepped in the lift. It took just seconds to get to the top floor and she was trying hard to keep control of her breathing.

She stepped out onto the infamous tenth floor, where all the directors sat, and then she halted momentarily. She must have been up here dozens of times, her desk was here, but she didn't recognise it at all. It was far classier than her floor.

She headed through the glass doors to find six men sitting at their desks. Not one of them acknowledged her presence. She glanced around and could see only one desk unoccupied. It had a laptop sitting squarely in the middle of it and a few papers scattered either side. It didn't seem familiar, but it had to be hers, it was the only one free.

She started walking over to it when she caught a glimpse of Mr Bird standing in his office. The door was shut, but she could see through the window that he was in the middle of the room talking to someone; although she couldn't see to whom.

She reached the unoccupied desk and looked across it, but she recognised nothing. The scrawled notes on the paperwork were not in her handwriting. She knocked the laptop awake and found that it belonged to a B Wolfe. Whoever that was.

'Where do I sit?' she finally muttered to the man next to her.

He looked at her like she'd gone mad. 'In there,' he said pointing to Mr Bird's office.

'Oh shit,' she mumbled under her breath. Why on earth was she sitting in Mr Bird's office? He really had been trying to keep an eye on her. Worse still, now she really did have no choice but to speak to him.

She slowly edged her way to the door that was emblazoned with a gold plaque saying "Simon Bird, CEO". She took a second to think if it was familiar. She must have known his first name, they were married. Did she call him Simon? Even if she had, she certainly wouldn't be now. She needed to keep her distance. He was nothing more than Mr Bird, her boss.

She hesitantly knocked on the door and waited, her heart echoing in her ears.

'What is it?' a stern male voice said.

She slowly opened the door to be greeted by two men staring at her. Mr Bird was standing tall, his six foot, well-built stature glaring down at her, not that she was much smaller herself in her stiletto heels. He'd been talking to the older man that had been in his house the night before. Paul, Beth suddenly remembered.

'Miss Lance,' Mr Bird said with an icy edge.

'Beth, come in!' Paul added from the sofa at the back of the room, seeming much happier to see her.

She walked in, ensuring that she kept the door behind her wide open, just in case. 'I'm sorry to bother you, Mr Bird.'

'Nonsense,' Paul replied. 'We were just talking about you.'

'My uncle was just informing me that he has our annulment well in hand,' Mr Bird finished.

A slot fitted into place as Beth realised that the man

sitting on the sofa before her was the owner of the business and the man ultimately in charge of Bird Consultants. She recalled Diane telling her that he also spent most of his time in New York. Maybe they'd both be going back soon.

'I don't want you two thinking about this marriage thing anymore. I'll take care of everything,' Paul assured them.

'Thank you, Mr Bird.'

'Paul, please,' he insisted. Beth just nodded. She felt quite comfortable calling him Paul. He seemed far easier to get along with than her supposed husband. She also suddenly felt convinced that whatever had happened to her, Paul Bird had not been involved with it. Maybe that's why younger Mr Bird was now pretending he couldn't remember? Maybe his uncle had found out and so he was trying to hide his evil ways? That would make a lot of sense. Either way, Beth felt it best not to push the subject. If she didn't muddy the waters then they'd both go back to New York soon and she could get on with her life.

'As well as the mix up with the marriage, Mr Bird,' Beth said, turning her attention to her line manager, 'it seems that I am now also the Administration Director and I've been working in your office.'

'So I've been told.'

'Do I still have that job?' she asked a little fearfully.

'Of course you do!' Paul declared. 'You were promoted on merit, you deserve the job completely.'

'Thank you,' Beth smiled, quite relieved. She turned to the desk in the corner of the room that she actually recognised as her own, and she took a courageous breath. 'Mr Bird, would it be okay with you if I moved my things back downstairs?'

'What?' Paul asked, although Mr Bird didn't flinch at all.

'It seems to me that it would make far more sense if I was with my team on a day to day basis. I will, after all, be working with them far more than yourself. I mean, I believe so. I mean, I guess so. I mean-'

'Fine,' Mr Bird stated, cutting Beth's ramble short. 'It is highly irregular for the CEO to share his office.'

'No, you can't!' Paul suddenly blurted out.

'Why?' Mr Bird asked him.

'It doesn't seem right.' Paul glared at the two of them, searching for his words. 'We can't have one of the directors sitting downstairs. What sort of message does that send out?'

'That we're about teamwork?' Mr Bird quickly replied, much to Beth's surprise. 'Besides, where else is she going to sit?'

'But she's the first woman to be a director in the history of the company,' Paul stated.

'Isn't that a good thing?'

'And the only one that sits downstairs. People will think we're discriminating. It'll make us look bad.'

'Please, Paul,' Beth pleaded. 'I know how it will look, but it also looks bad that the only female director is sharing the CEO's office. Of course, Mr Bird, I know it's simply been a space issue; I know that.' Beth's heart was racing again. 'However, I believe if we promote my move as the directors branching out to work more closely with their teams, surely that's a very positive message. As you quite rightly stated, Mr Bird, this is more about teamwork than anything else.'

Paul opened his mouth to argue, but he stopped himself. Then after a second he shook his head and simply said, 'Whatever you both think is best.'

'I'll just collect my things.' Beth walked over to her desk, eager to get away as quickly as she could.

'You'll need to speak to IT to get your computer moved,' Mr Bird informed her. She nodded again.

She started to grab her notebooks and stationery, when suddenly her pen flew across the room. She didn't know how, she must have knocked it. She looked to see where it had landed and her heart stopped. Of all of the possible places, it had rested right near Mr Bird's foot. Cursing her luck and taking another deep breath, she watched Mr Bird bend down to pick it up. He held it out for her.

She hesitantly walked over, trying to smile politely.

'Thank you,' she mumbled, then she slowly reached for the pen from his hand.

As her fingers touched the plastic, Beth felt a small surge of energy race through her. It was like something jolted inside of her and for the first time she dared to look directly at Mr Bird.

She stared into his deep brown eyes noticing, quite to her surprise, how vulnerable he seemed. In fact, Beth caught a glimpse of tenderness. Then suddenly it was like she was seeing him in a whole new light. A flutter of excitement tickled her as she thought to how staggeringly handsome he was.

As he let go of the pen, she came to her senses. How long had she been staring at him? She looked back to her desk, reminding herself that although he may be good looking, he was still one of the scariest men in the world. He was a killer and a manipulator, and he'd duped her into a life she can't remember.

Any pleasant thoughts that she'd had about him quickly vanished and she moved over to clear her desk once again. She grabbed her things as quickly as she could and then she headed straight for the door.

'I'll speak to IT,' Mr Bird suddenly said.

'Pardon?' Beth replied, not quite sure if she'd heard correctly.

'I'll speak to IT to get your computer moved. It'll get done quicker if I ask.' A ghost of a smile dashed across his lips and Beth quivered.

'Thank you, Mr Bird,' she nodded, not sure if she should be grateful or wary. Deciding it was probably best to be a bit of both, she quickly left, shutting the door firmly behind her. She scuttled back across the Executive

Floor and prayed that she wouldn't have to see that man again for a very long time.

THREE

Simon watched Beth go. What the hell had just happened?

Up until a few minutes before, Simon had been quite sure that this Beth was another one of those users, just like his ex-girlfriend. His ex had been nothing but a heartless gold digger. Since breaking up with her ten years ago, he'd learnt to be very careful about who he trusted. For ten years he'd kept everyone at arm's length, yet this girl had somehow managed to worm her way in.

He couldn't imagine ever wanting to share his office with anyone, let alone his life. He'd found it very easy to believe that she'd simply been trying to boost her way up the corporate ladder, and what better way to do that than to trick the CEO of a hugely successful company?

Although Paul had insisted that dark magic was probably the cause of the strange recent events, he'd also insisted that Beth was just as much a victim of this foul play as they all were. Paul had put it down to a cruel act carried out by a disgruntled Malant somewhere out there, but Simon had immediately assumed that Beth was the guilty party.

That was until, though, he'd handed her that pen. Up

close, there was something about her that made his heart pound. She was mesmerising. He'd never felt like that before. Just the smell of her perfume was intoxicating.

It didn't feel like magic. It felt genuine; real. Something about this girl weakened him and it made no sense to him at all. In fact, it scared him a little. Dark magic could do a lot of things, but it could never affect a person's emotions, and this Beth was most definitely stirring up something inside of him.

He moved back over to his desk, deciding that it was probably best that he steer well clear of this girl in the future. She blurred his thoughts too much. He'd had a lifetime of weird things happening to him, but recent events had been a little bit too bizarre. It was causing him a great deal of distress not being able to remember three months of his life and he needed to make sure nothing like that would ever happen again. He'd learnt years ago that women couldn't be trusted; he needed to keep that in mind.

'She's beautiful, isn't she,' Paul suddenly said, yanking Simon back to reality.

'I hadn't noticed,' Simon shrugged.

'I saw that look in your eye,' Paul smirked.

'I have no interest in women like her,' Simon lied. He really didn't want to admit to himself how much he was attracted to her. This wasn't just a crush, this was unnerving. No one had ever been able to stir up his emotions quite like Beth just had.

The more he thought about her, the more he decided that this Beth was clearly dangerous. One way or another, she was bewitching him, and he needed to put her out of his mind. And that's what he decided he was going to do right away. Well, as soon as he'd sorted out her computer.

Simon picked up his phone and dialled for the IT department. 'It's Mr Bird. Please can you arrange for someone to move Miss Lance's computer. She's moving back downstairs. And then I want her desk moved out of here as well.'

'Of course. Could I just ask who Miss Lance is?' the male voice on the other end of the line fearfully asked.

For a second Simon didn't know what to say. 'The Administration Director.'

The voice hesitated. 'Mrs Bird?'

'No!' Simon bit back. 'Miss Lance. It's Miss Lance. Please do it as a matter of priority.'

'Err... Of course, sir.'

Simon slammed down the phone and glared at Paul. 'Does everyone in this company think I'm married to that girl?'

Paul hesitated. 'No idea. Like I told you last night, it's all a blur myself. Where have those months gone!'

'I want this cleared up. I don't want us to rest until we've got to the bottom of what happened.' Simon felt his skin prickle at how horrifying it was to not be able to remember so much. Something very strange had been going on and he was desperately uncomfortable about it.

'You know I'm on the case. I don't want you worrying about it, though. You need to stay on top of business, let me take care of everything else.'

'That's another thing. What on earth have I been doing for the last few months? On the plus side, I can see that I've sorted out MB Solutions and have scored two new contracts with Layfields, but I've also managed to really piss off Flaremore. Then I've got about seven hundred emails that I've not even opened, let alone dealt with.'

'I don't know what to say.'

'And why was everyone asking this morning if they could work on contracts again? It's our core business, what else would they be doing?'

'I heard it was some sort of technical glitch. Like I've said to you already, don't worry about it. They're all getting on with things again now. It's all just business as usual.'

'It doesn't feel like it. I need to get back to the States.'

'No!' Paul snapped.

'What?'

'You're not going back to New York.'

'What are you talking about? That's our life.'

'Not anymore,' Paul announced. He took a deep breath and walked over to Simon's desk. 'I wasn't going to mention this yet, but I suppose it's as good a time as any.'

'What's going on?'

'I'm moving back to the UK.'

'What?' This was massive news to Simon.

'I've been considering it for a while. They don't need me over there and I like it over here. Things have changed.'

'Like what?'

'I'm not going to tread on your toes, don't worry, you're still very much the boss over here. I'm going to appoint a General Manager in the US to take care of things over there and then I'm going to take a step back. Let you youngsters take the reins. It's for the best.'

'I don't know what to say.' Simon hadn't seen this coming at all. Paul seemed so happy in New York. What on earth had been happening in the past few months? Simon had to get his memories back.

Then the reality of Paul's decision hit him. New York had been Simon's escape, his safe haven for years. His life in the UK was so exposed, he hated it. The UK was where things hurt. But could he still live in New York without his uncle? Paul was all that he had. They needed to stick together.

He decided to be honest. 'I need to get away, Paul. You know I hate it here.'

Paul gave Simon a sympathetic smile. 'I know how much you've suffered, mate. More than you should have. Look, give me a few weeks in the UK, let's see how it goes. Stay with me here for a few weeks, and if nothing changes, nothing gets better, then I'll go back with you.'

'A few weeks?'

'Do that for me, will you? Do it for your uncle.'

Simon knew that he could never deny his uncle anything. If this was what Paul needed, for whatever reason, Simon would have to support him. 'Okay. A few weeks.'

'Good. Well I better let you get back to it.'

'Get back to what? I don't even know where to begin. I suppose I should go and see Flaremore-'

'No!' Paul insisted.

'What?'

'Leave Flaremore to me. They were originally my client back in the day, I'll deal with them.'

Simon eyed his uncle suspiciously. Paul hadn't seen Flaremore for years, why was he suddenly so keen? But Simon decided not to argue. Paul did have the better people skills and it was one less thing for Simon to worry about. 'Fine. Just keep me posted?'

'Absolutely. You need to put that incredible mind of yours to other things.'

'Like the seven hundred emails I've got? What have I been doing?'

'You've been busy.'

Simon just shook his head. He was always on top of his work. Whatever had happened to him recently had been drastically out of character. He was just glad to be back to his old self.

Although deep down inside he knew he was far from the man he used to be. He couldn't quite put his finger on it, but something big had changed. For starters, he'd never felt so powerful. He'd always felt the magic within him, but it was now overflowing. It had tripled in intensity, at least. He felt more powerful than ever before, as if nothing in the world could beat him. It was most unusual and he really didn't know what to make of it.

'I'm off, then,' Paul announced.

'Where are you going?'

'I've got a couple of estate agents to meet with. If I'm going to be moving back, I'll need somewhere to live.'

'What?' Simon asked, yet again thrown by his uncle's behaviour.

'It's just to see what's out there. I won't buy anything until we know whether we're staying or going, don't worry. But I need the facts.'

'What's wrong with my house?'

'What?' Paul replied, clearly confused.

'Why do you suddenly not want to live with me?'

'You don't need me hanging around.'

Simon was utterly perplexed. Unless one of them was travelling, they'd always lived together; since Simon was fourteen. This change was completely out of the blue. 'But we've always...'

'Yeah, and now...' Paul's voice faded away and his expression became more sombre. 'You're right. It's us lads all the way. Let me just indulge, you know I like being nosey. But don't worry, Si, I'm looking out for you. It's all going to be all right. Trust me.'

'Okay,' Simon nodded, but the wariness inside of him was growing. 'I'll see you at home later.'

'No probs, mate. See you later. Take care.'

Paul headed off and Simon turned back to his laptop. He had a lot to think about. He didn't know where to begin. He supposed the first thing, though, was to try and get on top of his workload.

FOUR

In the Buckinghamshire countryside, back at Simon's house, Jim was pacing around the living room. He'd agreed with Paul that Paul would go to the office to find out how things stood with Beth, and then they'd reconvene back at home to start planning how they were going to sort this mess out.

Paul had phoned to say he was on his way and now Jim was eagerly awaiting his arrival. He was using the time to try and get his head around everything that had happened.

It had all seemed to be going so well the night before. He'd been incredibly relieved when Simon and Beth had finally agreed to cast the spell to keep the Malancy alive.

It hadn't been pleasant witnessing their agony as they'd performed the spell, and it had been quite horrific to watch them slowly and painfully turn into those bird-like creature things. But then it just ended.

Being a direct descendant from the original Malant family, Jim was used to seeing spells being cast and spells being broken. He knew that when a spell was normally severed, the magic dissipated. He'd seen spells break down in front of him many times and they were often quite a spectacle. It had been the strangest thing with Simon and

Beth, though. One minute they were these bird-like creatures, the next they were back to themselves. If you'd have blinked you would have missed it. Jim had never seen anything like it. It wasn't as if the magic had been severed, it was if the magic had just never existed in the first place. How he longed to know what had happened; but that was one of many questions he had at that moment in time.

Jim raced to the window when he finally heard the sound of a car. Much to his relief, he saw the black BMW of Paul's driver pull onto the driveway.

Jim paced back over to the middle of the room as he waited for Paul to join him. 'How did it go?' he asked, the second Paul opened the door.

'Same as last night,' Paul replied, shaking his head. 'It's like they're strangers. Beth's even asked if she could go back to her old desk and Simon seemed quite happy to oblige.'

'This is such a mess.'

'We need to figure out what's gone on here, and fast. They were so in love. They had such an amazing connection, and then suddenly they don't even call each by their first names.'

'It's like they know each other but they just don't remember each other.'

'And to add to it, not surprisingly, Simon wants to go back to New York.'

'Of course he does. What did you say?'

'I told him I'm moving back to the UK so he'd have to stay put.'

'That was quick thinking.'

'Maybe. Either way, I think we need to tell them the truth. Simon at least.'

'We can't.'

'You keep saying that, but why? Surely if we tell Simon what's happened then he'll help us fight back. He's always an asset, you know he is.'

'He's also unpredictable. You know how his anger fuels

27

his magic. How can we tell him that he really is married, that he's now in charge of the Malancy and he's finally found the happiness he's always dreamt of, but it's all been stripped away from him for a reason that we don't understand? He'll go mad. He'll go off the chart. We need to first at least figure out what's behind this sudden turn of events before we can even consider discussing it with him.'

'But we need Simon to figure it all out. Can't you see?'

'We can't take the risk. It could send him on a destructive path. To know that he's lost absolutely everything right at the point when he'd gained all that he ever wanted, it will eat him alive. And that will just push Beth away even more. We both saw how terrified she was when he was being calm.'

'What if we just tell him bits? Try and control how it affects him?'

'What do you suggest we tell him and leave out? It's been an overwhelming few weeks for both of them. How can we even start to explain it all in just a few minutes? How could we expect Simon to understand, and then, even if he did believe us, how could we expect it not to make him furious?'

'Maybe he has the right to be angry. He was happy. For just one fleeting moment he was genuinely happy. But some bastard keeps messing with him.' Paul thought for a second. 'Or was this always his fate?'

'Things should never have been as difficult for him as they have been.'

'No, I mean now, is this their fate? Like, what's the point in them being in love anymore? They've served their purpose, they've saved the Malancy. Are they just normal folk now, and this love that brought them together, has that just gone? Is this it for them?'

Jim shook his head. He remained silent for a minute. It was time to tell Paul the truth. He'd never meant to keep it a secret, he'd just wanted them to take it one step at a time. 'I think you better sit down,' he said, gesturing for Paul to choose a sofa.

Paul looked at him inquisitively, but did as requested. They both took a seat and Jim found his words. 'I am very, very sure that some dark force is at play here.'

'It would seem like it, but we can't be sure.'

'I can.'

This got Paul's attention. 'What do you mean? What do you know?'

'I know the Malancy isn't saved yet.'

'No. We saw them do the spell. They did it just here, in this room.'

'Yes, and that's the most vital part of it. However, there is one more step.'

'What are you talking about?'

'To breathe new life into something, sometimes you need to literally breathe new life into it.'

Paul shook his head confused. 'I don't know what you're going on about.'

'They've done the hard bit. My family has lost the power it had and that's not going to change. However, they now need to start a new line to seal the deal.'

'Start a new line?' Paul took a moment to cogitate on this. Then his eyes widened. 'As in a new family?'

Jim nodded. 'I'm afraid so. If they don't conceive a child in one year of the spell being cast then the Malancy will end forever anyway.'

'Are you serious?' Paul stood up and rubbed his head, trying to compute this new information. 'Have you always known this?'

Jim just nodded.

'Why didn't you tell us?'

'To add even more pressure to an already difficult situation? Beth's so young and so ambitious. I know children aren't even on the horizon for her yet. I didn't want to tell her until I absolutely had to. It's too much for her; for both of them. Their lives have changed enough without being forced to have children when they still barely know each other.'

'What if they were birds, though?'

'That was another layer of Damien's spell. As those horrible bird things they couldn't conceive a child. It was well thought through, I'll give him that.'

'What would we have done?'

'Whatever we had to. We would have found a way. Just like we'll find a way now. Someone out there - and it doesn't take a rocket scientist to guess who - has further messed with Mr and Mrs Bird. I don't know what they've done nor how they've done it, but we have to find a way to overcome it.'

'Well magic can't have done this. You can't change people's thoughts. It can't be done.'

'We have to consider that someone's found a way.'

'This is crazy. It's impossible. Do we need to go and see Damien? Find your brother?'

'They're not going to help us. They're more likely to make life harder. We can't let them know that we're even suspicious of their involvement. No, this is all on us now. We need to first find out what sort of magic this could be. We need to start thinking like Simon and start getting our facts together. In this instance, our only power is going to be our knowledge.'

Paul sat back down again. 'If only we knew where Jane was.'

'She's clearly connected somehow.'

'Connected? My guess is more like drawn into it unwillingly.'

Jim paused for a second. It hadn't escaped him how much Paul had spoken of and defended Jane ever since this situation had started. 'You think highly of her, don't you?' he noted.

Paul stared at the floor for a few moments and then said, 'She's my go to girl. We've always been there for each other. She'd help us now, you know she would. She has so much experience with magic, she'd know exactly what was behind this.'

Jim couldn't deny that Jane was very good at her job. He'd always trusted her as a colleague, but they had enough on their plates without worrying about extra problems. He would love to find Jane and solve at least one mystery, but they had more pressing matters to deal with.

'Right, we need to get started,' Jim announced, standing up. 'I have quite a few Malant books in my room that cover dark magic, I'd say that's a good place for me to start. Do you want to do an internet search?'

'Absolutely. What am I looking for?' Paul asked, standing up himself.

'See if you can find anyone ever breaking that one Malant constraint. Has anyone ever cast a spell that changes people's thoughts and feelings?'

Jim and Paul took a moment to consider what this might mean for the future of the Malancy, both silently praying that something else far different was at play here. This could be a very dark path, indeed.

Trying not to think too much about how dark this could get, they both set to work.

FIVE

Simon hadn't been able to shake off his tetchy feeling for most of the day. It was now well into the afternoon and he'd cleared a massive amount of backlog, but the uneasy feeling that he'd been left with ever since he'd seen Beth that morning still plagued him. At least her desk had now gone and there was nothing at all left of hers in sight.

He heard a knock at his office door. 'Yes?' he summoned.

Eric, one of the directors of the company, opened the door and stepped in. 'Sorry to disturb you. It seems there's something wrong with the boardroom.'

'What do mean something wrong?' Simon asked, glancing up from his laptop.

'It's... sort of sealed itself. The windows are all black and the door has vanished. Gus noticed it when he was in one of the other meeting rooms and he thought it best to let us know.'

'You'll have to get maintenance to look at it or something. What do you want me to do?'

'Simon, I don't mean it's bordered up, I mean it's magically sealed. I don't know what any of us can do. Could you take a look?'

Simon rolled his eyes. That was the problem of being back in the UK; he always got pulled into unnecessary things that were a pointless distraction. He never had to deal with such rubbish in New York.

He stood up and headed out of his office, locking the door behind him. Then he made his way to the first floor where all the meeting rooms could be found.

He approached the boardroom, expecting it all to be some sort of ridiculous misunderstanding, but he was taken aback when he saw, in fact, that it had been completely sealed shut. It was just as Eric had described. The windows were blackened and the door was nowhere in sight. It was just a solid wall stretching across the length of what he knew to be the boardroom.

Simon placed his hand against the glass to sense the magic. It wasn't a great surprise really that magic was involved, but he wanted to be sure. He then pinched his fingers ever so slightly and sucked all the power away, instantly restoring the boardroom to its former state.

He looked through the window and saw a man, who must have been in his thirties, sitting in the middle of the room looking quite fed up. Understandably.

Simon opened the door and the man shot to his feet. He looked quite weary, with red eyes and greasy hair, and his suit was crumpled, like he'd been in it for days.

'What are you doing in here?' Simon asked.

The man went to speak, but then he stopped himself. He screwed up his face with confusion. 'What?'

'Who are you? Why were you trapped in this room?'

Again the man remained silent. He was clearly thinking quite hard and then a small smirk etched up on the corner of his lips. So small, Simon barely noticed it.

'Well?' Simon nudged.

'Thank you, Mr Bird. I was wondering how long I'd have to be stuck in here.'

'Why were you stuck in here in the first place?' Simon's irritation level was increasing as his question still hadn't been answered.

'New boy prank. You know what Damien's like!' The man suddenly seemed far more relaxed.

'Damien? Please tell me who you are.'

'My name's Brian Wolfe. I'm the new Sales Manager here, Damien's new sidekick you could say.'

'And he trapped you in here, why?'

'Like I said, new boy prank. It's a sales thing. It's how we bond. He stitched me up good, I'll give him that.'

'Right,' Simon replied, irked by how Damien's childish behaviour had once again taken him away from his work. Sometimes he didn't know whether he actually liked the fact that Damien was good at his job. Yes, he brought in millions of pounds of work for the company each year, but he was incredibly difficult to work with, and part of Simon really wished that Damien would disappear.

It was then that Simon realised that he'd not seen Damien all day. In fact he could barely remember the last time that he'd seen him at all.

'Where is Damien?' Simon asked Brian.

'In Scotland. Did you not know?'

Simon didn't feel the need to answer this question.

'He'll be gone for a while, so he told me,' Brian continued. 'There are a few potential clients he's working on and you know how much he loves winning those jobs.'

Simon remained still. He had no interest in engaging with this man that he knew nothing about. Although, Simon deduced, he must definitely be Malant to accept being trapped in such a way.

'Damien's asked me to work from his desk for a few weeks, until he gets back,' Brian added. This was most unusual and Simon waited intently for an explanation as to why. 'Damien quite likes me sitting with the other directors. We work so closely together, you know, so he says it's like him being there himself. I can keep him in the loop on anything he needs to know. So you'll be seeing lots of me.'

Simon glared at Brian. He wasn't best pleased that this stranger had been given such freedom to mix with the directors of the business. He'd need to look into that. 'How long have you been trapped in here?' he then asked.

'Two days, I think,' Brian replied.

'Two days?' This surprised Simon, and for the first time he flinched. How had it taken so long for anyone to notice?

He quickly answered his own question when he rationalised that most people at the company weren't Malants and knew nothing about the Malancy, so how could they fathom the idea of the boardroom just disappearing? It must have seemed crazy, not a reportable incident. What was Damien thinking about being so careless with his magic? It was so drastically unprofessional and dangerous.

'You'd better go home and clean yourself up. Take the day and I'll see you tomorrow,' Simon ordered.

'No, it's fine,' Brian argued.

'It wasn't a suggestion,' Simon clarified firmly. 'And if you speak to Damien before I do, please tell him to contact me.'

'Anything I can help with?' Brian quickly asked. Simon noted a small sense of urgency in Brian's tone, but he assumed it was related to an eagerness to please rather than anything else. Now he had two Damiens to deal with. What joy!

'No,' Simon simply replied, then he walked off.

'I'll be sure to let him know,' Brian called after him, but Simon was already at the lifts.

* * *

No matter what Simon had been led to believe, Damien was nowhere near Scotland. Still very much sacked from Bird Consultants, he was about to enter George Malant's office at the Malancy Headquarters in

London to continue with the only job of any sort that he had.

'What did I tell you?' he beamed as he burst his way into the office.

George had been warned of Damien's arrival and he looked straight up from his desk with hope. 'So it's confirmed?'

Damien was a little confused. He thought George would have been the first to find out. It was the first thing that he'd checked at six o'clock the previous night. That was before he'd cracked open the champagne to celebrate. He might have woken up with quite a hangover, but it was well worth it to mark the occasion. 'I would say so.'

'Have you been to their house?'

'I thought it might be a bit too soon to gloat,' Damien chuckled.

'No, have you confirmed they're birds?' This brought Damien to a halt. 'I've been trying to get hold of Brian, but no one's heard from him since Tuesday.'

'Birds?' Damien simply asked.

'I don't mean to doubt you, Damien. I know the spell was pretty tight, but when it comes to Simon there are never any guarantees. I think we've all learnt that lesson recently.'

'Birds?' Damien asked again, trying to process George's line of thinking.

George's face grew sterner. 'Tell me you cast the spell properly, Damien.'

'The Malancy's ended. The spell's irrelevant.'

'The Malancy's ended?' George stood up. 'What... How?'

'I told you. There was no way Simon was going to let Beth become a bird. Our spell stopped them casting their spell.'

'What are you talking about?

'We won.'

'Since when? Is there something that I don't know

about?'

'Clearly just that the Malancy's ended.' Damien was getting bemused by George's strange reaction.

'I don't think so.'

Damien opened his mouth to reply, but he was brought to silence as his confusion turned into doubt.

'Damien, what makes you think the Malancy has ended?' George asked slowly, searching for clarity.

'Because it has.'

'What's changed?'

'The magic's gone.'

'No it hasn't. At least I don't think it has.' George walked over to the corner of his office where a rather large rubber plant stood. He touched it and focussed hard on some papers on his desk. Within seconds the paperwork flew off in a gust and scattered to the floor.

'I'd say the Malancy is still definitely in play,' George said, heading back to his chair. 'They've obviously cast the spell. Now we have to know if they're birds or not.'

'That can't be...' Damien argued. He made his way over to the rubber plant himself. He touched it and tried to move some books on George's bookcase. Although he'd not been a regular user of his magic, Damien certainly knew how to summon up the power to move things. But no matter what he did, nothing happened. He couldn't even feel it inside of him anymore.

He tried again and again and again, but still nothing happened. 'What have you done to me?' he snapped, pacing back over to George.

George looked bewildered. 'Your magic has gone?'

'How can it just have gone if the Malancy hasn't ended?' Damien's heart was pounding, he was so angry. Someone was messing with him and he didn't like it. He hated to be out of control.

George thought for a few seconds and then a smile curled up on his lips. In then turned into a small chuckle. 'You've lost your power?'

'That's impossible.'

'Remind me again how angry you made Simon Bird?'

'It's impossible!' Damien insisted.

'We told you not to go home, but you had to play your games. You had to flaunt the power you thought you had over him.'

'How could he have done this to me?'

The smile suddenly dropped from George's lips. 'Like it or not, Simon is now the most powerful Malant on the planet. The only people that could ever have equalled his power were the original Malants and they're long gone. That's why I never wanted it to get this far. We're in very dangerous territory.'

'That bastard!' Damien was fuming.

'And what are you going to do about it?'

'He better watch himself!'

George chuckled again at this. 'Listen to yourself, you pathetic little man. Simon is now enormously powerful and you're nothing more than a normal, average, non-Malant. What are you really going to do about it?'

Damien felt so enraged, his blood was surging through his body. How could Simon have taken away his magic?

Then a flash of Simon saying that he didn't need power to make Damien's life a misery shot through his head and Damien made a silent promise to himself. Simon had always been the all-powerful one, as long as Damien had known him. Damien might have never had equal strength but he'd certainly got the better of Simon more than once. Damien would have to think this through carefully, but just like Simon had said, there are other ways to make someone's life a misery. In that moment he vowed revenge, no matter what it would take.

'So we still don't know if they're birds?' Damien suddenly asked.

'No, I thought that's what you were here to tell me.'

'Don't forget we had two back-up plans - both courtesy of me, I'd like to add. I suppose we don't know where we're at with the other one either?'

'No, I don't, and I'm waiting for someone around here to find out,' George bit.

'What's Brian said?'

'Like I told you, no one has heard from Brian since Tuesday. God knows where he is. But I should be hearing back from Mr Taylor any minute. He's driven over to Bird Consultants to see what he can find out.'

'Isn't that a bit dangerous?'

'I'd say it's proactive, which is more than you're being at present. Besides, Simon never met him. He'll be fine. That's if Simon's even there. We can only hope.'

Just then George's phone pinged a text message. He read it and sighed angrily. Then he glared sternly at Damien.

'What is it?' Damien asked, although he wasn't sure he wanted to know.

'They're not birds. Mr Taylor waited around until close of play and he watched Beth leave the office.'

Damien rubbed his forehead. 'That spell was locked tight. You know it was.'

'Clearly it wasn't!' George snapped. Then George sighed. 'You cast the bloody spell, didn't you?'

'I certainly did!'

'Then it's not going to have worked as they've taken away your magic. That's how they've overcome it.'

Damien felt the surge of anger rise in him again. Just when he thought he couldn't hate Simon any more, his detestation of the man found a new depth. 'This isn't my fault. He could have taken away anyone's magic.'

George stood up. 'No, this is *all* your fault, Damien. You should have got someone else to cast the spell but you're too arrogant to let anyone else take the glory.'

Damien addressed George directly with a new level of determination. 'It wasn't about glory. It was about doing the job properly. And don't forget, we had two back-ups, George. The second is like nothing we've ever done before. They can't have seen it coming and they won't know what's happening. It has to have worked.'

'It better have done. The time is ticking, Damien. We have just three hundred and sixty four days now to stop them ruining my family's legacy. We must let the Malancy end.'

Damien breathed for a moment. He didn't really care that much about what happened with the Malancy. He never had. What he cared about was not going to jail and not being made to look like a prat again. And now he had the added drive of vengeance. Simon would pay for being such a smug, slimy git, Damien would make sure of it.

'Leave it to me. Give me one day and I'll find out for sure where we stand.'

'Your plan better have worked, Damien.'

'Believe me, George, one way or another they won't complete the spell. The Malancy will end.'

SIX

Sitting at her desk the next day, in the midst of the other administrators, Beth glared at her computer and her jaw dropped open.

Earlier that day she'd spent some time with the Finance Manager, learning about the accounts system and how it fitted in with the admin function. It was then that she'd realised she hadn't got a clue about her own finances. She'd suddenly become very worried that she'd not been her usual frugal self over the three months that had vanished from her mind. What if she'd left herself in a compromising financial situation?

She'd darted back to her desk the second the meeting had finished and she'd swiftly logged on to her internet banking. It was then that her jaw dropped open.

She'd never seen her account so healthy. She actually had money! Taking a quick look, she could see that this was clearly a result of her Bird Consultants salary. This promotion had indeed come with a very reassuring pay rise. No wonder she'd quit her job at The Rose.

She was most definitely in shock, but she didn't know whether it was related to sheer joy or grave concern.

Beth took a deep breath. She thought back to the

conversation she'd had with her parents on the phone the night before. She'd been heavily toying with the idea of going to the police. It wasn't right that she could lose three months of her life and be duped into marrying someone that she didn't even like – no, worse, hated and feared.

Much to her surprise, though, her parents couldn't have been more discouraging about the idea of her reporting it. In fact, they'd actually seemed quite distraught.

Their initial argument was that it all seemed so ludicrous. They said she might find herself being ridiculed rather than being taken seriously. She rationalised, though, that no matter how crazy the situation might be, it didn't make it any less a crime.

They then followed up that argument with the fact that she had no proof of any wrong doing. She'd married a millionaire CEO who had boosted her career quite prematurely. And, now it seems, he'd also provided her with an incredibly inflated bank balance. If anything, he could go on record claiming that she was a gold digger. Simon seemed far more the victim here than she did. Truth and lies: how could this all be riddled with such grey areas? Surely truth should always prevail, no matter what the circumstance?

Beth refocussed on the credit in her bank account. No matter what the truth may be, she suddenly found herself questioning, not what had happened to her, but instead how bad the fallout of the events actually were.

Yes, she was far from pleased about the idea of being married to that awful man, but she wasn't hurt in any way. Apart from the electrified sensation charging through her soul, and from feeling quite tired, she was actually in a very good state. Perhaps a better state than she'd ever known.

As much as she hated to admit it, rather than feel negative about missing three months of her life, maybe she should just be grateful? Things hadn't really taken the path that she'd expected, but she was still well on her way to the destination that she'd always dreamed of. So maybe she shouldn't be rocking the boat.

'Are you okay?' Diane suddenly asked from her desk, yanking Beth back to reality from her deep thoughts.

'Erm... yes, I think so.'

'You've gone ever so pale. You haven't had more contact with you know who, have you?'

'No, no. Nothing like that. Just trying to get my head around everything. So much seems to have changed in the time I can't remember.'

'I know. You've been treated very badly.'

'But have I?' Beth asked.

Diane seemed quite put out by this question. 'Of course you have.'

'I've been given a fantastic promotion, a pay rise. I mean, how have I been hurt?'

'Oh Beth, he's getting to you again, isn't he. Nobody has the right to manipulate you. No matter how bad or good the result, you should have been able to make your own mind up about everything. He's a bad man. An evil man. If he contacts you, I need you to tell me. Tell all of us. We've got your back, we'll look out for you.'

Beth felt so confused. Diane was right, she shouldn't have lost three months of her life, but nothing bad seems to have happened. Quite the opposite when she thinks about it. Except being married to that creepy, overpowering man.

Beth looked at the time and was happy to find it was after one o'clock. She needed a break. She grabbed her bag and pulled out her rather pathetic cheese sandwiches. That was all she'd been able to muster up after work last night. Then she thought to her bank balance again.

For the first time in her life, she could actually afford to splash out. So, putting away her unappealing Tupperware box, she made the decision to go out for lunch.

'I think I need to clear my head. Do you want anything while I'm out?' she asked Diane.

'No, you have a break. You deserve it. Just stay away from Mr Bird, we know he's in the office today.'

'I will do.'

Beth made her way out of the building and onto Heaningford High Street. She knew there was nothing but The Rose back in the direction of her flat, so she decided to head the other way.

Less than a minute on and she found a few little shops and a couple of restaurants. There were quite a few people milling around a convenience store, and then she saw a quaint little tea shop.

Beth noted what a delightful little place it seemed, nicely decorated with tea cups on the wall. She couldn't resist heading in. There was a small queue ahead of her, but she could clearly see the array of sandwich fillings in the counter at the front. With excited taste buds, she knew she'd made the right decision.

Just as she was making her mind up as to what she fancied, she heard a voice behind her.

'Hello Beth,' the man said.

She turned around to see a tall, lanky man smiling sweetly at her. She had no clue who he was, but considering recent events, that was no surprise.

'Hi!' Beth greeted, trying not to be rude. How could she explain not knowing who he was when he clearly knew her? She'd have to play this by ear.

'How are you?' the man asked.

'Really good, thank you. Especially as it's Friday.'

'It's good to see you.'

'You too!'

The man seemed to sigh. 'Now that's good to hear.' A strange, wicked smile then grabbed his lips. 'You look a little confused.'

Beth had to be honest, at least in some way. This was too difficult otherwise. 'You'll have to excuse me, I haven't been myself of late. It seems my short term memory has been a bit... compromised. I can't recall your name at all.'

44

'Oh no, that's a shame. Mind you, you did seem very tired the last time we met. I'm Damien. Damien Rock.'

'Do you work at Bird Consultants?'

'Yes, I certainly do. I'm the Sales Director.' He then hushed his voice ever so slightly. 'I'm not actually supposed to be in today. Nor any time soon. Mr Bird - you know what he's like – well he's been demanding so much of me of late. I've been all over the country, following up leads, converting sales. It's been exhausting.'

'He's quite a demanding boss, then?'

'The worst. He's been threatening me with the sack for weeks. I'm only here to collect a few files, then I'm going to have to shoot off again. So if anyone asks, you haven't seen me.'

'I'm so sorry. Of course.' Beth understood completely. Mr Bird was such a horrid man.

'What can I get for you, love?' the middle aged lady behind the counter asked, grabbing Beth's attention.

'Erm...' Beth scanned the fillings quickly. It was too hard to choose. 'Chicken salad, please.'

'Make that two,' Damien added. 'We had the same last time as well, didn't we.'

'Did we?'

'You don't remember that either?'

Beth just shook her head. At least he didn't seem to mind.

'We've had lunch together a few times. You bought last time, insisted on it. So this time it's most definitely on me.'

'Really?' Beth asked, now feeling quite uneasy that she'd forgotten all about this man and their apparent lunch dates.

'Don't worry about it,' Damien soothed. 'I know how it can be, working at this place. It messes with your head.'

'I'm starting to see that. You don't have to buy me lunch.'

'It's only fair. And it's my absolute pleasure. You know we really should meet up again sometime soon to talk about our Italy plans.'

'Italy?' Beth queried with confusion.

'Our trip to Florence. But you don't remember, do you?'

'That'll be five pounds sixty, please,' the sandwich lady said, giving Beth a second to process her thoughts. Damien handed over the money and Beth grabbed her lunch. Then they both walked out together.

'We were going to go to Florence together?' Beth asked.

'It was just an idea,' Damien uttered, shrugging his shoulders. 'We've both never been, so... Never mind.'

'No, no, it's a lovely idea. It's just...'

'I get it, Beth. It's fine.' Damien stopped and looked Beth squarely in the eyes. 'I know what it's like working with Mr Bird. Everyone gets confused at times. There's just one more thing I have to know before I go.'

'Anything.'

'Do you remember our kiss?'

'What?'

'I'll take that as a no.'

'We kissed?'

'Best moment of my life.' Beth didn't know how to respond. 'It's fine,' Damien said, squeezing Beth's hand. 'I'll always remember it.' There was an awkward pause for a moment as Beth still didn't know what to say.

'I'd better go before Mr Bird catches me,' Damien finally said, breaking the silence. 'Let's catch up soon.'

'Yeah,' Beth nodded.

Damien smiled one last time before heading off quite quickly, clearly in a rush not to be seen.

Beth turned on her heels and headed in the opposite direction, back to her flat. She needed some time before returning to the office. Had she really kissed that man? It sounded like they were starting a relationship. It had to be true, she supposed. Why would he lie?

She considered whether she found him attractive. He

wasn't bad looking.

Then a flash of Mr Bird's stunning features popped into her mind. She quickly tried to get rid of the image. Damien may not be as perfect, but at least he was honest. She could see why he would have turned her head. And at least it was one more piece to the jigsaw of what she'd been up to for the last three months. She was relieved to know it hadn't all been about scary Mr Bird.

It was also a relief that this Damien hadn't been overly shocked by her lack of memory. He seemed to know Mr Bird fairly well so this must be a regular occurrence for those who get involved with that terrible man. If only she could remember how on earth she'd got involved with him in the first place.

Still, whatever had happened, Damien had definitely made her feel a lot better about everything. Maybe seeing him again wouldn't be a bad thing. In fact, she was quite looking forward to it.

SEVEN

Down the road, not far from the tea shop, Damien couldn't wipe the smile from his face. That had gone better than he could ever have hoped for. Now they'd see who was the more powerful! He might end up with the girl after all. That would not only secure the end of the Malancy, it would also show Simon who really was the best man.

'Damien!' a voice suddenly called out. Before Damien could even see who it was, the person had yanked him away from the road to the side of a restaurant, completely out of sight.

Damien grabbed hold of himself, a little stunned, then looked up to see his attacker. It was Brian.

'Am I glad to see you!' Brian said.

'Where have you been?'

'Simon trapped me in the boardroom. He's taken away my phone and everything, I haven't been able to contact anyone. Then I just saw you. What are you doing?'

'Getting the best news of my life,' Damien grinned.

'You know, then?'

'Oh yes. And it's better than I could have wished for!'

'Great. Will you feed everything back to George? Let him know why I've been silent? I need a new phone and

48

everyone's numbers too.'

'Anything else you want? I'm not your slave, you know.'

'No, but you're the only one who can help me. Will you tell George?'

'I suppose I'll have to.'

'Oh, and Simon wants you to call him.'

'Why?' Damien asked, his heart suddenly pounding in his chest at this request.

'Because he thinks you still work for him.' Brian couldn't help but smirk at this.

'Of course!' Then Damien's happiness was halted. 'But all the other directors know I've gone.'

'I've got that well in hand. I've told Simon that you're in Scotland working on some new clients and I'm sitting at your desk while you're away. I've placed myself directly as the go between until further notice. Who else needs to know?'

'That's brilliant, Brian. Well played. Right, I'll give our supreme Mr Bird a call. This could not be going any better.'

'I better go. You'll get me that phone, right?'

'Yes, yes, whatever. Speak to you soon.'

Brian headed off back towards the office and Damien took a moment to grin. Maybe Simon had been right: you don't need magical powers to make someone's life a misery. He couldn't resist making that call.

He grabbed his mobile from his pocket and dialled Simon's number.

'Simon Bird,' the voice answered.

'It's Damien,' Damien replied, trying to downplay his smugness.

'Where have you been? And what phone are you calling me from? Why have you not been answering your mobile?'

'This is my mobile,' Damien stated, feigning confusion.

'I don't recognise the number.'

'Haven't you updated your phone yet?' Damien was

trying not to overplay his mock confusion. 'First you force me to change my number, then you don't even bother to save it.' Damien knew, in reality, that there was no sound reason as to why he'd have a new phone number, but he could easily play on Simon's lack of memory. He felt very sure that, unlike Beth, Simon would skirt around the issue.

'You've changed your number?'

'You insisted on it. That fraud thing. Why do I get the feeling you don't remember?'

Simon remained silent for a moment and Damien was dying to laugh. At least Beth had the guts to be honest. She was so much better than him. Then Simon finally said, 'Fine. This is your new number. Where have you been?'

'I'm in Scotland. Where you sent me. Simon, are you okay?' Damien was really trying not to laugh now, he was having such fun.

'All I need is an update. Do you think you can manage that?'

'It's tough, Simon, I'm not going to lie. It could be a few weeks yet before I crack any of these deals. They want the help but they're finding it hard to get over the ethics of it all.'

'Is it worth your time just focussing on them and nothing else?'

'Of course is it. You did too when we spoke last week.' Damien could hear Simon sigh and he knew he was getting to him. It was so much fun! 'Considering the fact that they're worth about fifty million each, I'd say it's worth me staying up here for a while longer, don't you?'

'Fifty million? We've never had a contract worth that much.'

'And that's why you put me in charge of sales. And why we hired Brian. He's doing a grand job of taking care of my other accounts until I'm back. He's a real asset to the team. Look after him.'

'I want regular updates, Damien.'

'Yes sir,' Damien mocked. He could almost hear Simon

sigh one more time before he hung up. It was far too easy to wind him up. He really wasn't the all-powerful Simon that he acted like. Damien had him wrapped around his little finger and now it was time for him to pay.

As Damien walked away smugly, a little too satisfied with the power that he was now sure he had over Simon and Beth, he didn't know that he'd just made his first massive mistake.

As he walked away to his car, trying to keep his distance from Bird Consultants, he had no idea that just a few minutes before, when he'd been speaking with Beth, Paul Bird had driven by.

EIGHT

Jim was sitting in the living room at Simon's house, virtually buried in books about the Malancy. They discussed magic, laws, history, traditions, just about every topic that he could think of, but not one of them mentioned anything about a Malant being able to change a person's thoughts or feelings.

He was pulled from his reading when he heard the front door slam shut.

'Jim!' Paul yelled as he opened the living room door to check.

'What is it?' Just one look at Paul's face told him it wasn't good news.

'That bastard!' Paul started pacing around the room, clearly agitated by something.

'Who?'

'Damien!'

Jim felt a throb in his stomach at the mention of that name. What could he have possibly done now?

'I saw him talking to Beth,' Paul explained.

'What? Where?'

'By the sandwich shop down the road from the office. I was driving by, purely by chance, when I saw the two of them just coming out of the shop. It was only brief, but it looked like a very friendly conversation. God, I wanted to smack the living daylights out of him.'

Jim placed the book he was reading on the coffee table and stood up. 'What were they talking about?'

'Who knows? Who ever knows with that bastard? The one thing that we can be sure of, though, is that he definitely knows that Beth's lost her memory. And whether he's behind it or not, he'll be using it to his advantage, there's no doubt.'

Jim searched his brain for some logic. Why would Damien be talking to Beth? Obviously it was in some way to keep her away from Simon, but what could he have said? What was his angle now?

'We have to stop him,' Paul stated.

'How? We can't approach Damien. In fact, does he know you saw him?'

'No. Definitely not. He was too engrossed in talking to her.'

'Then we have a small advantage. It's a rare thing nowadays. We need to keep the power here, no matter how small it is.'

'What power? What does that mean?'

Jim thought hard. 'Let's think like Simon again.'

'We can try.'

'What do we know? What are the facts here that we actually know?'

'That Damien's a little fucker that needs sorting out once and for all.'

'I think we've always known that. No, looking at the facts, we know that, for some reason, Simon and Beth have lost their short-term memories. They don't remember being married.'

'Or even really knowing each other.'

'Then you catch Damien, who is risking a lot coming anywhere near Bird Consultants, talking to Beth. He has to want something from her.'

'Of course he does!'

'Even if he didn't before, we have to assume that he now definitely knows that she's lost her memory. He's not going to let an opportunity like that go to waste. I think we have to consider that he's going to want to – no, need to – interact with her again. He's obviously got some angle and he'll need to speak to Beth to get it to work.'

'Most probably.'

'So to cause him issues, we need to stop him being able to talk to Beth.'

'So we tell her?'

'Tell her what?' Jim asked.

'Tell her to keep away from Damien.'

'For what reason?'

'Because he's a slimy bastard.'

'Think about it, Paul. We need to be defensive. For all we know, Damien was telling Beth that you're going to warn her away from him. He could have said that you are indeed the bad guy, not him. No, without knowing what Damien's angle is, we have to play it safe.'

'So why don't we ask her what he said?'

'Why on earth is she going to tell you? Again, if Damien's warned her off, you poking around will just push her away even more.'

'Then what do we do?'

Jim took a second to process his thoughts. 'We need to keep it neutral. We need to ensure that Damien is kept away from her but without Beth ever really knowing it. In fact, we need to make sure that she's kept away from all the anti-Malants.'

'You want to watch her twenty-four hours a day?'

'Precisely.'

'What?'

'We need someone to be watching over her twenty-four hours a day.'

'She might get a little suspicious if Simon's butler is hanging around all the time.'

'Not us!' Jim stated, shaking his head. An idea was now forming in his mind. 'We need someone neutral. We need someone with no connections to any of this.'

'Where on earth are we going to find someone like that? Everyone we know is involved one way or another.'

'That's not true. I can think of the perfect person right now. He's got experience, he's trustworthy; he lives in Manchester so he's completely away from it all. He's never even been to London. And he loves the Malancy, so he's definitely not involved with George.'

'You want to get some stranger to keep an eye on Beth?'

'No. I want to hire him as Beth's bodyguard!'

It didn't take long for Jim to convince Paul that this was the best idea for everyone. They'd both get peace of mind that Beth was being looked after and it would interfere with whatever plans Damien had up his sleeve.

Jim made the phone call to his friend and then on Saturday morning he and Paul drove up to Manchester.

They'd told Simon that Paul had to visit a friend in need and Jim's help was required. They were quite cagey about it and this clearly agitated Simon. But, thankfully, always trusting his uncle, Simon didn't ask too many questions.

By early afternoon, they were sitting in a coffee shop in Manchester City Centre, awaiting the man's arrival.

'You really think we can trust this guy?' Paul asked, sipping on his Americano.

Jim regarded Paul. He could see how recent events were taking their toll on him. He was looking wearier by the day. He had ever since Beth's disappearance. It felt like the stakes were getting bigger with every passing minute, but so was Jim's determination. Jim knew he wouldn't rest until they'd found a way to end this torment once and for all. It wasn't just about saving the Malancy now. It was about the welfare of his friends, and his own personal sanity.

'I've known him for years,' Jim replied. 'I definitely trust him. And being that he's the brother of a friend of a friend, he's so far removed from any of the chaos going on down south, it's the safest option we've got. I haven't seen him since a Stag Do I went on two years ago, but that's the beauty of social media, you can always keep in touch.'

'He seems so young, though.'

'Twenty-six is old enough to know what he's doing.'

'He doesn't have a lot of experience.'

'He's been working as a security guard for five years. He's been through his training, and he's got a good worth ethic from everything I know about him.'

'They made him redundant!'

'Paul, they made hundreds of people redundant. They virtually closed down the site, it was no reflection on his skill set. Think of it as fate. He's needs a job, badly, and we need him.'

Their conversation was cut short as suddenly a tall, well-built man with light brown hair and sparkling blue eyes approached them. 'Jimmy, great to see you again!'

Jim stood up and shook the man's hand. 'It's been a while. Paul, I'd like you to meet Toby Gardner. Toby, this is a good friend of mine, Paul Bird.'

'Good to meet you.' Jim had forgotten how strong Toby's Mancunian accent was.

'Likewise,' Paul replied.

'You want tea or coffee?' Jim asked as Toby sat down.

'Yeah, coffee. Black, no sugar would be great. Cheers pal.'

Jim quickly ordered the coffee and came back to find Paul and Toby chatting about football. At least they seemed to be getting along.

'I think we better get down to business, if that's all right with you?' Jim said, taking his seat.

'Yeah, course,' Toby replied. 'What's this job offer, then?'

'It's a bit delicate. But we'll make it well worth your while.'

'I'm listening.'

'Paul's niece is caught up in something... difficult. I don't want to say too much. Let's just say she's caught the attention of a few undesirable characters and we're worried for her safety.'

'Right,' Toby said, looking concerned.

'So we want to hire you to be her... well sort of her bodyguard. Until we can get this thing resolved.'

'Her bodyguard?' Toby seemed to be impressed by the idea.

'We just need you to keep an eye on her. Wherever she goes.'

'But she can't know we've hired you,' Paul added.

'She'll go mad,' Jim explained. 'You know what control freaks women are. She'll think we're just being overprotective. We really haven't told her how much danger she's in.'

'It would worry her way too much,' Paul finished.

'Yeah,' Toby nodded.

'We'll pay for your expenses, of course. We've already rented the flat opposite Beth's flat so you can live there,' Jim explained.

'And just so you know, her flat's been protected,' Paul said. 'No Malant can enter, not unless they're part of her family. So might be interesting to see if anyone tries it on.'

'Yeah,' Toby nodded.

'We were thinking, we'll cover all your food, travel and rent, and then five hundred a week on top?' Jim offered.

'Five hundred pounds a week?' Toby almost spat out his coffee. Jim and Paul just nodded in reply. 'I'm in!' Toby said, holding out his hand for them to shake.

'Brilliant,' Jim said.

'The most important thing is that you can't let anyone, and I mean anyone who is not a Bird Consultants employee or a member of our family speak to or interact with Beth in any way,' Paul said.

'What about her friends?' Toby asked.

'She hasn't lived down south for long. So if they're not a member of our family or they don't work for the company, then she doesn't know them and they shouldn't be talking to her,' Paul replied.

'We'll support you in any way we can. Just keep in touch, and if anything out of the ordinary happens, you need to tell us straight away, okay?'

'For five hundred pounds a week, with expenses, I'll do owt you ask.'

NINE

At the same time as Jim, Paul and Toby shook hands, back in Central London Damien had called a meeting with George and Mr Taylor. He wanted to share the good news about Simon's and Beth's lack of memory, and, more importantly, gloat.

'Very well done, Damien,' George said, sitting at his desk.

'At least this plan isn't quite as unethical as turning them into birds,' Mr Taylor said, flashing Damien a stony glare.

'Is the Malancy ethical?' Damien threw back.

'Who said we need to fight fire with fire?' Mr Taylor replied.

'That's enough,' George warned. 'Thank you for your help, Damien.'

Damien smiled smugly. 'I saw Brian as well.'

'So he's finally made contact!' George exclaimed.

'Seems good old Simon had trapped him in a room. He said he needs a new phone. His was confiscated, like he was a naughty school boy.'

'When did Simon do this?' George asked.

'I'm guessing before they cast the spell.'

'Nothing gets by that man, does it?' Mr Taylor observed.

'Or Brian is just a useless spy,' Damien countered.

'It's always Mr Bird, and you know it,' Mr Taylor replied. 'I mean look at you. I can't remember ever hearing of a Malant losing their power before. Simon is clearly not a man to be messed with and you're living proof.'

Damien felt sickened at this jab. 'Fuck off.' It had yet to truly sink in that he'd lost his magic. Truthfully, he'd never really used his power that much, but it was always nice to have the option. It was his birth right. How could Simon do such a cruel, inhumane thing as strip someone of their very nature? Simon really was a cold-hearted bastard

'Everything else aside, Damien,' George said, 'it has to be acknowledged that the Malancy would now be in the hands of a very dangerous man were it not for you.' As George uttered the words, Damien felt his head swell. 'We'll always be grateful.'

Damien nodded. Then he got a niggling feeling that there was something finite about George's words. 'What's next then?' he asked, trying to put his doubts to rest.

'You've given us a great foundation to work on. Thank you very much.'

'Why do I get the feeling you're asking me to leave?'

'It's not personal, Damien. Things have changed. Let's be honest.'

'You couldn't have done any of this without me!' Damien snapped.

'And I told you we'll always be grateful.'

'What the fuck?' Damien was fuming. Why were people constantly dumping on him? It was so unfair. Everywhere he went, everyone he met, people were always being nasty to him. He'd lost everything, absolutely everything, and now the people that he thought were allies were taking away all that he had left.

'Have a bit of dignity,' Mr Taylor muttered.

'Is this because I've lost my power?' Damien asked.

George sighed. 'There is nowhere else you can help, and we need to focus. We can't have extra people tagging along for the ride.'

'But it's a ride that I made possible! You just said it. The Malancy would be Simon's if it wasn't for me.'

'And I've stated that we're very grateful,' George said through gritted teeth.

'You were just using me-'

'That's enough!' George snapped.

'Mr Taylor's not a Malant. How come he gets to stay and I'm thrust out?'

'Do I have to call security?'

'Security?' Damien asked, shocked and hurt.

'You have five seconds to get out or I'll have you taken out.'

'Dignity,' Mr Taylor said.

Damien glared at the two men around him and then shot to his feet. Saying nothing, he took a deep breath and then he walked out, trying to keep his head held high.

They had no idea who they were messing with. He knew Simon better than any of them. If they wanted to play this game without him, then that was their choice, but he knew there was no way they could win without someone being able to think like Simon. This was a great loss to George and his team. He hoped they'd lose everything now themselves. It would serve them right.

* * *

By Monday morning, Paul and Jim had moved Toby to London and he was set in place to start guarding Beth. He was happily sitting in his car outside Bird Consultants ready for action.

To help, they'd arranged for the footage from the CCTV camera near the front door of the building to be sent to Toby's mobile phone. It also sent him an automated ping every time Beth went in or out of the building, just to make sure nothing would be missed.

Feeling peace of mind that Beth was in safe hands, Paul and Jim carried on with their research. They were still no closer to finding out what had happened to Simon and Beth, but they weren't losing hope.

Paul had finished his morning check on Simon and the office, and he was now back in Buckinghamshire in Simon's study trawling through pages on the internet. He was searching through forums that discussed unusual magic performed by Malants, but nothing useful was cropping up. Jim had popped out for a short while to run some of Simon's errands, still very much playing his butler role.

It was approaching midday when Paul's mobile phone started to ring and they were finally to get some answers.

He looked down to see who it was, but it wasn't a number he recognised. It was a number starting with 01228 and Paul didn't even know where that was.

'Paul Bird,' he answered.

'Paul, thank God. It's Jane!'

TEN

After another morning of disturbances from the office, Simon's irritation levels were soaring. He hated being in the UK. He'd been drawn into so much crap that he never had to deal with in New York and all he could think about was jumping on a plane and getting as far away from this life as he could. It was utter torture.

How could Paul do this? What was he thinking? How could he suddenly decide that he wanted to move back permanently to the UK? He'd always seemed so happy in America, and he knew that Simon preferred it there too.

Maybe, Simon decided, if he was going to be stuck in the UK for a while he could work from home. He looked at the directors outside of his office. They always wanted a piece of his time while he sat at his desk, yet when he was in New York they managed perfectly well on their own. He didn't need to be there.

He flicked to his calendar and his heart sank. He had two internal meetings the next day, three customers to visit later in the week, and he'd been considering going up to Scotland to check on Damien. That summed up the problem completely: he could get no peace and quiet at all.

He flicked back to the contract he was working on. He

was editing a document that Brian had drafted up. It was quite poor and needed a lot of amending. Simon was seriously questioning how good this Brian really was. He made a mental note to query it with Damien the next time they spoke.

'Simon!' The panicked voice of his uncle startled Simon as Paul burst into his office. Paul slammed the door behind him, charged across the room and then glared at Simon from the other side of his desk.

'What's the matter?' Simon said.

'I need your help.'

'Anything.'

Paul took a moment to catch his breath as he grabbed one of the spare seats in the office. He sat down opposite Simon and then took a few moments more to consider his words carefully. 'You can't ask me too many questions about this,' he finally said. 'You trust me, don't you?'

'You know I do,' Simon confirmed.

'I need you to cast a spell for me.'

'What sort of spell?'

'A difficult one. You're ten times more powerful than me - than anyone - you're the only one that can do this.'

'Are you in trouble?' Simon asked. He'd never seen his uncle so agitated before. Simon felt quite uneasy about what was to come next.

'It's Jane. You know, Jane Parker?'

'Your friend from Malancy HQ?'

'Yes, the Senior Law Enforcement Director.'

'What about her?'

'She's in trouble. A lot of trouble. I can't tell you any more, and she's done nothing wrong, but we need to protect her.'

'Protect her how?'

'I need you to cast a spell that hides her. We need to make sure she can't be located and we need to do it now.'

'Located? What do you mean?'

'From location spells. Someone very nasty is looking

for her. I can find her a safe place to hide, but you need to make sure that it stays a safe place.'

'I don't know if I can do that.'

'Of course you can, Simon.'

'I've never heard of anyone doing that before.'

'Well I have. And it worked really well. Now you need to do the same.'

'Even if I could, that would take incredible strength.'

'It would be a walk in the park for you, Si, and you know it.'

Simon thought for a second. It was very rare that his uncle asked for anything, the least he could do was try. He owed his uncle everything. More than that, he'd never seen Paul so desperate, Simon knew he had to help.

'I suppose... if I reversed a location spell,' Simon mused. 'Rather than imagine the person to try and find them, I could block them out instead. I don't know, it could work.'

'Will you try?'

'It's so specific, though. I've only ever done a location spell on someone I know really well. Remember that time I thought I'd lost you when you'd gone on that three day binge?'

Paul had always smiled at that memory, but this time his face didn't flinch and Simon knew things were serious. 'You know Jane,' was all he said.

'Not really,' Simon stated. He couldn't even remember the last time he'd seen her; it must have been years ago. 'If I was doing a location spell, I'd have to summon up clear images of her. I don't think I could do that with Jane.'

'I could tell you about her.'

'It doesn't work like that.'

'There has to be a way around it!' Paul insisted.

Simon thought again. 'The only way I can see of getting around it is if I had something personal of Jane's. Something I could tap into. That maybe has a chance of working, but-'

65

'Like what?' Paul interrupted with desperation.

'Anything. From her hairbrush to her socks, it wouldn't matter. As long as they were connected to her.'

Paul took a moment to scan his brain. Then he turned back to Simon. 'Would a photo work?'

'A photo?'

Paul grabbed his wallet from his jeans pocket and pulled out a small photo. 'Would that work?' he asked.

Simon looked at the scruffy photo in Paul's hand. It was of a young woman posing sweetly against a beautiful, scenic backdrop, and Simon vaguely recognised it to be Jane. He took it from Paul, but he wasn't thinking about the spell anymore. 'Why do you have a photo of Jane in your wallet?' he asked.

Paul glared at Simon but said nothing. After a few moments he walked to the window that looked out across Heaningford. Simon had never seen that look on his uncle's face before but he immediately recognised the sentiment, and it was quite a surprise.

'I love her,' Paul uttered.

'What?' The surprise turned into shock as Simon processed his uncle's words. Simon had never heard his uncle say anything like that.

'I think I have all my life.'

'Isn't she married?' Simon asked, worried for his uncle. This seemed like dangerous territory.

'It's complicated. We're not just having a sordid affair. There's a lot more to it.'

'She feels the same way about you?' This was big news for Simon. He was normally so on the ball, he couldn't believe that he'd missed it.

'Yes. Anyway, we haven't got time to talk about that now. Can you do the spell or not?' Paul made his way back over to Simon's desk. Simon had so many questions about this unexpected revelation, but he knew better than to push his uncle when he'd closed a subject. It would have to wait for now.

'It's worth a shot, I suppose. I can't promise anything, though.' Simon felt more than ever that he had to try. He wanted his uncle to be happy and he knew that he had to help Jane for Paul's sake, whatever she was going through.

'Just give it all you've got.'

Simon stood up. 'I'll need to get a stone or something. And we'll need somewhere quiet to do it.'

'We haven't got time for this, Simon. They're probably already looking for her!'

'Paul, you're asking me to do quite a difficult spell. I'll need to augment it somehow.'

'No you won't.'

'I think I will.'

'Just try it without, Si. Trust me. You've been getting stronger every day, I've seen it.'

'You've seen it?'

Paul addressed Simon very directly. 'Trust me. More than you've ever trusted anyone. You can do this spell all on your own and I know it. I know you Simon, you're my boy, and I know you have far more power at this moment than you realise. Use it. Use it now for my sake and for the sake of the woman I love.'

Simon looked inside himself. He had been feeling stronger and more powerful. Something had most definitely happened to him in those three months that he couldn't remember. Did Paul know what had happened? Or could he just sense Simon's increased power too?

Then Simon thought to the aura that he emitted. He knew it scared people and that he was chilly to be around. Maybe that had increased in potency along with his sudden surge in strength. He wanted to ask, but then he realised he didn't want to know the answer. He was already difficult to be around. Did he really want to know if it had got worse?

Choosing to put that aside in his mind, Simon turned to face Paul. He knew he had to give it a go. The worst that could happen was that the spell didn't work. No bad could come of it.

He looked out across the Executive Floor. He wasn't quite in the mood to perform a spectacle for everyone, and he knew Paul wouldn't allow him to find somewhere quiet, so there really only was one option left. Simon clicked his fingers and all the windows to his office went black. He then stared at his door and the lock clicked shut.

'Let's give it a go,' he then said to Paul, sitting back down at his desk. 'You might want to close your eyes.'

'I know the drill,' Paul replied. A small flash of curiosity sparked in Simon's head as he couldn't recall ever performing such a spell in his uncle's presence before; but he didn't dwell on it for long. He had more pressing matters to deal with.

Simon picked up the picture that Paul had laid on the desk and he drew the image into his mind. It felt so weird that he was about to cast such a spell without an element for support, but he was willing to give it a go.

He didn't quite know how to process the idea of it working. It would be amazing if he really did have boosted power, but he also couldn't help but worry about the consequences. His already powerful state caused him enough issues without it increasing even more.

He didn't have time to think about that now, though. He put all his other thoughts to the back of his mind and he once again looked at the picture in his hand. Then slowly he closed his eyes.

When casting a location spell, the start was the same as with any spell. He'd summon up all of his emotion and concentrate it all like a ball in his chest. It was at the point when the power started to formulate that he'd begin the process of trying to locate the person that he was searching for. He'd simply just picture that person in his mind. This time, though, he needed to try and do the opposite.

He thought to the picture of Jane in his hand and he imagined it being deleted from existence. He scratched away at the image in his mind until all that was left was blackness.

As he did this, he channelled the force within him. His instinct told him that he needed to draw strength from an external element, but remembering what his uncle had said, he instead tried to increase the force of his own strength. He intensified the ball of power that was building up inside of him. He'd never felt anything like it. He felt on fire there was so much power surging through his body.

As the blackness in his mind thickened, Simon's body started to glow. It was at first a bright, golden glow, before quickly transforming into a fiery red blaze that smothered every inch of him. He felt the power climax and then dazzling beams of light choked his office, leaving nothing in sight untouched.

Simon could feel it. The spell was over. There was nothing more he could do. He simply dropped the photo, letting it fall to his desk, and the light instantly vanished.

He opened his eyes to find Paul staring at him, a little startled. 'Is it done?' he asked.

'The spell completed. I don't know if it worked but I did everything I could.' Simon then sat forward and addressed his uncle very directly. 'How did I do that without an element?'

'I told you, Si, you're more powerful than you know.'

'It's only been the past few days. I've felt so... electric.'

Paul nodded. 'I know, mate. And we'll talk about it later. For now, though, we need to see if the spell worked.'

'How are we going to do that?'

'You need to do a location spell. Find Jane.'

'Are you kidding? I've just done a massive spell.'

'And it's not even touched the surface. You're incredible Simon. Embrace it.'

Simon did have to admit that even though he'd just wielded in a few seconds more power than he'd ever done in his whole life, he didn't even feel a pinch of tiredness. It was very odd. He couldn't decide if it was a good thing or a potential warning, but he did take comfort in the fact that Paul didn't seem the slightest bit concerned about his new found strength. In fact, Paul was very encouraging. Maybe Paul was right. Maybe it was time that he truly embraced his power.

'Okay, let me try and find her.' Simon picked up the picture of Jane again from his desk and he closed his eyes.

He once again summoned the strength from within him, but this time he pictured Jane instead of blocking her.

As the image of Jane became more vibrant in his mind, the golden glow that signalled the spell was working once again lit up Simon's frame. Within seconds it became a fierce red beam, before developing into a scarlet sheen that swallowed Simon whole.

Like a flash, a bright blaze illuminated Simon's office, covering everything in sight, and both Bird men knew the spell was complete. Simon dropped the picture and the dazzling beams instantly vanished. He looked across at Paul.

'Well?' Paul asked.

'That was so weird. I know I did the spell right, but I saw nothing. I don't mean blackness, I mean nothing at all. It was just emptiness.'

'That's right. The spell's worked!' For the first time Paul smiled. He moved around the desk and hugged Simon awkwardly, his excitement taking over. 'Thanks mate, thank you so much.'

'I can't believe I did it.'

'You need to have more faith in yourself. Right, I've got to go.' Paul grabbed the photo of Jane and carefully placed it back in his wallet.

'You're off?'

'I've got to go and take care of Jane. Don't tell anyone anything.'

'Where are you going?'

'I'll keep you posted.' Paul walked to the door and then turned around. 'I'll be taking Jim with me.'

'Again?'

'I can't do this without him.'

'He's meant to be *my* butler.'

'I'll explain it all as soon as I can, but for now Jim's coming with me and we'll be gone for as long as it takes.'

'But what about me?' Simon was getting a bit fed up. Not only was he being completely left in the dark - when even his butler was privy to the secrets - but he was being left in a place that he really didn't want to be. The thought of sneaking off back to New York quickly crossed his mind.

'You've got work to do.'

'I mean, what about the stuff that Jim's supposed to be helping me with? The stuff I pay him for?'

'Get a takeaway, Simon. You're more than capable of looking after yourself. We've both just witnessed that you're the most powerful person on the planet. I'm sure if you put your mind to it you can cook yourself something nice for dinner. Magic something in the oven. There's no end to the possibilities.'

Paul went to open the door but it was locked. He turned back to Simon. Simon sighed and then, with just his mind, he flicked the lock.

'When will you be back?' he asked Paul.

'When we're ready. I'll be in touch. Don't worry, Si, you'll hear from me. I'll see you really soon. And I'll look after Jim.'

'Okay. Have a safe trip.'

'Oh, and we're taking the Lexus,' Paul added as he opened the door. 'See you.' Then he was gone.

Simon couldn't believe it. What was going on? He didn't know whether he wanted to be part of it or not. Actually, he was probably glad that he wasn't. It all seemed to be quite messy and he'd helped Paul out where he could.

Then he turned his mind to his increased power. Where had that come from? It can't just have occurred overnight. There must have been a catalyst. He needed to get his memories back, but he had no clue how he was going to manage that.

He couldn't help but think that some time on his own, away from the office and away from his family, would do him the world of good. Clarity of thought would be a massive help. He just didn't know how he was ever going to get that stuck in the UK, being bothered by everyone all the time.

Then he remembered that he wanted to speak to Paul about these fifty million pound jobs that Damien was working on. What on earth could anyone need fixing that was worth fifty million pounds? It all seemed really peculiar and he needed Paul to shed some light on it.

Obviously Simon had known all about this at some point, but he wasn't going to admit to Damien that he'd lost his short term memory. The last thing he needed was to show any sort of weakness where Damien was concerned, that was always a bad mistake. No, he'd just have to wait now until Paul was back and then he'd make a point of speaking to him about it.

At that moment so much seemed to be going on and Simon felt completely out of it all. There was a massive gap somewhere that he needed to fill. Maybe some time alone tonight might be the best thing for him, to try and gather some perspective.

He looked at his windows and noticed they were still black. He went to click his fingers to make them transparent once more when he suddenly decided not to. He looked to his door and locked it again with his mind. If he had to be stuck in his office, the least he could do was block out the world around him.

It was a small attempt at getting peace, but it was all he was going to get for now. He then looked back down as his laptop and he got straight back to work.

ELEVEN

It took Jim and Paul about six hours to drive up to Carlisle where Jane was. The only information they had was that she'd been held against her will somewhere in Scotland but she'd managed to get away. She'd got as far as Carlisle but she was soon to run out of petrol and she was terrified that they were coming to find her.

Paul had thought quickly. She'd described where she was and he'd booked her into a nearby hotel. Then he'd dashed into London to get Simon to cloak her, and now they were on their way to help.

'She gave you no other clues?' Jim asked, sitting in the driver's seat.

'It was only a two minute phone call. She sounded desperate, scared even. I've never heard her like that.'

'I suppose we can be quite confident in assuming that this relates to the anti-Malants,' Jim said.

'She must have been locked up in the same way as Beth. We should have known. We should have done more to save her.'

'We had quite a bit on our hands as it was, Paul.' As much as Jim liked and respected Jane, he couldn't bring himself to find the same level as concern as Paul had. With

Paul it went far past general concern for Jane's welfare, his reaction felt almost personal. Jim didn't know what to make of it. 'Simon and Beth had to be our priority, along with saving the Malancy,' Jim added, trying to rationalise Paul's apparent guilt. 'At least we know Jane's all right now.'

'I'm just relieved that Simon's managed to block her.'

Jim couldn't help but smile at this. He finally had an advantage over his brother. He imagined George trying to do the location spell and finding nothing. All the way through this fight he'd felt one step behind, even though he'd managed to get Simon and Beth to do the spell. Being in the controlling seat for a change gave Jim a big boost. Jane would no doubt have plenty of answers for them; answers they desperately needed.

Jim's fortitude may never have faltered, but he couldn't deny that he'd also been very worried as to how they were going to succeed in saving the Malancy. This new little triumph was definitely starting to strengthen his hope that maybe they could win this battle after all.

After an exhausting journey, they finally reached the Premier Inn where Jane was hiding, just off the M6. She'd called them from the hotel to say she was in room number two twelve and they were now knocking on the door waiting for her to answer.

'It's Paul,' he called through the door to reassure her.

Within seconds Jane opened the door and Jim and Paul quickly entered. Jim noticed how messy she looked, her normal sharp self a million miles away.

Then he was brought to a complete standstill. Jane wrapped her arms around Paul and they started kissing. Jim didn't know where to look. This was quite unexpected. Suddenly Paul's grave concern for Jane's welfare all fell into place.

The couple broke apart and Paul looked to Jim. 'None of my business,' Jim said, although he really wanted to know what was going on.

'It's a long story, Jim,' Paul said.

'And one I'm afraid you're going to have to hear,' Jane added.

'What?' Paul asked, surprised. 'You know Jim, don't you?'

'I know James Malant, yes,' Jane replied. 'It was only a few weeks ago that I heard of him as Jim, Simon's butler, though. But then I've learnt quite a lot over the past few weeks. You'd better take a seat.'

'I'll make us a cuppa,' Jim said. His years as a butler had left him always with an urge to look busy. He'd got very good at making tea when times were difficult.

He turned round to the tea tray in the corner of the room and noted there were only two cups. 'Does someone mind having theirs in a glass?'

'I will, Jim,' Paul said. 'You've driven us all this way, you deserve a proper cup of tea.'

Jim walked into the bathroom to fill the kettle up. As the water poured, he grabbed a glass from the shelf. Then he moved back into the bedroom to place the kettle on its base. He flicked the switch to turn it on and then turned around to ask Jane how she took her tea, when he was halted. He suddenly felt completely out of place as he witnessed Jane and Paul locked in an embrace on the edge of the bed.

Wishing he could disappear, he focussed back on the tea making task. He carefully set the glass down next to the cups, taking his time to place it very neatly. Then he started to fiddle with the tea bags, slowly placing them one by one in the cups and glass. He then picked up one of the two tea spoons and he examined it for cleanliness. It was spotless, but he spent a few seconds double-checking, just in case; just for something to do.

Now really not sure what to do with himself, Jim pulled out the chair from the desk next to him and he sat down. They needed to get on with saving the Malancy and he needed this loving exchange in front of him to stop.

'What's going on then, Jane?' he suddenly asked, desperate to get back to the issue at hand.

Paul and Jane broke apart and Jane turned to Jim. Jim noted the pair were still holding hands but he tried to concentrate on Jane's face. She was clearly searching her mind for where to start and Jim could see how sad she looked.

'You need to know, I haven't meant to cause anyone any harm,' she started. 'I didn't want to be a part of any of this. I had no choice.'

'It's fine, Jane,' Paul soothed, squeezing her hand. 'Tell us what happened. Were you kidnapped like Beth?'

'It's probably easiest if I start from the start. It's all such a mess. I don't know what we're going to do.' Jim had never seen Jane looking so broken. She was always so professional, so precise. Whatever had happened had clearly knocked her about.

'Take it a step at a time, sweetheart,' Paul said.

Jane took a deep breath. Then she looked to Paul. 'We need to tell Jim everything. Is that okay with you?'

'Of course,' Paul said, kissing Jane on the head. 'Whatever you think is best.'

'Okay,' Jane breathed. Then she turned to Jim. 'Three weeks ago, just after Simon and Beth got married, Paul and I spent a few days together in the Lake District. Romantically.'

Jim just nodded, trying not to react. Part of him didn't want to know about this at all, then on the flipside he had about a million questions. Although none of them seemed relevant at that moment in time.

'I got back to work on the Tuesday and I was on top of the world. Then, when I went out for lunch, Damien just appeared out of nowhere. I was shocked. I thought he was locked up.'

'You weren't part of letting him out, then?' Jim asked.

'I had no idea. He pulled me aside and said that I had to help them. He said George Malant needed my help and if I didn't go willingly then they were going to tell my husband about my affair with Paul.'

The kettle clicked off and Jim immediately stood up. He felt a sudden bolt of anger. There they were trying to save the future of the Malancy whereas Jane was clearly just trying to save her marriage. She only had herself to blame, gallivanting around the country with another man. How could she be so careless, so selfish?

Jim focussed his attention on the tea making as Paul carried on questioning Jane. 'They knew about the Lake District?'

'I have no clue how,' Jane replied.

'I'm so sorry. We're so stupid.'

'It's very clear that you are,' Jim suddenly said. He threw tea bags into the bin and glared at Jane. 'How can you put the future of the Malancy at risk just to save your marriage?'

Jim slopped milk into the cups and glass, visibly annoyed. He picked up the drinks, not caring to be that steady, and then he thrust the glass into Paul's hand and a cup into Jane's. Then he sat back down, ready for answers.

'It's not as simple as that, Jim,' Jane explained. 'If it was, I'd gladly give up my marriage to save anything.'

'Then tell me, what's more important than saving the Malancy?' Jim asked.

'Saving my sister!' Jane threw back at him.

'It's okay, Jane,' Paul soothed, squeezing her hand again.

'Your sister?' Jim asked as his mood softened. Maybe he had been a bit hasty with his assumptions.

'Yes.' Jane replied. She turned to Paul before saying anymore and he seemed to nod his consent. Then she said, 'About twenty years ago, I was training to be in the police. The normal police, nothing to do with the Malancy. There I met Darren, my now husband. I knew he liked me but I wasn't really that interested. We were friends, though. Then I found out about a job on the law enforcement team at Malancy HQ and my head was turned. I was so excited. I quit police training and started working straight away with the Malancy. It suited me extremely well.'

'It was at a Malancy charity ball one night that I met Jane,' Paul said.

'Even before Bird Consultants, Paul always had his hands in everything. So we met, fell pretty much straight away in love, and within a few months we were ready to get married.'

'I proposed to her in Paris. A little clichéd, but we loved it.' Paul and Jane shared a loving look and Jim felt awkward again.

'Then it all fell apart,' Jane said, the atmosphere instantly tensing. 'My sister was involved in a hit and run. She's not a bad person, she wasn't drunk or anything, she was just young, very young, and she didn't know what to do. She should have stopped, but she didn't. The victim pulled through, and although he'd suffered from quite a few injuries, there was no long term damage. No one but Lily at the time knew she was involved. That's when I had the visit from Darren.'

'What did it have to do with him?' Jim asked.

'Being a Malant means he's always one step ahead of everyone else in his team. He found out that there was a CCTV camera right near where the incident had happened and he knew Lily was driving.'

'So?' Jim said.

'To cut a long story short, Darren said that if I married him instead of Paul then he'd make the footage disappear along with anything else they had on Lily. Basically, if I married him then Lily would be fine. He'd make sure of it.'

'What?' Jim asked, shocked.

'He's been holding it over her ever since,' Paul explained.

'Lily is my little sister and I need to protect her. I know what she did was wrong, and I'm supposed to uphold the law and all that, but it was just an accident. She didn't mean any harm and I know she's been looking out for the victim ever since, magicking a few good deeds his way. He's doing really well from what I hear and it all happened so long ago. But it doesn't seem to matter, I know Darren will make sure they push for the toughest sentence possible. He's got a hell of a lot more power now. He's climbed up the ranks at a great pace. I don't know what he's really got in that file. Who knows how much of the truth has been twisted over the years, but he'll make sure she goes to jail; I know he will. He'll find a way. She won't get a fair hearing and I can't let that happen.'

'I don't get how he has this power over you? Can't you just get rid of the file yourself?' Jim asked. 'You're powerful Malants, both of you. Surely together you could outwit him.'

'How are you supposed to get rid of a file that's hidden so well you don't even know where to start?' Jane reasoned. 'Darren's very clever, he's made sure I'll never find it. You can't just do a location spell for paperwork. You know it doesn't work that way.'

'We're in love, Jim,' Paul stated. 'We wanted to – we still want to spend the rest of our lives together. That bastard has ruined everything. That's why I moved to the States. As soon as Simon was old enough, I had to get away. It hurt too much to be near Jane and know that I could never be with her.'

'And she's the reason you want to move back?' Jim asked, remembering what Paul had said last week.

'We've barely spoken in years. I thought I was dealing with it,' Paul said. 'Then Simon turned into a bird and I knew Jane was the only one that could help.'

'Seeing Simon and Beth so in love, seeing them get married, it brought it all home,' Jane said.

'We knew we had to find a way to be together,' Paul said. 'We decided that we needed to talk, to gather our thoughts. We had to see if we could find any way around this situation, so we took a few days away in the Lake

District.'

'I thought it was far enough away that it would be fine. And Darren hasn't mentioned Paul in years.'

'I spoke to him a couple of weeks ago,' Paul announced.

'You did what?!' Jane was clearly very unhappy.

'Things had got bad, very bad, and Simon was desperate for help. He asked me to call you at home. What could I say to him? How could I explain that I couldn't help him, that *we* couldn't help him? Anyway, I think it was for the best as it proved to Darren that I wasn't with you. I felt sick. I hate that bastard.'

'Oh God,' Jane sighed.

'Now you've escaped, won't they just tell Darren?' Jim asked.

'No, I don't think so. Not now. It's the only card they have.'

'What did they want you for?' Paul asked.

'To protect their secret. They knew that when Beth disappeared you'd turn to me. They knew I'd be able to dig deep enough to find out what was going on. I think they decided that it was more advantageous if, not only could you not get my help, but you actually believed that I was part of it all. Make life even more difficult for you.'

'How could they think that I'd ever doubt you?' Paul asked.

'You didn't?'

'Far from it, Jane,' Jim answered. 'He's been a wreck worrying about you. At least it now makes sense.'

Jane smiled at Paul and they kissed again. Jim was getting very fidgety now with this continuous love scene playing out in front of him.

'So do you know?' he interrupted. 'Do you know what's happened to Simon and Beth?'

Jane nodded. 'I know everything. That's why I know George and his team will be looking for me. I know why Beth was kidnapped, I know why they almost turned into birds and I know why they don't remember a thing about each other. The only thing I don't know is how the hell we're ever going to get them back together. Damien's really done his homework this time. I'm very scared that this could be it.'

TWELVE

Paul couldn't take his eyes off Jane. She was so beautiful. Even despite her clear weariness, he still couldn't believe how attractive she was.

The picture he always carried of her in his wallet had been taken about fifteen years ago, so the Jane that he'd got used to looking at was much younger. But when he'd placed his eyes on her again at Malancy HQ, when Simon had just turned into a bird and they were seeking help, he'd been lost for words as to how much her beauty had only increased with age. How did he ever think he could get over her?

Darren had ruined both of their lives. In every way, Paul viewed Jane as his soulmate. He'd met his perfect match but she'd been stolen away from him in a cruel and heartless manner. How was he ever supposed to move on? Of course, he'd met other women, plenty of them, but none of them had compared to Jane. She was the only person that he wanted to share his life with. It hadn't been a deliberate decision from the outset, but it had transpired over the years that if he couldn't have her then he didn't want anyone.

As worried as Paul was about Simon and Beth, and

about the future of the Malancy, he couldn't help but feel tinges of delight about being with Jane. They were together. That was all that he'd ever wanted. He couldn't let himself think about the future, even just one day ahead. He knew, all too soon, their time together would all be over with again. He just had to focus on the here and now and enjoy every second with her as it really was a blessing. Even if it had all come about in such terrible circumstances.

Although they'd hardly spoken in so many years, as Paul looked to the worry on Jane's face he knew what she was thinking. He knew there was no way that she'd want the Malancy to end. Getting that job on the Malancy law enforcement team had meant so much to her; it was her life. She was incredibly dedicated to the Malancy and Paul knew that it would break her heart to see it end.

'What's Damien been up to, then?' Jim asked.

'I hate to say it, but he's really excelled himself this time,' Jane replied. 'He showed everyone why he was worthy of the Sales Director role at Bird Consultants.'

'I don't know if I want to hear this,' Paul said.

'We know Simon and Beth have lost their memories. They don't seem to remember anything about the last three months,' Jim said.

'Has he found some way of doing the impossible?' Paul asked with a sickening dread. 'Has he found a way of using magic to change their thoughts?'

'No, you're quite right,' Jane said, 'that still remains impossible. But Damien, being Damien, has managed to find a loophole.'

'What sort of loophole?' Jim asked.

'He's used what he knows best. He's used a contract.'

'What?' Paul and Jim turned to each other with bewilderment.

'He had fifty Malants working on it around the clock. No stone was left unturned, trust me. They brainstormed every tiny detail, making sure any possible loose end or any angle that Simon could come up with to break the contract was neatly tied up. They sealed it so tightly. It's the biggest, most complex contract that I've ever seen.'

'What does it say?' Paul asked.

'Basically, when Beth signed the contract she set into play certain actions. The details are long and complicated, but it comes down to the fact that if and when the spell was cast to continue the Malancy, Beth signed to say, that with immediate effect, she wanted both herself and Simon to forget all about each other.'

'That's crazy!' Paul blurted out.

'I guess not,' Jim responded.

'Why would Beth sign that?'

'She didn't know what she was doing. I saw it all. They had a camera on Beth all the time, watching her every move. They kept her awake so she wouldn't have the dreams and know how to cast the spell, and it also served to completely wear her down. Damien was so cruel. He was so manipulative, you'd almost be in awe of it if it didn't make you sick.'

'He certainly convinced her of Simon's treachery,' Jim said.

'He played on all her fears and doubts but never actually committed to anything. He just kept putting words in her mouth and making her believe that it was all her own thoughts. It was despicable.'

'Did you see them kiss?' Paul suddenly asked.

'So Simon did see that?' Jane asked, to which Paul just nodded. 'Yes. It was just before Simon threw Damien across the room. I'll admit I did enjoy watching that. The kiss was all Damien, though. Beth barely seemed to notice he was there. She was so drowsy, she couldn't stop crying.'

'So what did he say to her to get her to sign the contract?' Jim asked.

'She didn't even have chance to read it. Damien told her that George was going to kill her and this contract was the only thing that could save her life; but she only had seconds to sign it as he was on to them. She was already confused because of the lack of sleep, then to be told her life was in danger. She really thought it was a life or death situation.'

'Bastard,' Paul hissed.

'I don't suppose we have much choice now but to tell Simon,' Jim said. 'If there's a contract involved-'

'No, you can't. It gets far more complicated,' Jane warned.

'What else?' Paul asked, dreading the answer.

'The contract stated that Beth wanted her memories of Simon to be wiped away. It did give reasons as to why, but I didn't get chance to look at it closely. Then it was layered with small print. I'm sure you've noticed that Beth and Simon are still fully aware of each other, it's only their relationship that's been tampered with.'

'Yes, another weird part of it,' Paul confirmed.

'That's because the contract stated that Beth didn't want to completely wipe Simon from her mind. Instead she apparently just wanted to forget anything good about him. She wanted to forget that she loved him, she wanted to forget all the time that they'd spent together, that they were married, and anything else even remotely positive. And it would be exactly the same for Simon. Then a very small clause was added to Beth's memory loss. One that she apparently felt was absolutely vital.'

'A clause?' Paul asked, again fearing the answer.

'Upon signing the contract Beth instructed that she forget all the good things about Simon, but she also instructed that she wholly remember all the bad things. She wanted to remember, with absolute clarity, all of the awful rumours about Simon and the terrible things that people have said about him.'

'What?' Jim was shocked.

'More than that, she wanted the awful things that stuck in her mind to be magnified. She basically determined that she would not only dislike Simon, but she'd actually fear him.'

'Sorry, I can't get my head around this,' Paul stated with disbelief. 'Are you telling me that Beth not only no longer remembers loving Simon, but she's actually scared of him?'

'Terrified. You know the rumours. He's portrayed as a cold-hearted killer with serious social issues.'

'Thanks to my brother,' Jim said.

'Why has Damien done all that?' Paul asked, shaking his head. 'How low can one person go?'

'It's not just about being cruel,' Jim replied. 'You're right, Jane, he's thought it through this time. Just forgetting Simon would still mean that they could fall in love again. But if she wakes up hating him, then you've pretty much eradicated any chance of them ever getting back together.'

'Because if Beth never encourages him, Simon will never think of her in a romantic way,' Paul muttered as the pieces slotted into place. 'He pushes everyone away. Beth's the only person who has ever changed that.'

'So if we tell Simon the truth, we run the risk of him trying to get Beth back and then scaring her off even more,' Jim said.

'Scaring her off for good,' Jane finished.

'I really think we need to tell him,' Paul said.

'He'll go mad, Paul. You know he will,' Jim said. 'This is more than just about losing everything, this is about someone trying to control their relationship. He'll want to kill Damien for starters, and we don't know what Damien has already said to Beth. We need to stay one step ahead here and telling Simon will open up a huge can of worms that could cost us everything.'

'Then what are we going to do?' Paul asked. 'Without Simon, we have no chance of breaking the contract.'

The three of them fell silent as they contemplated their options.

'I need to sleep on this,' Jim said, rubbing his eyes.

'This has been a lot to take in and it's been a long day.' Paul glanced at the clock at the bottom of the television and he saw it was just after ten pm. 'I'm going to go and get myself a room.'

'I'm paying for it,' Paul interjected. 'I'll sort it out with you tomorrow.'

'That's very kind of you,' Jim replied. 'I don't think I'll sleep, but maybe we'll all have clearer heads in the morning. I'll see you at breakfast. Eight o'clock?'

'Perfect. Just get some rest.'

As soon as Jim left, Paul turned to Jane. She was still sitting next to him on the bed. He gently brushed her hair away from her face with his fingers so that he could properly see her. She looked so tired and so afraid. He kissed her gently on the lips. 'Are you okay?' he asked.

'I've been better. I really hope we can sort this out.'

'You're not alone there.'

'Not just to save the Malancy, either. I can't believe this has happened to Simon and Beth. I've never seen a couple so happy, so in love. I hate to see them kept apart like this.'

'The way we are?' Paul whispered.

'No one deserves the misery we've had.' Jane looked deep into Paul's eyes. 'Not one day has gone by when I haven't thought of you.'

'Same here. Every day for years. You have to know that I'll never stop thinking about you.'

'So many times I've questioned if we've-'

'She's your sister,' Paul insisted. 'When it comes to family, I understand very well about making sacrifices. Even more so in recent days.'

'Why doesn't it feel right, though? How can it be that we feel like we've lost, no matter what we do?'

'I don't know, Jane. I wish I knew. I wish I had more answers. I know I love you, though.' Paul kissed her again.

Jane then took a moment to look at his face. She skimmed her fingers across his cheeks, his lips, his forehead, like she was studying him, trying to commit every pore to memory.

'I love you too,' she whispered after a few moments. How Paul needed to hear those words. At the moment they left her lips he felt a bolt of desire shoot through him.

He kissed her again, this time more passionately. He gently pushed her towards the bed and their kissing grew in intensity.

Before they knew it, they were both removing each other's clothes and exploring each other's bodies. With such tenderness and so much longing, they smoothly interlocked and made love. Nothing felt more natural for both of them and they both held on to every moment as if it could be their last.

When they'd both climaxed, Jane curled up next to Paul and he wrapped his arm around her. He felt so in love. He thought back over the years that he'd had without her, praying to have a moment just like this one. There had been occasions when he'd wished that he'd never met her, and that he'd never had to endure such heartache. At that very moment, though, he knew that he was honoured to have known such a love. No matter what had happened over the years or what would happen in time to come, he knew, with no doubt, that their love would last forever. There was no escaping it.

Then a realisation hit him. He sat up straight and Jane turned to look at him. 'Are you okay?' she asked.

'Damien's contract. It only stated that Beth and Simon lose their memories. Good, bad, whatever, just memories, though.'

'What are you getting at?' Jane queried.

'Because that's all it could say. In effect, we do this sort of thing all the time at work. We're always changing situations to persuade people to think in a different way. But that's all we ever do. We just change the way people perceive things, we never - in fact we can't - actually change the way someone feels about something. We change fact not emotion.'

'So?'

'We change what's in the head not what's in the heart. That's where the limits are, even for Damien.' Paul shifted to address Jane directly as he saw a glimmer of hope. 'The contract might have persuaded Beth that Simon is scary, and Simon is naturally too afraid himself to get involved with anyone, but it can't have stopped them loving each other. I mean, nothing about them has actually changed. In every way they're still the same people; the same people that they both fell in love with. All we need to do is persuade them differently. If we can change their minds in a different way, I bet we could overcome the contract.'

'What are you suggesting we tell them?'

'Nothing. That's the point. We need this to be natural. Jim might be right, they're too emotionally involved to handle the truth, or any sort of truth. But if they don't know the difference and they just fall in love, for what they believe is the first time...'

'So we're not going to tell them anything?'

'No. We just need to subtly push them together until they start to realise their feelings again.'

'What if Damien's thought about that?'

'What if he has? He can't do anything to change how they actually feel about each other. It's impossible. All he's been able to do is change how they remember each other.'

'But Beth is terrified of Simon and Simon's terrified of getting close to anyone.'

'I've seen them together, Jane. It's still there. They still look each other up and down, they still have that glint in their eyes. It only needs a gentle push. All we have to do is remind them of how compatible they are. They may never get their memories back, but if they can fall in love again, if they can get married again. If they can start a family.'

'But what if Beth becomes even more terrified of Simon. It could push her away even further.'

'It's only rumours and negative gossip fuelling her fear,

none of it's based on fact. If we show her the real Simon, the man that's so different to the hearsay, I'm sure it will start her questioning things. You can't be scared of something that's not scary.'

'I suppose. But we'd have to be careful. You know I like Simon, but he can be cold at times. He keeps people at a distance.'

'I know. I wish I knew how Beth had got round him in the first place.'

'That's it!' Jane's face lit up.

'What do you mean?'

'They've already done this. They've already met and fallen in love, all on their own. Nobody else interacted with them. In fact, quite the opposite, George and his gang were already trying to keep them apart. They beat the odds once, so all we need to do is encourage history to repeat itself. Whatever they did the first time around, when Simon was CEO and Beth was junior admin, something made them feel a connection. Beth fought the rumours once and Simon let her in. All we need to do is get them to do it all over again. How did they meet?'

'In the office.'

'No, but how? How often do admin girls rub shoulders with the CEO? Something must have happened; a catalyst must have thrown them together and got them talking.'

'I don't know. Simon just said they met at work.'

'Oh you boys never gossip. See how dangerous it is!'

Then a spark of genius hit Paul. 'Boys don't, but girls do. I know how we can find out. We're heading back to London tomorrow and we're going to get Simon and Beth back together!'

* * *

Being a bodyguard wasn't quite as exciting as Toby had imagined. He'd waited around all day while Beth sat in the office, then he'd followed her home, which took all of ten minutes, and now she was in her flat and hadn't moved all night. Talk about boring!

He was sitting by the window in his own flat, opposite Beth's, desperately waiting for something interesting to happen. The highlight of his day had been finding some new games to play on his phone. Surely it had to get better?

At that moment, being unemployed and living back with his parents again was starting to seem like the better option. He thought this was a huge opportunity to escape all that and start afresh, but he was seriously questioning how much more of this boredom he could take.

He didn't want to seem ungrateful, he was being paid extremely well for this gig, but so far it had turned out to be mind-numbingly dull.

His thoughts of how long he'd give it before telling Jim where to stick the job were cut short when a car suddenly pulled up on the opposite side of the road. A tall, smartly dressed man stepped out and he walked towards the front door to Beth's block of flats. This wasn't the first person that night to approach the front door, but Toby grabbed his binoculars anyway, praying that this might at last be someone of interest.

And, at last, it was! He watched the man press a buzzer and, although he couldn't be sure it was flat two, he'd definitely pressed the top row of numbers. Toby, at least, had to check this out. Finally, the potential for some action!

With a thrill energising him, he swiftly grabbed his keys and raced out his flat. He jogged across the road and, within a minute, he was at the man's side.

'Hello,' a female voice said through the intercom with caution. Could that be Beth?

'Sorry, love,' Toby said, jumping in before the strange man could say anything. 'Think I might have the wrong flat. Are you flat three?'

'No, flat two,' the female voice replied. Yes! It was

Beth!

'Sorry to bother you then.'

'No problem,' the female voice answered.

'What do you think you're doing?' the stranger demanded to know.

'Who are you?' Toby asked, forcefully leading the man away from the front of the building.

'None of your business.'

'Are you looking for Beth?'

'What has it got to do with you?'

'Beth's under my protection now. So unless you give me a very good reason why you need to see her, I'll have to insist you leave.'

'How dare you!'

'Thirty seconds and counting,' Toby warned, standing up tall to show he meant business.

The man went to argue, but then he stopped. He glared at Toby for a few seconds and then turned away. He headed straight back to his car and quickly drove off.

Toby felt a rush of excitement. Maybe being a bodyguard wasn't so bad after all.

THIRTEEN

Early the next morning, straight after breakfast, Paul, Jim and Jane all piled into the Lexus and they headed back down south. It took them just over five hours to make the journey, and by the time they reached Simon's house in Buckinghamshire, Paul was itching to get on with his plan.

After quickly settling Jane into her temporary new home, he grabbed a slice of toast for lunch before jumping back in the Lexus. He then made his way straight to the Bird Consultants office.

Not half an hour later, he was entering the reception. Margaret greeted him with a warm welcome, but he barely noticed, he was far too focussed on what he needed to do. He headed straight to the lift, pressing for the ninth floor, ready to officially start mission "get Simon and Beth back together".

Reaching floor nine, he made a beeline straight for Gayle's office. He glanced quickly across at Beth sitting at her desk. This wasn't where she belonged. This was all so wrong. This plan had to work.

'You got a second?' Paul asked, closing the door behind him.

Gayle looked up from her typing, a little surprised.

'Hello stranger. I've always got a second for you.'

Paul looked out across the office floor. He knew what he had to do, but he hadn't really thought it through in any depth. Seeing so many people about and considering the sensitive nature of what he was about to tell Gayle, he suddenly felt concerned about how unpredictable her reaction could be. He thought maybe it might be better to go somewhere a little more private. 'Will you join me in the boardroom?' he asked.

'Now?'

'Is that okay?'

'Of course.'

Gayle picked up a notepad and pen and followed Paul to the lifts. They made their way to the first floor and headed straight into the boardroom, with Paul firmly shutting the door behind them once they'd entered.

They sat down at the far end of the room and Gayle poised herself ready to take notes.

Paul had spent so much time thinking about how this plan would get Simon and Beth back together, but he hadn't once considered how he was going to talk to Gayle. He suddenly didn't know where to start. Best to take it a step at a time, he thought.

'It's about Beth and my nephew, Simon,' he began.

'Okay,' Gayle said, clearly not expecting this.

'I take it you know they're married?'

Gayle hesitated. 'Yes.'

'Has Beth said anything to you about that in the past few days?'

Gayle thought carefully before responding. 'She told me and the girls that she couldn't remember marrying him. I think she's under the impression that the marriage has be annulled.'

'It most definitely has not!'

'Okay.'

Paul took a breath. 'You've been Admin Manager for a few weeks now, haven't you?'

'Yes, about a month.'

'So you've had your knowledge escalated?'

'What do you mean?'

'Gus is your manager, right?'

'Yes.'

'So you've sat with Gus and he's taken you through the next steps. He's escalated your knowledge.' Paul could tell that Gayle was deeply confused. 'Surely he has?'

'Knowledge of what? You mean me having more responsibility?'

'No, the Malancy.'

'The what?'

Paul couldn't help but feel a little peeved as he realised that even though Gayle was now a manager of the company she knew nothing of the Malancy. What had Gus been playing at? How was she meant to do her job properly without an escalated understanding of what the company really did? Of course she would only be on knowledge level one, but it was vital that she have some appreciation for the true nature of Bird Consultants. He most definitely had to speak to Simon about this. This was not acceptable.

But that would have to wait. Paul had quite a lot to deal with at that moment and Gus's inability to do his job properly was way down the priority list. Even though it now meant that Paul's current task in hand was going to be even harder than he'd anticipated. Now he'd have to do everything himself.

As the founder of Bird Consultants, Paul had escalated the knowledge of many employees over the years, but this was going to be different. When he'd first thought of bringing Gayle into his mission, he'd immediately assumed that she was in the know. He'd taken it for granted that she'd already come to terms with the Malancy and that she'd had time digest what it was all about. That way telling her about Simon and Beth would have made so much more sense.

Now he was going to have to tell Gayle everything, and fast. And he'd have to make sure that she not only believed him, but she was in a fit state to help him. He needed her help to eliminate a major problem that was threatening the future of the magical community that she was yet to learn even existed. This was going to be overwhelming for both of them.

'Right,' he said, knowing there was no way now to soften the blow. He had to just come out with it all. 'What I'm about to tell you might come as a shock. You should have already been told some of this, and I'm really sorry that hasn't happened. I'll look into why, but for now you're going to have to listen.'

'All right,' Gayle said with a hint of concern in her voice.

'Myself, Simon and all the other directors of this company are different. We're what are known as Malants.' Gayle just stared at him blankly. 'We're part of a group of people known as the Malancy.'

'Do you mean like an official body or something?'

'No, it's not an organisation, it's something you're born into. It started off with a very powerful couple five hundred years ago. It's hard to explain. In fact, I'm not sure even I know the full story myself anymore. But basically, they had magical powers and they've passed these powers on through generations ever since.'

'Magical powers? Is this a joke?'

'Far from it, Gayle. I have never been more serious.'

'I don't know what you're talking about.'

'I know it sounds strange, but we have actual magical powers.'

'What does that even mean?'

'Myself and virtually every other Malant alive can only use our magic through the power of another item. We call them elements. It could be anything, as long as it's not manmade. So, for example, we could touch a tree or pick up a stone from the ground and we can utilise the strength of that element to cast a spell.'

'What?' Gayle looked utterly stupefied.

'The only Malant who is different is Simon. He was born with a different power; he can do magic all by himself. It runs through him. He's the most powerful man ever to be born. That's why people fear him, they can feel the energy oozing out from him and it scares them.'

Gayle rubbed her head. 'You know I think a lot of you, Paul, but this is ridiculous. Is this some sort of wind up?'

Paul sighed. He hadn't got time to walk her through it stage by stage as normal. He had so much more to tell her. Then it occurred to him that seeing was believing. He looked around the boardroom and saw a plant in the corner.

'I'll show you,' he said, walking over to the dracaena by the window. He touched the plant and went to close his eyes when he realised he felt nothing. There was no power in it. Or maybe there was no power in him. Maybe the Malancy was over. Maybe it was all too late.

Panicking a little, he knew there was only one option. He grabbed his mobile from his pocket and called Simon.

'Hi mate, can you pop down to the boardroom please... I need your help with something... No, now... It's urgent Simon, I need you now. Good.'

Paul walked back to his seat. 'Give me five minutes and I'll show you just what the Malancy is all about. If I still can.'

Gayle just nodded, not at all trying to hide the disbelief from her face.

Neither of them spoke as they waited, and the few minutes it took Simon to reach them dragged on forever.

Finally the boardroom door opened and Simon stepped in. He immediately hesitated when he saw Gayle, then he turned to Paul. 'How can I help?'

'I'm in the process of escalating Gayle's knowledge and I need you to do a little demonstration.'

Simon glared at his uncle. Paul knew this was far from

standard procedure and he had no reasonable explanation as to why he was asking Simon to do this; not without revealing the dreaded truth. But it was tough luck.

'Are you serious?' Simon asked.

'Do I look like I'm joking?' Paul was determined to stay strong.

Simon then turned to Gayle. 'I'm not sure we've met?'

'She's our new Admin Manager. Replacing Trisha,' Paul replied.

'When did Trisha leave?'

'It doesn't matter. I need to escalate Gayle's knowledge, and I need to do it now.'

'Surely Gus should be doing that?'

'You'd think, and we need to talk about exactly why he hasn't, but for now I'm stuck doing it.'

'What's the urgency? This is quite peculiar.'

Paul knew Simon had every right to ask these questions and he felt awful for not being able to give his nephew a straight answer. Without being able to justify his actions, though, all Paul had left was to be irrationally demanding. He hated it, but it was for the greater good. It was for Simon's own good.

'Just do as you're told,' Paul snapped. 'Spin the chair, pick up the table, I really don't give a shit what you do, but Gayle needs a little encouragement. And we need to do it now.'

Paul felt the daggers shoot across from Simon's icy glare. There was no way Paul would ever normally speak to his nephew like that in front of an employee, but they were in desperate times. Perhaps even more so now as he felt niggled by the worry that the plant hadn't been powerful. What if the Malancy was really all over with? Why couldn't Simon just get on with it?

Simon took a deep breath. 'If you say it's that important,' he simply said, then he turned his attention to a chair at the other end of the room. Paul knew he wasn't happy, but they could deal with all that later. At least he was finally complying.

Within seconds the chair lifted high into the air and Paul sighed with relief. Simon spun it around a few times quickly, with just his mind, and then he set it carefully back down in its original place.

'Will that be all?' he asked, once again glaring at Paul.

'Thank you, Si. You did good.'

Simon turned his glare to Gayle and then he left. Paul exhaled, that hadn't been pleasant for anyone. He focussed his attention back towards Gayle, immediately seeing how ghostly pale she'd become.

'How did he do that?' she asked.

'We're Malants. We're magical people. We can do all sorts of things. And that's what Bird Consultants is all about. We work with companies who have issues that can't easily be solved. They pay us very generously to magically take away their problems, whatever they might be. Think about everything you've ever known since working here. It does make sense, doesn't it?'

Gayle remained silent for a few moments and Paul could tell she was thinking things through. Then she said, 'Okay, I'll play along. It seems utterly crazy, but you've got my attention.'

'Thank you, Gayle. Just keep thinking it through. It all does make sense. This is all the truth.' Gayle just nodded. 'So I told you that Simon is the most powerful Malant ever to live. As you've just seen, he can move objects with only his mind. I can't. Nor can any other Malant. Except one.'

'Who?' Then it clicked with Gayle. 'You don't mean Beth?'

'We've always thought that Simon was cursed somehow. He had incredible power but it meant that no one could ever get close to him. I'm sure you've heard the rumours about him and felt the coldness in his presence.' Paul stopped for a second as something suddenly dawned on him. 'Although that seems to have changed in the past week.'

'Yes, he's... an intimidating man.'

'I think you mean he scares the crap out of everyone.'

'I wouldn't-'

'I know what goes on, Gayle. But there are solid reasons why. Reasons that I found out about just last week. Simon was born for a purpose. He was a chosen being that was born with extra strength so that he can cast a spell to continue the future of the Malancy.'

'What?' Gayle was shaking her head with confusion.

'Just stick with me. There was one other chosen one born. Someone who he was destined to be with; destined to love.'

'Beth?'

'We've only just found out that she's a Malant. Her parents hid away her powers so that she was protected.'

'Protected from Mr Bird?'

'No. No! They're in love. They're so good together. No, her parents wanted to protect her from the people who wanted to stop them casting the spell. Some people want the Malancy to end.'

'Why would they want to do that?'

'It's such a long story. All you need to know is that Simon and Beth cast the spell successfully. But it wasn't enough. There's one more thing they need to do.'

'Hang on, tell me about this spell again.'

'The Malancy would have ended if Simon and Beth hadn't cast a spell together. But that was only part one.'

'So what's part two?'

'They don't know this. No one knows this. I'll tell you because I need your help, but you have to keep this a secret. In fact, keep all of this a secret. I'm supposed to get you to sign a contract, but I trust you Gayle. Do you trust me?'

Gayle looked away for a second. Then she said, 'I can't believe I'm saying this, but yes. This is all too crazy to be made up. I can tell you're not lying.'

'Thank you.'

'Go on then, what else do they need to do?'

'Have a baby.'

'What?'

'They need to conceive their first child - the first of the new line of Malants - in one year of the spell being cast or the Malancy will end forever.'

'What? Bloody hell, Paul! Please tell me you're making all of this up.'

'I wish.'

'So what's the problem? Can they not have children? Is that why they've spilt up? Hang on, no. When Beth came in last week and moved back downstairs, she seemed properly scared by Mr Bird. How does that make sense?'

'This is why I need your help. This is the crux of it all. Someone has made Beth and Simon forget all about each other. No, it's more complicated than that. Beth can't remember loving Simon, she only remembers the horrible things that people have said about him. Like where someone might have told her that Simon is a killer...' Gayle looked at Paul awkwardly. 'It's all right, I know what people say about my nephew.'

'So this someone has done this so they'll split up and then not have children?'

'Basically,' Paul nodded.

Gayle chewed on the facts again. 'I suppose it explains Beth's sudden change of heart about Mr Bird. It was so out of the blue. I knew it didn't make sense.' Gayle addressed Paul directly. 'So you want me to help stop the rumours?'

'No... Well actually that won't do any harm. Probably a lot of good.'

'Diane's the worst. She keeps filling Beth's head with so much crap about how Mr Bird must have drugged her and-.'

'What!' Paul felt his blood pressure soar. 'How dare she! Who does she think pays her salary?'

'Calm down, Paul. I'll deal with her. I'll make sure this

is all nipped in the bud.'

'You can't tell her any of this.'

'No, I won't. I'll just play her at her own game. I'll tell her that Mr Bird has hidden a microphone in the office. That'll soon shut her up.'

'Simon would never do that.'

'He also doesn't drink blood, I'm guessing. Doesn't stop Diane.'

'Drink blood?'

'I think she's a closet devil worshipper, I wouldn't take it personally.'

'I had no idea. I'm glad you're going to be taking care of her. Thank you. But there's something else I need you to do as well.'

'Do you want me to talk to Beth?'

'No! She'll never believe it. It could scare her off even more. No, we need to go back to basics. I realised last night that all this spell could have done is wipe away their memories. It couldn't have changed how they feel about each other; no Malant has that power, not even Simon. All it's done is made them both forget that they ever had loving feelings for one another; but the feelings must still be there. So all we need to do is reconnect them so they fall in love all over again.'

'How do I fit into that?'

'Do you know how they first met? Do you know what first brought them together? Jim confirmed that Simon used to go and visit Beth in the pub after work, but something must have happened before that; something that got them speaking in the first place.'

'Who's Jim?'

'Simon's butler. Well, he was his butler. It's complicated.'

Gayle raised her eyebrows. 'How the other half live, eh.'

'Watch it, I'm part of that other half you know.'

'Do you have a butler?'

'No. But Jim is far more than a butler. Jim is Simon's saviour, trust me.'

'Okay. I won't judge.'

'Do you know how they first met? Were you there or did Beth ever tell you?'

Gayle took a moment to think. 'The first time I ever saw them talking was when he came to ask for teabags. I'll never forget it. We'd never even heard his voice yet he was chatting to Beth like he'd known her for years. I suppose I should have known then something was going on between them.'

'But when did they first meet?'

'Tea!' Gayle suddenly said. 'It was all related to tea. She said she'd made him a cuppa. They must have met in the kitchen.'

Paul smiled. 'That's so Beth. I bet she saw him fumbling with a teabag and she couldn't resist taking over.'

'So we get her to make him another cup of tea?'

'We need to get them alone in the kitchen again and we need to let history repeat itself.'

Gayle looked at the clock on the wall. 'We'll all be going home soon.'

'Okay, first thing tomorrow morning. No, when is it quietest in the kitchen?'

'Mid-morning, I suppose.'

'Right, mid-morning tomorrow, we're on.'

FOURTEEN

Damien practically skipped into the Malancy Headquarters first thing the next morning. He'd still been in bed when George had called him and had summoned him back in. It hadn't taken him long to get up and get ready, and now he was full of his own praise as he headed into George's office.

'Can't live without me, then?' he said, shutting the office door behind him. He saw Brian and Mr Taylor sitting opposite George, all looking quite cosy. He grabbed a chair from the back of the room and pulled it up next to Brian.

'Thanks for joining us,' George said.

'I knew you'd need me back.'

'Something unforeseen has happened and we thought you might be able to help,' Mr Taylor said.

'Shouldn't you be selling something?' Damien asked Brian.

'I'm doing just that as far as anyone knows,' Brian replied.

'Mr Taylor went to pay Beth a visit last night,' George said.

'You lucky thing!' Damien smirked as he felt the stab of

jealousy.

'Someone's watching over her. I couldn't get past the doorbell. I don't know who he is, he just said that she was under his protection.'

'It's got James written all over it,' George stated.

'So what do you want from me? You want me to get rid of him?' Damien asked.

'First things first, we need to know who he is,' George replied.

'So we draw him out,' Damien said.

'How? The second any of us go near Beth, he'll escort us away. He's a big man,' Mr Taylor said.

'I can go near her anytime I like. I work with her,' Brian said.

'A work meeting! That's what we need,' Damien said.

'What good is that going to do?' George asked.

'An off site work meeting. Brian could take Beth and meet me somewhere. This bodyguard man is bound to follow and then we can flush him out; find out more about him. Everyone has weaknesses.'

'What sort of meeting requires just the Sales and Admin Directors?' Mr Taylor asked, cynically.

'A fake one,' Damien dryly stated. 'I don't know, a sales meeting where they need someone to take the minutes.'

'Admin Directors don't take minutes,' Mr Taylor responded.

'Not real Admin Directors, no,' Damien said. 'But Beth hasn't got a clue what she's doing. She won't question it. Not at all. Especially if we make it out to be a top priority and super important meeting. She loves all that crap.'

'I'm on board with that,' Brain enthused.

'Just hang on, though,' Damien added. 'If I help with this and get you intelligence on this bodyguard, what do I get in return? Or are you just going to fling me out again when you're done with me?'

'Fair question,' George said. 'Okay, if you help us to overcome this new issue and you ensure that Simon and

Beth never get back together, I'll look out for you. How about when the Malancy has ended once and for all, I promise you a job for life with the aftermath support group. You can be Chief Consultant or something. Does that suit?'

'I want a contract. I want it next time I'm here. Then I might tell you about this bodyguard.'

'Fine. You've got yourself a deal. Right, you two, get to it,' George said to Damien and Brian. 'I want this threat gone and I want it gone yesterday.'

'Yes sir!' Damien smirked, standing up.

'When can I get a replacement phone?' Brian asked.

'I'm working on it. I've got a lot on my plate at the minute. Oh that's another thing, Damien,' George added.

'What?'

'Jane's escaped.'

'Escaped? From Scotland?'

'She played us, then she took one of the cars and vanished.'

'Haven't you done a location spell?' Damien asked.

'Of course, but someone's blocked her. That can only mean one thing.'

'I told you those Birds are trouble. Are you going to tell her husband?'

'Not yet. That's the only leverage we have. For now just keep an eye out, all of you. Jane must have made contact and so we have to assume that they now know about the contract. It's well hidden, we don't need to worry about that, but our advantage has weakened.'

'Don't worry,' Damien declared, 'hell will freeze over before any of that family get one over me again.'

* * *

Simon sat in his office feeling utterly downbeat. The night before had been particularly difficult. There was a new addition to his household and for some reason he felt very bitter about it.

He justified his sourness as a reaction to Paul keeping him in the dark about what was really going on. Simon hadn't got a clue as to why Jane was now living with them, what had happened to her husband, and why he'd had to do that reversed location spell. There was something massive going on, but Paul was refusing to share the truth. He just kept repeating that Simon had more important things to worry about.

Sitting on his own now, reflecting on the night before, Simon couldn't help but feel that something else was bothering him, though. He'd seen a new side to his uncle. Paul seemed happy, genuinely happy. He clearly loved Jane, and they'd not even attempted to downplay their feelings for one another. Kissing and cuddling and holding hands; all night long.

Simon didn't begrudge his uncle a single ounce of happiness, but seeing them together had unnerved Simon for reasons that he just couldn't fathom. He'd seen Paul with dozens of women, although none of them that he'd really cared about before. But there was something about seeing Paul and Jane together all loved up that left Simon winded.

He'd become so uneasy with the situation that he'd opted to have an early night and he'd worked on two contracts in bed. Even then he'd found it hard to concentrate. Why did this bother him so much?

He needed to get away. Forget what Paul said, he'd just have to go back to New York on his own. Even just for a week. He needed that clarity of thought and he needed it badly.

Simon was suddenly pulled from his thoughts when his office door opened and Paul breezed in.

'Morning Si! You okay today?'

'Yes.'

'You left so early this morning.'

'I had work to do and I thought you'd probably want to

spend time with Jane.'

'We had a nice breakfast, thank you. But I'm here now.'

'Good. I need to speak to you about something. About those jobs in Scotland.'

'Scotland?' Paul asked, but Simon could tell that he was already distracted, looking at his watch.

'Yes, the fifty million ones.'

'Of course,' Paul nodded, but Simon knew he wasn't really listening. 'Let's walk and talk, shall we?'

'Walk where?'

'I need a cup of tea, don't you?'

'I've just had one.'

'If you want me to listen, then join me in a cuppa. I promise, I'll be all ears.'

Simon sighed, then he stood up. 'All right.'

The pair left his office and Simon made sure he locked it behind him. They walked across the Executive Floor and headed to the lifts.

'What do you know about these jobs?' Simon asked.

'What jobs?' Paul replied.

'The ones I've just been talking about!' Simon was becoming frustrated.

The lift doors opened and Paul pressed for the ninth floor.

'I like tea, don't you?' Paul stated as the lift started to move.

'What are you talking about? Can we talk about Scotland?'

'Scotland?'

The lift doors pinged open again and Paul headed straight for the kitchen. Simon noticed a little urgency in his footsteps, it was most peculiar. He followed his uncle into the kitchen, only to stop in his tracks when he saw Beth and that other woman that Paul had been speaking with yesterday. Gayle; yes, Gayle.

Beth was just popping a teabag into her mug when she locked her eyes directly onto Simon. The pair of them just glared at one another for a few moments and it took Simon's breath away.

He didn't know why but this girl mesmerised him. It was as if she'd cast a spell over him and he was at her mercy. He'd never felt like that before and he really didn't like it.

Forcing himself to reject any warm feelings that he might even possibly start to feel in the presence of this girl, he stood in the corner. He didn't want a cup of tea. He'd already had three that day.

'Gayle!' Paul chimed.

'Look at that,' Gayle smirked. 'I was just thinking about you and here you are. I need to talk to you. Do you have a second?'

'Of course,' Paul nodded.

Simon felt his frustration increase as he watched his uncle place down the two mugs that he'd taken out from the cupboard and move over to the other corner of the room to speak to Gayle. She, he clearly had time for.

'Si, mate, would you be all right to make us a cuppa? I'm going to be a minute.'

Simon went to argue but Paul was already deep in conversation with Gayle. He didn't want to make a scene, therefore he was left with little choice but to make the drinks.

He watched Beth carry on with her tea-making and he hesitated before stepping over to where Paul had left the mugs. Directly next to Beth, you might know.

He slowly walked towards the mugs and he felt his heart start to pound. Trying to ignore Beth next to him, he opened the jar of teabags and placed one in each mug. What was going on? Why did she make him so on edge?

He couldn't look at her as she finished with the urn, but he could smell her alluring scent. It was driving him wild and he hated it.

He stepped over to pour hot water into the mugs himself, not daring to look as Beth went to get milk from the fridge. He knew she hadn't looked his way either. Not that that was unusual, no one ever engaged with Mr Bird.

Suddenly he heard a smash and Beth let out a tiny shriek. He looked down and saw tea and shattered mug all over the floor.

'I'm so sorry, Mr Bird,' she said with a look of horror in her eyes. 'I didn't even touch it. I don't know what happened.' He followed her gaze and saw that a few splashes had hit his perfectly polished black shoes.

'No problem, Miss Lance,' he said, really not bothered at all.

'We'll be back in a minute,' Paul shouted as he and Gayle suddenly left the kitchen. Simon felt even more frustrated. What was going on with his uncle today?

Simon turned back to see Beth grabbing the kitchen roll off the side and then she froze. After a second she slowly tore off a few sheets and again she hesitated. Then, slowly and cautiously, she held out the sheets for Simon.

He reached out to take the kitchen roll from her hand, and the instant his skin touched the paper, a spark of lust shot through him. It vanished as quickly as it came, and he tried to put it out of his mind as he curled the roll up in his hands. It was most unnerving. She was clearly bewitching him somehow and it had to stop.

He bent down to wipe his shoes and Beth grabbed a few more sheets to start cleaning up the floor. Then her mobile phone rang.

Beth grabbed her phone that she'd left on the kitchen side and answered it. 'Beth Lance... Oh hello... Of course. What, now? I'm in the middle of... I can't...'

'If you need to leave, please leave,' Simon said. 'I can clear the mess.' As the words left Simon's mouth, he couldn't quite believe that he'd said them.

'No...' Beth said to Simon, moving the phone away from her face.

'It's fine. Work must come first.'

'Are you sure?'

'Positive.'

Beth nodded and then she spoke back into her phone. 'I'll be there as soon as I can.'

Beth hung up and once again they locked eyes with each other. What was happening to him? Not only had he not felt anything even remotely caring towards a woman in a decade, he certainly didn't think the CEO should be mopping up spilt tea from the floor. But he found himself in new territory and he couldn't resist it. It was like something deep inside of him was controlling his emotions, not his head like normal.

'I'll just...' Beth fumbled.

'Please, Miss Lance, I insist. You clearly have a lot of work to do. It would be my pleasure to help.'

Beth hesitated. 'I do have to rush to a sales meeting. Are you sure?'

'It's fine.' Simon held out his hand for the kitchen roll and after another small hesitation Beth handed it to him. Again a lustful spark raced through him as their hands met through the paper. Then Beth, with clear urgency, dashed straight out of the kitchen.

Simon watched her leave, the kitchen roll firmly squeezed in his grip. The door shut behind her and he was alone. He felt a breeze of energy leave with her, like all that was left in her wake was an empty vacuum of isolation.

Simon was no stranger to being alone, but at that moment he'd never felt so lonely.

FIFTEEN

Beth quickly scuttled to her desk to pick up her bag and a notepad and then she turned straight back round towards the lifts.

'Where are you going?' Paul suddenly asked her, poking his head out from Gayle's office.

'I have a meeting to get to. Got to dash.'

'Where's Simon?'

'He's still in the kitchen.' Beth didn't know why, but Paul looked very displeased. She forced a smiled. 'See you later, I really have to go.' Then she raced to the lifts as quickly as she could.

The lifts were right near the entrance to the kitchen and Beth prayed that Mr Bird wouldn't come out. He made her shudder.

On the one hand he was absolutely gorgeous and when she looked at him she couldn't help but get lost in his velvet eyes like a giddy schoolgirl. But then she pulled herself together, remembering all the awful things that he'd done. She couldn't abide people with absolutely no morals. More than that, his behaviour was criminal. He was one of those that put himself above the law with his excellent contacts and sneaky ways. She despised him.

The lift finally pinged its arrival and she sighed with relief as she'd managed to evade him. She pressed for the ground floor and her mind thought to how Mr Bird had been so surprisingly kind to offer to clean the mess of the tea. Although, in reality, she didn't see why it was her duty, she hadn't knocked the tea over. She'd at first thought it was him, trying to keep her in her place. But then he'd looked as shocked as she was.

Why was he constantly so nice to her? He'd organised the moving of her computer downstairs and had not put up a single objection to her changing desks. And then, at that very moment, he was probably on his hands and knees wiping up tea from the kitchen floor just so she could get to a meeting.

It had to be a trick. It had to be his way of luring her back in again. He definitely had some power over her. The incredible wave of energy that had shot through her as he grabbed the kitchen roll from her hand had to be some force that he was casting over her. He was clearly trying to weaken her again so he could have his wicked way. But not this time! This time Beth would stay strong.

She got out the lift and walked across reception, her head held high. She refused to waste any more time thinking about that horrible man. She had a very important meeting to go to.

Beth headed out of the building and saw a silver Audi A5, just as promised, waiting for her at the end of the pathway. She strode straight towards it, saw Damien in the driving seat as expected, and then got in the back.

'Hello!' she smiled as she shut the door behind her.

'Hi, Beth. Nice to see you again so soon,' Damien replied. 'I hope it's no trouble pulling you away at such short notice, but this meeting really couldn't wait.'

'Not at all, that's what I'm here for.'

'Oh, by the way, this is Brian,' Damien said as he pulled away.

'Nice to meet you,' Beth said.

'Hi. I'm the new Sales Manager. Nice to meet you too.'

'Sorry we're having to go off site like this,' Damien explained. 'But as I told you before, if Mr Bird catches me in the office again, I'm a dead man.' Then Damien lowered his voice, but still loud enough so Beth could hear. 'Or just sacked if I'm lucky.'

'Why would he sack you? You said this related to a major deal,' Beth argued.

'It's the biggest single project this company has ever seen. Potentially worth fifty million pounds.'

'Fifty million!' Beth gasped. 'Well surely Mr Bird should be happy. Why is he making life so difficult for you?'

'Mr Bird's exact words to me a few weeks ago were: get your arse up to Scotland and close that deal and I don't want to see you again until the contract's been signed. I didn't think he was being absolutely literal until I came back a week later. My mum had been taken into hospital so I had to come back. Anyway, Mr Bird saw me in the office and threw me out. I mean, grabbed me round the collar and threw me out.'

'Oh my God!' Beth gasped again.

'I told him why I'd come back and he said he didn't care, this was my last warning.'

'That's so horrible. I'm so sorry. How can he be like that? He can't banish you up to Scotland. No one has the right to do that.'

'Tell me about it.'

'Well, you know you can always rely on me. I won't be saying anything to anyone.'

'You're so kind, Beth.'

Beth smiled, but it didn't stop her feeling deep indignation about how Damien was being treated. 'Surely we could do something about Mr Bird? Does the other Mr Bird, Paul, know what he's like?'

'Paul's not much better. It's their way or the highway. I've thought about leaving so many times, but it pays so well, and ultimately we help people. That's all I've ever wanted to do really, help people.' Beth felt a warmness towards Damien as he said this. She could see why they'd become friends.

Then a new thought occurred to her. 'Are we safe? Am I safe in the office?'

'I don't know, Beth. I hate to say it, but maybe not. I'm guessing he's the one that's wiped your memories?'

'Do you think he drugged me? That's what a few people have been saying.'

'I don't want to comment, Beth. I can't say for sure, and you know I don't like putting words in people's mouths. All I know is that you're not the first person in the office over the years to make these claims.'

'Really?'

'One woman tried to report it once, but Mr Bird's above the law. He took care of it and then he took care of her.'

Beth's mouth dropped open at this and her heart started to pound. 'What do you mean took care of her? He's been so nice to me of late. Do you think he's trying to draw me in again?'

'I don't know what happened to her, but I never saw her again. Look, this is wrong. It's bad for us to speculate. I don't want to scare you unnecessarily. All I can advise is that you keep your distance.'

Beth sat back in the car, now absolutely terrified. The more she learnt about Mr Bird the more she feared for her life. The idea of quitting her job really did seem appealing. Perhaps she could just wait a week or two to see if he returns to New York first, though. The job was so good and paid so well. But this could be life or death.

'We're almost there,' Damien announced.

Beth looked out the window. She'd not been paying any attention to where they were going. All she could see was that they were on a very busy road. As they moved along with the traffic, Beth saw a big hotel in front of them. 'Where are we?' she asked.

'Ealing,' Damien replied. 'I've got us a small meeting room in that hotel.'

Finally getting through the traffic, Damien parked his car round the back of the hotel and they all got out. They walked into the reception, waited for someone to show them to their meeting room, and then they all made themselves comfortable.

'Tea?' Damien asked, moving over to pour from the flasks that had been set up on the side.

'That would be lovely,' Beth said.

'I'll have coffee,' Brian replied.

'Still milk no sugar?' Damien asked. Beth looked up to him. Whatever she may or may not remember, there was no doubt that this man knew her. She definitely felt a connection with him.

'Thank you very much.'

Damien poured them all drinks and then sat down to begin their meeting.

Suddenly the meeting room door jolted, as if someone was trying to get in. Then there was a loud bang on the door.

'Beth!' a male voice shouted. 'Beth, are you all right?'

Beth could have sworn she saw a sly smile on Damien's lips as he went to open the locked door.

'Come in,' Damien said as the man pushed his way through.

'Beth, are you all right?' Beth hadn't got a clue who this man was.

'Yes,' she replied, a little confused.

'Sorry, Beth, we should have explained. This is another member of our sales team,' Damien stated.

'Oh,' Beth commented with surprise. He was dressed so casually in jeans and a polo shirt, he didn't look like a sales person. Although Beth did notice how attractive he was. His crystal blue eyes, that had such concern for her welfare, instantly caught her attention.

'Who are you?' the attractive man asked Damien. Beth

scanned his frame. He was tall and strong and must have been about her age.

'I'm the Sales Director of Bird Consultants. You must know my colleague,' Damien said, pointing to Brian.

'We know all about you,' Brian said. 'Don't worry, we're up to speed.'

'Right,' the stranger answered.

'We were expecting you,' Brian said. 'Sorry, we should have let you know sooner, but this was a very last minute meeting.'

'So you all work for Bird Consultants?' the man asked.

'As will you very soon,' Damien replied. Beth could have sworn she saw Damien wink. She wasn't really sure what was going on.

'Beth, will you just excuse us for a second,' Brian said, opening the door and gesturing for the man to exit with him. Hesitantly, the stranger left the room with Brian.

'What was that all about?' Beth asked Damien.

'New boy. He's very eager.'

'Why was he so worried about me?' Beth asked.

'I don't know,' Damien said dismissively. 'We'll have to ask him. It was a bit weird, wasn't it? Anyway, is this your first time to Ealing?'

'I think so,' Beth replied.

Damien flashed a dazzling smile at her and sniggered. 'That's a helpful answer.'

Beth grinned. 'I mean... I can't really remember.'

'Of course. Well, I like it here,' Damien commented. 'I lived here for a while when I first started working at Bird Consultants.'

'How long have you been working for the company now, then?'

'Oh I don't know. Forever,' Damien smirked again. 'Feels like a life sentence most days.'

Brian and the man came back into the room and he looked a lot less puzzled. 'Sorry about that,' Brian said. 'It seems Toby here was a bit daunted on arriving at his first ever Bird Consultants meeting.'

'Your first meeting?' Beth asked.

'Yes,' Toby nodded. 'I don't start for another few weeks. But we thought it best I join this meeting as I'll be working on this project moving on.'

'Oh right. Well, welcome on board,' she smiled. 'Can I just ask, though, why were you asking if I was okay when you came in?'

Toby looked at Damien and Brian nervously. Then Brian suddenly said, 'He's got a soft spot for you.'

'What?' Damien asked, seeming to be even more shocked than Beth.

'Sorry Toby, she's bound to find out eventually,' Brian said. Then he turned his attention to Beth. 'You were on the interview panel. I guess you don't remember.'

As soon as Brian suggested that Beth had forgotten it, she immediately believed it. And Toby definitely seemed to know her.

'When the door was locked, I were worried,' Toby mumbled. 'I thought I were early and you was trapped in here somehow. I don't know.'

'Well thanks for caring,' Beth smiled. She felt incredibly flattered that he was so concerned about her. She was definitely developing a soft spot for him in return.

'I think we should get down to business,' Damien suddenly said, quite sharply.

'Of course,' Brian nodded, and they all took their seats.

For the next hour, Damien and Brian talked heavily about the troublesome fifty million pound deal. There were so many complications and Beth eagerly jotted down the minutes, learning more and more about how important this sale could really be for the company.

She'd noticed that Toby had not said a single word and his contribution to the meeting had been non-existent. All he'd done, pretty much, was stare at Beth. Not that she'd minded.

The meeting ended and Damien summed up the action

points. Then he turned to Beth. 'Are you all right to type up the minutes and send them to Brian? I suspect that Mr Bird has started to monitor my emails, so it's best just to send them to Brian for now.'

'He can't do that!' Beth argued.

'He can do what he likes, Beth. He's the boss.'

Beth's heart was pounding again. Mr Bird made her blood boil. Every time she heard his name he managed to get under her skin. She couldn't stop thinking about him. 'Whatever you need me to do,' she nodded. 'I want to do what's best for the company. That's all I care about.'

'You're a real team player, Beth. I admire that,' Damien smiled.

They all stood up and started to put away their paperwork.

'Do you two gentlemen mind if I grab Beth for five minutes?' Damien said. 'There's a delicate matter that I need to discuss.'

'No problem, we'll wait downstairs,' Brian nodded. 'Come on Toby.' But Toby didn't move.

'Is there a problem?' Damien asked.

Toby didn't take his eyes off Beth for a few moments. Then he turned to Damien. 'No, guess not. We'll be downstairs. We won't be far.'

Toby slowly followed Brian out of the room and Damien closed the door behind them, double checking that it was securely shut.

'There are a couple of things that I want to talk to you about,' he started, moving back round the table to stand next to Beth.

'Okay.'

'I didn't want to say anything in front of Brian. He doesn't know anything about this yet. I wanted you to be the first to know. I'm probably going to be leaving soon.'

'I don't blame you!'

'There might be an opening at my new place. A senior role; something that I'd know you'd be fantastic at. Would you like me to put a good word in for you?'

'What?' Beth asked with surprise.

'I'd feel so much better if I could get you away from Mr Bird. I'm very worried about you.'

'I'm worried about me too. But I don't really have much experience.'

'It's a start-up company, they're just looking for someone who shows flair. And believe me, Beth, you show tons of it.'

'That would be amazing. Would you really put in a good word for me?'

'I'd find it hard to say something bad about you.'

Beth suddenly felt a little awkward. 'Do you need my CV?' she asked, trying to keep it focussed. 'I'll need to update it.'

'Let me speak to them first. I'll be in touch.'

'Thank you so much. It's so kind of you.'

'It's not just kindness.'

'What do you mean?'

Damien leaned more casually on the side of the table. 'I miss the time we used to spend together. If I move, I know I'll miss you. Yes, I really want to get you away from Mr Bird and I want to know you're safe, but there are selfish elements to my plan as well. I hope that doesn't offend you?'

Beth smiled. It didn't offend her at all, although it was frustrating that she couldn't remember anything about their time together. They clearly had some sort of connection. 'Of course not. It's very sweet.'

'Look, I don't need to be back in Scotland for a few days. How about we go out for a drink tomorrow night? Like we used to.'

Beth didn't know what to say. Was he asking her out on a date or were they going out as friends? She really wanted to find out but she also felt so stupid having to ask. If it was going out as they'd done before, then she really should already know the answer to her question. Asking might make it very awkward indeed.

She didn't think that she wanted to go out on a date with him. He seemed nice and friendly, and they certainly seemed to get on very well, but she didn't have any romantic feelings towards him. If she hadn't been sure before, the way that Toby had caught her attention told her that Damien really wasn't the one for her.

Beth toiled with her predicament, cursing her memory loss. What if she was to say no and then all he had meant was to go out as friends? That could ruin their friendship. She didn't want that. She had so few friends, and even fewer that were sympathetic to what she'd been through.

Thinking to her memory loss again, she made her decision. If they'd gone for drinks before, then maybe that's exactly what she needed to do. Getting back on track was surely the best way to jolt her memories. And, ultimately, what did she have to lose?

'Okay, that would be lovely,' she finally said.

'Really?' The grin spread so far across Damien's face that it almost covered it. 'Fantastic. Okay, shall I pick you up at seven? Perhaps I could bring you back to Ealing, show you some of my favourite places?'

'That sounds great. Will be nice to go somewhere different.'

'It's a date,' Damien said, still through his enormous grin.

Beth's heart stopped as he seemed to confirm what she didn't want to hear. 'You know where I live, don't you?' she asked, deciding not to dwell too much on the details. She'd just take it as it came.

The grin disappeared and he addressed Beth far more seriously. 'Do you not remember that, either?'

Beth just shook her head slowly.

Damien softly touched her hand. 'We had a very special night in your flat, Beth.'

Beth felt sick. 'Have we...?' She couldn't say it.

'It was just foreplay,' he grinned coyly. 'We didn't want

to rush things.'

Beth was stunned. They clearly had been on dates before. She must have had romantic feelings towards this man once upon a time. How could she feel so differently now?

Before she even had time to contemplate that line of thinking, though, something else quickly occurred to her. If she'd been drugged by Mr Bird, had been forced to marry him, and then had spent three months under his control, how is it that she'd found so much time to spend with Damien? They'd clearly been more than just friends, but why would her so-called husband have allowed that?

Just as she was going to ask that very question, the door jolted and there was a familiar bang. 'It's Toby, let me in.'

Beth headed straight for the door and opened it. 'Are you okay?'

'Are you?' he asked, looking quite concerned again.

'Of course. Did you forget something?'

'Erm... yeah. Oh, it's in my pocket. I thought I'd forgot my phone! I'm an idiot.'

'I seriously doubt that,' Beth smirked. 'Are you going back to the office?'

'No, I've got somewhere else to be. But I'll see you soon, Beth. Don't worry.'

'I'm glad to hear it,' she said, feeling a sudden urge to flirt. 'Welcome to Bird Consultants.'

'Come on, Beth,' Damien said, quite harshly. 'I'll drop you back off at the office.'

'Great, I'll just grab my stuff.'

Beth took one last look at Toby and she couldn't help the grin that spread across her face.

SIXTEEN

Toby got back to his car without hesitation, keeping a close eye on the Audi that Beth was in. As soon as they started moving, he promptly followed them.

He felt agitated, but he couldn't quite put his finger on why. Maybe it was just the fact that it wasn't a very professional end to the meeting.

He'd told that man he'd left with - whatever his name was - that he needed the toilet. Then he'd headed straight back to the meeting room to listen to what that other man was saying to Beth. It was his job. He needed to make sure Beth was safe.

He'd heard that man asking Beth out and he'd gathered that they'd been on dates before. Then it went all quiet. That's when Toby's agitation flared up. What were they doing? Were they kissing? Was he touching Beth? Toby had been hired to look after her. He had no choice but to knock on the door and check everything was all right.

Toby's phone suddenly started to ring. He flicked the Bluetooth connectivity in his car and answered it hands free.

'Hello.'

'Toby, where have you been?' Paul asked with urgency.

'I've been doing my job.'

'Where's Beth?'

'Don't worry, she hasn't left my sight.'

'But where did she go?'

'She's been in a sales meeting.'

'A what?'

'It's fine. As instructed, I've not seen her interact with a single person that isn't a Bird Consultants employee. Oh, except for that old granny in the tea shop. But I figured she was okay.'

'Are you sure? It's definitely all work related?'

'Yes. She was with your Sales Director.'

'Right.' Toby could hear the relief in Paul's voice.

'We're on our way back now,' Toby said. 'She'll be back in the office really soon.'

'Good. I'll head home then. You have to keep me posted.'

'I will, I promise.'

'Thanks, Toby.'

'So you'll definitely want to know that she's got a date tomorrow night, then?' Toby added.

'A date?' Paul said it so loudly, Toby's car almost shook.

'Is that a problem?' Toby hadn't quite expected that reaction.

'Who with?'

'The Sales Director. I've just heard him ask her out.'

'What?!' Toby didn't know what to say. This was a severe response. 'Are you sure?'

'Yes. He asked her out for a drink.'

'How could he? This isn't good.'

'Sorry, I-'

'We need her to be safe,' Paul stated quite firmly. 'The more she interacts with people, the less safe she's going to be. We can't have her going out on dates.'

'I don't know what I can do.'

'Where are they going?'

'He's taking her to Ealing, I think.'

'Right. I need to think about this.'

'Do you need me to see if I can stop them?'

'No, you don't need to worry about it. You just keep an eye on Beth and keep reporting back. I'll take care of everything else.'

'No problem.'

'Catch you later.' Paul hung up.

That conversation had surprised Toby quite a lot. He knew Beth was in danger, but the stakes suddenly seemed so much higher. Toby couldn't help but feel a little shot of adrenaline. It had been a boring start to this new job, but he was getting a growing sense of importance with every minute that this role developed.

He focussed his attention sharply on the Audi ahead of him and smiled. Being a bodyguard was becoming quite enjoyable.

* * *

Paul arrived home half an hour later in a rage of anger. He headed straight into the living room to find Jim scouring his books again and Jane watching the television.

'What's the matter?' Jane asked with concern.

'That bastard, Brian, he's only gone and asked Beth out on a date!'

'What?' Jim placed his book down and gave Paul his full attention.

'Brian? As in the new Sales Director?' Jane asked.

'Yes. Didn't you get him the job?' Paul asked in reply.

'He's the son of a friend of a friend,' Jane explained. 'He was desperate to work at Bird Consultants. I was nagged into introducing him to Simon. I wasn't so sure at first, but when I saw his track record, I thought it would be a great fit for both parties. I had no idea he was such a Casanova, though. What did Beth say?'

'Yes! She agreed. They're going out tomorrow night.

Toby's just told me. There's us thinking we've got enough to worry about. I thought she'd be safe in the office.'

'This is far from expected,' Jim said.

'She's married to Simon. She can't.' Paul paced over to the window, he was so angry. Jane stood up and moved over to his side. She slowly reached down and squeezed his hand for support.

'Let's look at the facts. It's just one date,' Jim reasoned. 'It doesn't mean anything.'

'It's one step further away from Simon and Beth getting back together,' Paul argued.

'How did operation tea-making go?' Jane asked.

'It was a disaster. They could barely even look at each other.' Paul took a stone out of his pocket. 'I even used an element so I could flick a mug off the side to get them talking. But Beth just disappeared to a meeting. That was it. I went back in the kitchen and Simon was on his hands and knees mopping up the floor.'

'What?' Jim queried, now standing up himself.

'He was tidying up the spilt tea,' Paul clarified.

'That's great news!' Jim smiled.

'Is that a dig at him?' Paul asked, feeling quite defensive towards his nephew.

'Of course not. But when have you ever known Simon do anything domestic? I mean even at home, let alone at work?'

'Okay, so there's a first time for everything,' Paul snapped. 'But he's also never needed to. Even before you, he's had cleaners, and we have help in New York as well.'

'You're not understanding, Paul. Simon would never, in a million years, for anyone else, even you, get on his hands and knees and clean the floor. Yet he did it for Beth.'

'Oh, you're right!' Jane smiled. 'That's so sweet.'

'What are you saying?' Paul asked, although he was starting to see a glimmer of hope.

'Simon must definitely have feelings for her still,' Jim clarified. 'Just as you thought. You know how much he believes in playing the boss role. He never shows weakness, ever. But he has with Beth.'

'You know what, this date could be a really good thing,' Jane said.

'How do you figure that?' Paul asked with surprise.

'We can make Simon jealous.'

'Jealous?'

'We can use the date to our advantage,' Jane explained. 'This could actually be the best thing that could have happened.'

'I'm not so sure,' Paul countered, shaking his head.

'We've got proof now that Simon hasn't lost his feelings for Beth,' Jane argued. 'And nothing jolts the heart into action like a bit of jealousy. It's the oldest trick in the book.'

'I don't know. What are you suggesting?'

'Wherever Beth goes tomorrow night, you meet Simon at the exact same place. Just happen to invite him for drinks.'

'They're going to Ealing. Why would I go for drinks with Simon in Ealing?' Paul asked.

'Make something up!' Jane said. 'Come on, say you need a lad's night out and you've heard how great Ealing is. Say you're meeting a friend that happens to not show up. Tell him you're looking to invest in property there. I'm sure you can think of something convincing.'

'That's it!' Jim suddenly announced. 'Tell him you're looking to buy the bar, wherever Beth and Brian go. Simon won't turn down a business meeting like that.'

'That could work,' Paul nodded, starting to see how it really could. 'Except all we know is that they're going to Ealing, we don't know what bar.'

'But you have a man following her every move,' Jim added. 'Go for dinner with Simon and then get Toby to text you wherever they end up. You just happen to go there after.'

'Okay, that could really work,' Paul nodded.

'Are you kidding!' Jane smirked. 'This could be it. Tomorrow night, this could all be over.'

That night, over dinner, Paul set the ball rolling. Sitting around the table with Simon and Jane, tucking into Jim's stir fry, Paul casually began to speak.

'By the way, Si, you fancy joining me in Ealing tomorrow?'

'Ealing?' Simon queried.

'There's a bar there that I heard was going on the market. I thought I might check it out.'

'To buy?'

'Why not?'

'Since when have you been interested in buying a bar? And why Ealing? Is it Malant?'

Paul had to be careful what he said as he didn't actually know what bar they'd end up in. It was all down to where Brian took Beth. 'I'm not saying I've made any decisions yet, but if I do end up staying in the UK then I'm going to need a hobby. I don't want to be treading on your toes at the office all the time, and New York won't need me, so I thought a new venture like this would be a good investment.'

'You really are serious about this, aren't you?' Simon clearly tensed a little as he asked this.

'Anything's possible.'

Then Simon turned to Jane, although he was still talking to Paul. 'Is your new relationship affecting your decision?'

'There's no relationship,' Paul said, trying to hide the pain in his voice.

'I'm married,' Jane stated.

'What's going on, then?'

'That's not for you to worry about,' Paul warned. 'Yes, I will admit that I wish Jane wasn't married, but she is. And marriages aren't just easily flicked off like a light switch.'

'None of my business,' Simon nodded, looking back down at his food.

'Come with me tomorrow, mate. Let's look at this place together. If nothing else, it will be nice for us to go and have a drink, like we used to.'

'Ealing?'

'Cheaper than Central London, not too far from here nor the office, and it's got a buzz about it. The perfect place if you ask me.'

'If you say so,' Simon shrugged.

'Great,' Paul smiled. 'What's your diary looking like tomorrow?'

'Unfortunately I'm in meetings for most of the day. Have you been to see Flaremore yet?' Simon suddenly asked.

'I don't want to talk business in front of Jane,' Paul warned. It's not that he really minded, of course, he just didn't want to engage with Simon on anything that could get back to his memory loss.

'Well, when can we talk?' Simon asked, clearly miffed. 'I have things that I need to discuss with you. You know, what with you being the owner of the company and my boss. But you never seem to have time for me.'

Paul didn't need this. If only Simon knew the far more pressing matters that he was trying to deal with at that moment. How could anything at Bird Consultants ever compare to Simon's marriage, or to the future of the Malancy? The last thing Paul needed to think about was work. 'If it's work related,' he said, trying to put it off for as long as possible, 'then let's schedule in a work meeting. You're out tomorrow, so-'

'Friday?' Simon quickly asked.

Paul could think of no reason as to why Friday wouldn't suit. He supposed he'd have to talk work with Simon at some point, just to make out everything was normal. 'Friday is perfect.'

'Friday morning it is then. I'll send you a calendar

invite. This is really important.'

'I'm sure it is,' Paul agreed. 'And we'll get to that on Friday, where you'll have my full attention. For now, though, back to tomorrow night. Why don't I meet you at the office at five and then we'll go into Ealing together? We could grab some dinner first and then head to the bar after?'

'Okay. Fine. Are there Malant places to eat in Ealing?' Simon asked.

Paul sighed. 'I'll find out. Just relax, Si. We'll have a good night.'

* * *

The next day, Toby was given strict instructions to follow Beth everywhere she went and to report back exact locations to Paul via text. Everything was in place and everyone was feeling quietly confident.

That was, though, until about half past four in the afternoon. Paul had been collected from the house by his driver, the man he could always rely upon when needed, and they'd headed up the motorway towards the office. Then they came to a complete stop.

'What's the hold up?' Paul asked, looking at the gridlocked traffic around them. Then his answer came on the radio and Paul started to panic.

He quickly dialled Jim on his mobile.

'Hello.'

'Jim, we have a problem,' Paul stated. 'There's been a multi-car pile up. They're talking about helicopters. They've shut the bloody motorway. We're stuck.'

Jim was silent for a moment. 'There's no need to panic. Let's think this through. Worst case scenario, you don't need to be there, only Simon.'

'How can I not be there?'

'Simon's the only one that needs to see Beth with Brian.'

'But I need to get him to the bar.'

'And you can still do that. Give him a call and tell him you'll meet him in Ealing.'

'What? He won't do that.'

'He'll do it for you.'

'Then what?'

'I think we're just going to have to play this by ear. For now, tell him to get some dinner and you'll meet him in Ealing as soon as you can. Meanwhile, I'll get on to Toby and will tell him to be as prompt as possible with his contact.'

'I guess we have no choice. For fuck's sake, Jim, this was our one shot. We can't have Beth falling for anyone else. Simon needs to stop this. We need to stop this.'

'Stay calm, Paul, it's not over yet. This could still work.'

SEVENTEEN

Beth had got home from work just before half five that Thursday. She made a quick omelette for dinner before getting ready for her so-called date. Although she couldn't be less enthusiastic.

She had a quick shower, flicked a bit of make-up on and tidied up her hair. She knew she should be making more of an effort, but she just couldn't find it in herself. It had been a particularly hard week at work, though. She was probably just tired.

She justified the butterflies in her stomach as nerves of going out with a man after such a long time. Although she'd clearly been out with Damien before, she couldn't remember any of it. This all felt like strange new territory. No wonder she was nervous. Anyone would be.

Promptly at seven o'clock, her intercom buzzed. 'Hello,' she answered.

'Hi babe, it's Damien.'

'Won't be a sec.' Beth had no intention of inviting him up. She quickly grabbed her black cardigan, threw it over her blue summer dress, and then left her flat.

'Wow, you look gorgeous,' Damien smiled as he led Beth to his car in the car park.

'Thanks.' She looked at him in his jeans and a shirt. He looked okay, but she wouldn't call him gorgeous. As it wasn't in her nature to lie, she took a second to find something honest that she could compliment him on. She felt she had to. 'Look,' she smiled, 'your shirt is the same colour as my dress. How about that!'

'Peas in a pod. I've always said it of you and me.'

They got in the Audi and Damien started to drive on towards Ealing. She listened as he rambled on about himself during the half hour it took to get there. She really wasn't that interested, despite the fact that she felt like she should be. He talked about work a lot. She did question what else he had to his life. He was starting to seem quite boring.

They finally arrived at Ealing. Damien parked the car and Beth jumped out. He then grabbed her hand and led her on towards their destination. She didn't fight the touch of his skinny fingers. She felt too awkward to a make fuss. Although something about his hold sent shivers through her.

She followed him towards the Broadway, where all the life of the town could be found, and they headed straight towards a bar not too far from the Underground Station. It was strange as Beth would barely have noticed it had Damien not pointed it out, yet it was actually quite a large place once you'd got inside.

'I love the cocktails in here,' he said as they headed towards the bar.

It was a dimly lit place with lots of cosy corners and candlelight. She could see how it could be very romantic.

'I'll order for us,' Damien stated, trying to catch the attention of the barman.

Beth felt a flare of anger shoot through her. Why wasn't she allowed a choice? Who did he think he was? She took a deep breath and decided not to argue. She consoled herself with the thought that the next round would be hers and then he'd have to have whatever she wanted. Two could play at that game.

'I don't like bourbon,' she replied through a forced smile.

'I've tried them all, I'll pick us a good one.'

Two long, very yellow cocktails were served up and Damien, holding Beth's hand again, led her to one of the corners of the room where there was a red sofa. They sat down and took their first sips.

'Interesting,' Beth smiled, talking about her drink. 'A little sweeter than I'd normally have, but not bad.'

'It's fruity,' Damien smirked. 'Like a date should be.' Beth felt herself instantly tense as he said those words. 'Shall we talk about Italy again?' Damien then asked.

'Italy?'

'We were in the midst of planning our trip to Florence last time we went out.'

'Of course, I remember you saying. When were we going?'

'Next month,' Damien smiled. 'Before the kids break up from school, though. You'd done quite a bit of research on hotels, if I remember correctly. Shame you can't remember it.'

Then that burning question hit Beth again. She had to ask. 'If I was married to Mr Bird and he was drugging me and controlling me, how did we get away with spending so much time together?'

Damien took a long sip of his drink and Beth waited patiently for his answer. 'The honest truth?' he asked.

'Yes,' she nodded.

'I don't know. We'd started going out for lunch and we were getting closer. Then we had that magical night together. Then the next time I saw you, you said you were married. You seemed so unhappy about it, but it was like you'd just resigned yourself to that fate. We still met for lunch and that's when you said you wanted us to go to Italy. I'm not one to steal another man's girl, you need to believe me, but I knew you weren't happy. And I had seen you first. I think Italy might have been your way of escaping.'

'That must have been why Mr Bird sent you to Scotland!' Beth was starting to see everything click into place. 'To get you away from me.'

'Of course!' Beth could virtually see the lightbulb sparking in Damien's head. 'That's why he was so mad when I came back. He's jealous of us. Maybe that's why he got his claws into you in the first place?'

'Does Mr Bird really hate you that much?' Beth asked.

'Can I tell you something honestly? I didn't want to ever say this, I knew it would upset you, but I feel I have to be honest. We can't start a relationship on lies.'

'You know how much I value honesty above everything,' Beth stated, choosing not to register the part where he mentioned them in a relationship.

'As do I. This is absolutely true, I swear. Last time I saw Mr Bird he told me that if I ever went near you again, then he'd kill me.'

'What!'

'Another reason why I try and stay away from him. He has no right to dictate who I can and cannot see. Especially when...' Damien looked away.

'Especially when what?'

Damien turned back to Beth and stroked her hair. He stared into her eyes. 'Especially when I'm falling in love.' He then moved in closer to Beth and kissed her.

As his lips touched hers, a cold shudder raced through her. Suddenly every bone in her body told her to leave. The feel of his dry, lifeless lips was chilling, and waves of warnings crashed through her body. She pushed him away. 'Don't!'

'What is it?' he asked, quite surprised.

'I can't.'

'Come on, babe. It's not our first kiss.'

'I'm sorry Damien, I can't. This doesn't feel right.'

'It's that bastard getting into your head again, isn't it?'

135

'I don't know what it is. Maybe I should leave.' Beth went to stand up. She knew there were buses to Heaningford from Ealing. She could get home.

'No!' Damien shouted, grabbing her wrist and pulling her back down.

Beth suddenly felt terrified. More frightened than the situation warranted. Warning signs were flaring through her as his skinny fingers grasped her wrist tightly.

'Don't leave me, Beth. We were having such a lovely time.'

'Let go of me.' Beth tried to struggle, but his grip was fierce.

'Babe, come on. We're meant for each other.'

Suddenly a man walked in front of them and Damien was thrust to his feet. He instantly let go of Beth as he was hurled up. She rubbed her very red wrist for a second and then looked up to see who had joined them; who had saved her. It was Toby!

Toby had grabbed Damien by the collar and was whispering in his ear. He then pushed Damien away and Damien put his hands up in surrender.

'Are you all right?' Toby asked Beth.

'I just want to go home.'

'No problem.' He turned and glared at Damien. 'I'll take her. I think you'd better leave.'

Damien went to argue, but Toby's stature was not one to be argued with. Damien just straightened himself up and then slowly walked away.

'Do you want to finish your drink?' Toby asked.

'Not really. It's not even that nice.'

'Then let me get you something else. Whatever you want. It'll calm your nerves. Then I'll get you home.'

'Are you sure?'

'It would be my pleasure.'

'Okay. Can I just get a glass of wine?'

'Absolutely.' Toby headed to the bar and a couple of minutes later he brought back a large glass of white wine for Beth and a coke for himself.

'Thank you,' Beth said as he sat down next to her. She was still rubbing her wrist, it hurt so much.

'Can I see?' he asked. She felt so comfortable in his presence. He really had been her saviour.

Then she thought to Damien. As much as he'd hurt her, she could understand his confusion: one minute she must have been all over him, the next she can't remember a thing and isn't really that bothered anymore. She must have been sending him mixed signals like no one's business. Although he really shouldn't have hurt her.

Toby gently took Beth's hand and he studied her wrist. 'I can't believe he did that,' he said. Then he ever so softly placed his lips on her skin and kissed her red patch better.

Beth felt a little rush of excitement. She definitely fancied this tall, handsome man. And it was so nice to feel admired in return. It had been a long time since she'd actually met anyone she liked.

'You have healing lips,' she smiled, taking her hand back.

Toby smiled in return. He had such a beautiful smile, Beth felt that rush of passion again.

'I'm not sure you can make such a statement without properly testing my lips out,' Toby stated with a glint in his eye.

'You might be right,' Beth giggled. 'I might have been a bit rash there with my judgement.'

'Shall we test it out?'

'Would be rude not to.'

Toby kissed Beth on the cheek and then he looked back at her. She was glowing with excitement. She was loving this attention, and from someone so attractive.

'I'm not sure. It was hard to tell,' Beth stated, feigning confusion.

'One more?' he asked. Beth just nodded.

He kissed her on the cheek once more quickly, and then, without any warning, he placed his lips directly onto hers and they kissed deeply. It was amazing and Beth felt tingly all over.

'You better drink up,' Toby smiled as he broke away.

'Maybe I could stay out a bit longer,' Beth shrugged.

Beth and Toby stayed out for a few more hours. They mostly just talked, with a couple of kisses in between, then he dropped her off home just before midnight. It had been an unexpectedly good night for Beth and she went to sleep with a smile on her face.

EIGHTEEN

It was seven o'clock before Simon left the office that night. He'd been hopeful that Paul would get on the move again, but the motorway was still gridlocked. Paul had called him and he'd insisted that Simon go and get something to eat and then he'd meet him in Ealing as soon as he could.

Reluctantly, Simon had done as requested and he'd driven to Ealing alone. Feeling irritated that he was having to waste his time and not that hungry anyway, Simon had just grabbed a quick burger for dinner. It made a huge change from his usual culinary treats. Then he'd gone back to his car where he'd sat and waited for further news from Paul.

It was about quarter past eight when Paul was finally on the move. He'd texted Simon the details of the bar and told him to meet him there. Finally relieved to get to see what this bar was actually like, Simon made the short walk to it and headed straight inside.

He'd only taken about five steps in, though, when he was immediately brought to a halt. There, in the corner, was Beth. She was with a man. And just as Simon placed his eyes on her, the man placed his lips on her.

As Simon witnessed the kiss, his breath extinguished. He felt winded. His head fuzzed up and the world around him seemed to stop.

He quickly turned and fumbled out the bar. He stopped outside and leaned against the wall, trying to get a grasp on his breathing, trying to calm himself down. For reasons that he just couldn't fathom, it felt like his world had just ended.

What on earth was going on? He couldn't take it. He'd never felt like this before. He recognised the emotion as heartbreak, but it just didn't make any sense. He barely knew the girl, how could she have such an adverse effect on him?

He stood up tall and made a beeline to his car. This had to end. He hadn't felt like this three months ago. Something had happened, something that he couldn't remember, and he needed to get his life back on track.

Without hesitation, he pulled out of the car park and made his way home. Suddenly realising that Paul was on his way to meet him, Simon dialled his mobile through his in-car Bluetooth.

'I'm nearly there, mate,' Paul said as he answered.

'I'm on my way home.'

'What? Why?' Paul asked.

Simon didn't know what to say. How could he explain it? He didn't even know what was going on himself. 'I've just had enough. It's been a long day. I'll see you later.'

Simon hung up and very quickly made a second call. Sod Paul, sod what he thought was best, sod the business, sod everything. There was only thing that Simon needed and that was escape. He was suffocating in this country, around these people; he had to get away.

'Good evening, Mr Bird,' Jim answered.

'I have to go back to New York, Jim. I need you to get me on the next flight. I don't care what time it is, get it booked.'

Jim was silent.

'Did you hear me?' Simon pushed.

'You want to go back to New York?'

'Yes. As soon as humanly possible.'

'Will Mr Bird be joining you?'

'No. Just get a ticket for me. First possible flight.'

'Erm...'

'Do I have to do it myself?'

'Not at all, sir. Forgive me. I'll get on to that right away.'

Simon hung up. He told himself that he was starting to relax already, but the reality was very different. Beth had got so far under his skin, it hurt. He actually hurt. Why was he so bothered?

Beth plagued his thoughts during the forty minute journey home. No matter what he did, she popped into his head, kissing that other man. It was as if Simon knew what kissing her was like and it drove him wild with jealousy. He hated that he'd let himself get into such a state.

Simon had only been in one relationship in his life and that had ended in heartbreak. He'd refused to ever let himself fall for a woman again. How could he have let Beth get into his head like this?

Then Simon thought back to that fateful night when he'd walked in on his ex with that other man. That had hurt. That had been heartbreaking. But the pain he remembered having then was nothing in comparison to now. It made no sense.

Back then he felt more angry than anything. And maybe a little embarrassed. He certainly couldn't remember feeling like he wasn't able to breathe and he'd lost all his senses. He'd felt utterly overwhelmed with grief at seeing Beth with that other man. This was some sort of strange witchcraft.

Finally the gates to his house came into view and he felt like part of his nightmare was over. He ditched his car right outside the front door and let himself straight in.

'Jim!' he shouted as he walked through the hallway.

'Yes, sir,' Jim said, coming out from the living room.

'When's my flight?'

'There aren't any more flights tonight, but there is one at nine o'clock tomorrow morning.'

'Fine. We'll leave here at five. I can't afford to miss it.'

Jim just stared at Simon, as if he really wanted to say something.

'Is that a problem?' Simon challenged.

'No, sir. Five it is.'

Simon headed straight upstairs to pack. He couldn't wait to get on that plane and to get out of the country. He could almost taste the solace that was to come and he needed it more than ever.

He grabbed his suitcase from under his bed and started to throw his clothes into it. Then he heard the front door slam shut.

'Simon!' his uncle shouted from downstairs. Simon chose to ignore it. 'Simon!' Paul called again.

Simon knew that he had to speak to his uncle. He could hide from most things, but not his uncle. He moved to the top of the stairs and looked down at Paul. 'You called?'

'Get your arse down here now!' Paul demanded.

Simon went to argue, but he could see Paul meant business. He walked down the stairs slowly and stopped right in front of him.

'Why did you come home?' Paul asked.

'I'd had enough.'

'Is it true that you want to go back to New York?'

Jim and Jane suddenly appeared from the living room to witness the action. Simon glared at Jim. 'What gave you the right to tell anyone else about my plans?' he snapped.

'Leave him out of this,' Paul responded. 'He's only looking out for your welfare.'

'I'm a grown man, I'll do whatever I like.'

'And you want to go back to New York?'

'Yes. I'm leaving first thing tomorrow,' Simon

confirmed.

'Well no, you're bloody well not,' Paul argued.

'It's not your choice.'

'What happened?'

'With what?'

'What happened in Ealing?'

'Why did something happen?'

'Is this to do with Beth?' This made Simon's heart stop. What did Paul know about him and Beth?

'Who?' Simon pretended.

'Cut the crap, Simon. Is your sudden need to leave related to Beth?'

Simon had no desire to discuss this. Let alone with Jane and Jim watching. They didn't need to know about his mixed up emotions, it was none of their business. The only thing that could help him now was getting the hell out of the country.

'Why are you living with a married woman?' Simon threw back at his uncle, changing the focus.

'That's got nothing to do with this.'

'And what I'm going through is nothing to do with you.'

'Talk to me, Simon. You need to talk to me.'

'But you don't talk to me. She's living in my house, hidden by a spell that I cast. Don't you think I have a right to know what's going on?'

'Stop it, Simon. You can't help me and Jane. But we can help you.'

'The best thing you can do for me is to let me go.'

'No it's not.'

'I haven't got time for this. I need to go and pack.'

'No.'

'I have an early start.'

'Stop it.'

Simon realised that this conversation was going nowhere, so he turned on his heels and headed straight back upstairs.

'Simon!' Paul called.

'You can stay here if you want, but I have no reason to.'

'Yes you do!'

'Believe me, I don't.'

'But you love her!' Paul's words halted Simon. 'You love Beth.' Simon refused to move. What did Paul mean? 'You love her, Simon. That's what you can't remember.'

Simon turned round and looked down on his uncle. 'What are you talking about?' He could see Jim shaking his head, trying to stop Paul talking, but Paul was determined.

'You asked Beth to marry you. I've never seen a couple so in love. We were all there at the wedding. You were barely able to take your hands off each other. You're madly in love with Beth.'

Simon felt the hurt pound inside of him as he remembered Beth kissing that man. He walked back down the stairs so he was at Paul's level again.

'Don't be ridiculous,' he argued, although his heart told him Paul might be right.

Paul hesitated. Then he said, 'It's her ex-boyfriend. At least we think. He's a Malant. Look, someone has cast a spell on you making sure you've forgotten all about each other. It's got to be her ex-boyfriend, she said he was jealous. But we're looking into it.'

'What?' Simon asked, trying to process this new information. Then he felt a surge of anger rise in him. 'Why are you just telling me this?'

'We thought we could figure it out. We thought if we could break the spell then you'd never need to know.'

'I don't believe it.'

'And we don't know anything for sure,' Jim suddenly chipped in with.

Simon stepped back awkwardly. He had totally forgotten Jim was there. What must he think of all this Malant and spell talk?

'Jim's a Malant,' Paul said, reading Simon's face.

'What?' Simon asked, adding more shock to his already unstable state.

'It's true, Mr Bird. I didn't know it of you, and you didn't know it of me. But when you suddenly couldn't remember your wife, Paul and I got talking.'

This was all a lot of information to absorb in such a short space of time. Simon decided that Jim's Malancy status was probably the least important, so he put it aside in his mind. Instead, he focussed again on Paul.

'I can't believe this. How can someone cast a spell to make me forget my wife? That's not even possible. There's got to be something else going on. I mean if that was the case, why would you lose your memories too?'

'I was lying,' Paul said. 'We didn't know what to say. One minute you're declaring your undying love for each other, the next minute you barely know each other's names. What would you have done?'

Simon was lost for words. His heart told him that this made perfect sense, but his head just couldn't believe it.

'Let's go and sit down,' Paul said, calmly.

They all made their way into the living room, a far more comfortable environment for such a serious discussion.

'You're right, a spell shouldn't be able to change a person's memories, so we did some digging,' Paul began. 'Whoever did this got Beth to sign a contract. It stated that she wanted to forget knowing you. Well, actually, no. The contract stated that she wanted to forget all the good things that she'd ever known about you and just remember the terrible lies that people spread. I think she's pretty scared of you at the minute.'

Simon felt that wave of pain again at the thought of Beth wanting to do this. The thought of his wife wanting to do this. 'Why would she sign such a thing? Doesn't she love me?'

'Of course she does!' Jane insisted.

'She was tricked, Si,' Paul continued. 'She doesn't even

know that she signed anything. Believe me, believe all of us, that girl is crazy about you. You were both very much in love.'

'And you still are,' Jane added.

'That's the thing, Si. This spell could only affect your memories, not your feelings. As we can all see, quite clearly, despite anything you might remember, you're still very much in love with Beth. You know it, don't you?'

Simon felt completely mixed up. On the one hand he felt pure joy at the knowledge that he'd got married and that he'd found a companion that loved him in return. But then he also felt sick with grief. He hurt so much, he'd never felt anything quite like it. He could swear his heart was actually aching.

'I need to think about this,' he said standing up. 'I need to be alone.'

'Of course, Si. We're here if you need us.'

'Are we still leaving at five?' Jim asked.

Suddenly New York was the last place on his mind. 'No. Cancel the flight.'

'Of course, sir.'

Simon went to leave, then he turned back as a final question haunted his thoughts. 'Did you annul our marriage?'

'No,' Paul smiled. 'As much as anything, I don't think I could get it annulled anyway.'

'What do you mean?'

'You were under the impression that I should be able to annul the marriage based on the fact that you hadn't consummated it,' Paul explained. Simon just stared at his uncle as the realisation dawned on him. 'You were very much man and wife, Si.'

Simon suddenly thought to Beth in a more sexual way and his breathing quickened. 'I don't think you even left the house the weekend after you got married,' Paul added.

Simon swallowed. He couldn't imagine letting anyone in like that, what had he been thinking? Relationships always led to pain, as this experience was proving.

'See you tomorrow,' was all that Simon said as he left the living room and headed upstairs. He certainly had a lot to think about.

NINETEEN

When he got to his bedroom, Simon threw his suitcase on the floor and lay on his bed. The only thing on his mind was Beth.

He'd made his peace with never having a sexual experience again. He wasn't thrilled about it, but it was far easier than dealing with the heartache that went along with having any sort of relationship, no matter how serious it was. He'd never been able to believe that anyone would ever actually want to be with him for him. And now he was being told that he'd had that very thing just days ago.

He sat up. He'd had a woman in this bed. He'd had sex in this bed. He turned around to smell the pillows, just in case Beth's scent was there. They didn't seem to smell of anything, though.

He tried to imagine her naked body. He must have seen it before, more than once, but it was as if it had never happened. How he wished he could remember.

Then he realised that he actually must be able to remember or he wouldn't be feeling the way that he did. Paul was right. The spell had only blocked his physical memories, but his body still yearned for his wife. His body and soul were still filled with the love that he had for her.

For the first time, a warmth radiated his soul. It was like nothing he'd ever experienced before, or at least to his memory. He had a wife. He was in love and he was loved in return. It had happened for him.

Simon stood up. He didn't quite know how he was going to process it all. It was amazing and tragic all at once.

He moved to the bathroom and brushed his teeth, then he got undressed and slipped into bed. He could think of nothing else but having Beth next to him. A smile crept up on his face when he thought to how she must have been there next to him for so many nights.

He didn't even realise he was doing it, but he moved aside in the bed, as if to give Beth room. It made him feel less alone, imagining she was there. He needed that.

He stayed awake for ages, trying to think of all the things that they could have done together, trying to imagine all the time that they'd spent together. As the hours ticked by, he slowly drifted off to sleep, but the small smile was still fixed to his lips. Through all of his dreams, not a single memory returned to him, but Beth's eyes, her body and her heavenly scent dominated this thoughts.

When he finally woke up at six thirty, he had no doubt as to his feelings. He was in love. He was in love with the most incredible woman. He'd spent his life believing he was going to be alone and he finally wasn't.

But he was.

He was alone.

Then the stark reality hit him. It was as if he'd had a lovely night of escapism only to wake up to have to face the truth. He'd found true love, but here he was alone again. He had a wife, a partner, a true companion, but they'd been cruelly torn apart.

Then he felt sad. The realisation settled in his mind that nothing had really changed. This was just what he'd always been afraid of, and it was just how he knew his life was always going to play out. He thought he'd found a companion and it had all be taken away from him. And, just as before, she'd met another man. He'd had to witness his partner with another man.

He was now eager to stop thinking about it and eager to put the pain to the back of his mind. He needed to make peace with the fact that he'd had some enjoyment, but it was now all over with. Forcing himself to dwell on it no more, he quickly showered and dressed.

He didn't seem to notice that he'd chosen his purple tie and sharpest black suit to wear, subconsciously dressing to impress. He then splashed his favourite aftershave on and spent a few extra minutes tweaking his hair before heading down to breakfast.

Paul was already chatting to Jim in the kitchen when he arrived.

'Morning,' Simon said, taking a seat at the breakfast bar.

'How did you sleep?' Paul asked.

'Okay.'

Jane suddenly appeared fully dressed. She kissed Paul gently on the cheek before helping herself to coffee. Other than that there was an awkward silence.

Jim brought over Simon a mug of coffee and some cereal and Simon focussed intently on his bowl, trying not to engage with any of the three people now staring at him.

'How are you feeling?' Paul asked him.

Simon refused to look up. 'Okay.'

'Have you had any more thoughts about Beth?'

The truth was that Simon still couldn't stop thinking about her, even when he was deliberately trying not to. But he wasn't going to admit to that. 'Not really.'

'Oh,' Paul replied.

The silence appeared again and Simon could still feel the three pairs of eyes glaring at him.

'You've not thought of her at all?' Paul nudged.

'Perhaps.'

'But you love her!' Jane insisted, suddenly quite angered.

'Nothing lasts forever.'

'What are you talking about?' Jane really did seem quite angry.

'Si, you know you love her.'

Simon stared hard at his cereal. He didn't want to have this conversation. 'People move on,' was all he was willing to say.

'Move on?' Paul queried.

'How can you have moved on since last night?' Jane asked.

Simon looked up. 'Not me.'

'How has Beth moved on?'

'Quite quickly,' Simon all but whispered into his cereal.

'Are you talking about her date last night?' Paul asked.

Simon looked straight up at Paul suspiciously. 'What do you know about last night?'

'We do our homework,' Jim replied.

'We want you two back together just as much as you do,' Paul explained. 'It's not the end, Si, far from it. I mean, think about it. If you still feel love for her, then it goes without saying that she still has feelings for you. You just need to remind her.' Simon shook his head. 'Si, you do know that it's not over, don't you?'

Simon focussed back on his bowl of cereal.

'She loves you, Simon,' Jane encouraged.

'Then why was she kissing another man?' Simon asked this quite to the point. Saying it quickly was like ripping the plaster off, and Simon managed to get through it without too much anguish.

This silenced the room again. Then Paul asked, 'Kissing another man?'

'I saw it myself.'

'She was kissing him?' Jim asked.

'It means nothing,' Jane insisted.

'How can it mean nothing?' Simon glared right at her.

'You're a logical man, Simon, you need to start thinking logically.' Jane was getting quite fiery now.

'What does that mean?' he asked defensively.

'Put yourself in her shoes. Suddenly, out of the blue, she wakes up next to a man she thinks she's terrified of and is then told that she's married to him. You might have been able to accept something that bizarre happening. Weird things do happen when you're a Malant. But she doesn't remember being a Malant. None of this makes even the remotest bit of sense to her, and that makes her even more scared.'

'How can she not remember being a Malant?' Simon asked. 'You either are or you're not.'

'Her parents chose not to tell her,' Jim answered. 'Seems strange but that was their choice. They had to tell her, though, when she met you.' This seemed most peculiar to Simon.

'So you can see now how scared Beth must be feeling,' Jane said. 'Married to the terrifying boss of her company with no recollection of it, and no possible way to reason how she could have lost her memory.'

Simon suddenly felt the barriers that he'd put up that morning break down. He was starting to see things in quite a different light.

'She's all alone, Simon,' Jane continued. 'You were her family. She knows no one else down here, she left her life back up in Staffordshire. You were her new family. She's got no one now. She's going through a very strange time and no one understands.'

'She's been talking to her friends at work, but they've just been making it worse,' Paul said. 'All she hears is negative gossip about you. She can't remember the real you.'

Simon felt a flash of anger. He'd never been bothered before by the gossip at work. He'd just seen it as silly people with silly rumours and he'd always had bigger things to worry about. But just at that moment he felt like throttling everyone that had ever whispered some nasty lie about him.

'Don't worry, I've dealt with it. The gossip won't be continuing, but it does show you what Beth's been going through. She knows no different.'

'See?' Jane said. 'She's afraid, alone and utterly confused. So what does she do? She turns to the first man who shows her interest. Being with him no doubt makes her feel protected from you and it helps her make sense of the feelings of love she must have circling around her body.'

Jane's words echoed in Simon's mind. It all made so much sense. Simon had been so confused and he'd wanted to escape to New York. Beth is alone and confused, so she takes solace in the first man that comes along and shows her interest.

Then he felt the urge to fight. She wasn't really interested in this man. Simon hadn't lost her. It should be him who's comforting her, not that other stranger.

'So what do I do?' Simon asked, now driven by new hope.

'Remind her of how much she loves you,' Paul said. 'Your memories haven't come back, but you know it all to be true. You believe us because you know it in your heart. As will Beth. Talk to her, make her see sense. Your mutual love will beat this. Then the last three months won't matter as you'll fall in love all over again.'

Simon then felt sick. He'd not spoken to a woman about anything other than work in a decade. Or at least that he remembered. How was he supposed to have a romantic discussion with Beth? How on earth had he managed it last time? How could someone take away his memories like that? They were his memories, and it was his right to have them!

'I want to know who it is that's torn us apart,' he demanded.

Paul looked to Jim and Jane. 'Let us worry about that.

We're the ones with the memories. We're in a much better place to figure it out.'

'I want to know.' Simon was now ready to fight just about everything.

'We'll tell you as and when we find things out. Trust us,' Jim said.

'They will pay,' Simon stated.

'Yes they will,' Paul nodded. 'But you have much more important things to worry about right now.'

'You're right,' Simon replied, knowing in his heart that winning Beth back came before everything. Then he remembered something else that no longer seemed as important. 'Oh, you know we've got that meeting this morning?' Paul just nodded. 'Can we postpone?'

'Of course.'

'Good. Cause I've got a wife to win back.'

TWENTY

Toby had watched Beth go to work that morning and he was now sitting in his car, waiting while she carried on with her day.

He thought to the previous night and smiled. He hadn't really intended on kissing her when he sat down. It had taken him by surprise himself how overwhelmed with jealousy he'd been when that absolute bastard had tried to kiss Beth. Before he knew it he'd found himself on top of that prat and was close to knocking him into next week. What did Beth see in him?

Then, when he'd got them their drinks, he just couldn't resist a bit of flirting and one thing led to another.

He'd quickly justified his actions. Paul had told him that he didn't want her dating anyone as it might cause her further issues; make her unsafe. But if she was dating her bodyguard then that was actually about as safe as a person could possibly be. She also, then, wouldn't be dating anyone else. So, in fact, he was doing the best thing for everyone. In every sense, he was doing exactly what Paul and Jim wanted him to do.

His phoned beeped and he saw a text message from Beth. He'd already texted her good morning with a cheeky smile. She replied:

Had a great night last night, can't wait to see you again tonight. The weekend at last! xx

He found himself smiling. He was due to pick her up at six thirty, then who knows where the night might take them.

On the tenth floor of the office block just down the road from where Toby was parked, Simon sat at his desk. It was now mid-morning and he was finally getting the courage up to speak to Beth.

He'd been a wreck all morning, it was quite unlike him. He'd dealt with some of the biggest companies and most powerful people in the world without batting an eyelid, but telling a woman that he loved her, that was the scariest thing he'd ever had to do.

He knew if he didn't just get on with it, then he'd never do it. It was time to be brave.

He looked on the company's intranet for Beth's internal details and then picked up his landline. He dialled her direct line and waited.

'Hello,' she answered nervously.

'Beth... Miss Lance... Beth. It's Simon here. Simon Bird.' His heart was pounding and his mouth had dried up. Being in love really wasn't enjoyable.

'Hello.'

'Can you come up to my office, please?' he asked. There was nothing but silence. 'Beth?' he said, checking that she was still there.

'Now?' she asked. He could hear the worry in her voice. She really was scared.

'Yes please.'

'In your office?'

'Yes please.'

Again there were a few seconds of silence. 'Of course.

I'll be right up.'

Simon placed down the receiver and waited. Then the nerves really did kick in. He shifted his laptop and shuffled some paperwork on his desk, anything just to have something to do while he waited.

A few minutes later there was a soft knock at his door. This was it. He felt sick. He took a deep breath and then said, 'Come in.'

Beth slowly opened the door and, after a small hesitation, she stepped inside.

'Could you please shut the door?' he asked, not relishing in the idea of any of the other directors hearing his declaration of love to... well, to his wife.

Beth's eyes widened at this request. He could sense her fear and it saddened him. There was an awkward moment when he wasn't sure if she'd even stay, but after a few seconds she did as he asked. Then she moved over to the middle of the room.

Simon looked at her from behind his desk, for the first time allowing himself to enjoy her beauty. She was absolutely stunning. She had such a pretty face, with silky soft hair and a thin, shapely figure that was flattered so much by her purple dress. Then, to top it all off, he had to admire her undeniably strong demeanour. Even now, when he knew she was scared, she still stood up tall and tried to find confidence. It was very much like himself. He was starting to see why they were such a good match.

'Beth,' he said, then he didn't know what to say. Where should he begin? He'd practiced this so many times that morning, but now it was time for action he felt lost. He shifted in his seat.

He took a deep breath and looked straight into the green eyes that were staring right back at him. Then he saw it. She was questioning it. He could see a drop – just a small drop, but a drop nevertheless – of doubt as to what she was feeling. Jane had been right: Beth must still love him. He felt a new sense of confidence.

Just then her phone pinged. She was grasping her mobile tightly in her hand, and like a knee jerk reaction she went to look at it. Then she quickly stopped herself, as if she was worried about being told off.

'Please, Beth. It might be important,' Simon said, gesturing for her to check her message. If nothing else, it gave him a second to pull his thoughts together.

He watched her check her phone, and he witnessed the slight smile that curled up in the corner of her lips as she read the message that had been sent to her.

'Good news?' he asked.

'I'm sorry, Mr Bird,' she said, putting her arms down by her side again, instantly losing her smile.

'Simon. Please call me Simon.'

Beth glared at him. Then she nodded. 'Simon.'

'Your message seemed to make you happy,' he said.

'I'm terribly sorry, I shouldn't have looked. It was personal, not work related.'

This caught Simon's attention. She was his wife. What personal stuff was she talking about that didn't involve him? He felt the rumble of jealousy again.

'We all get personal messages, Beth. If we don't get our work life balance right, then I don't believe we can be productive.'

This statement clearly surprised Beth. Then her look turned to one of suspicion. 'So you wouldn't mind me taking a personal call during the day?'

'Of course not,' Simon replied, surprised himself by this question.

'Because it was my boyfriend, not just any old person. That's okay, then?'

Simon felt the walls around him close in and the floor below him vanish. He felt like he was falling; falling hard into a dark, cold, lonely hole. He lost his breath, but he knew he needed to grasp onto all of his strength to make sure that he didn't react. She couldn't see him react.

'Boyfriend?' he simply asked, holding on to his

composure like his life depended on it.

'Yes.' Beth seemed very confident in her response.

Simon tried to control his breathing. He wanted to be alone now. He hadn't expected this. How could he tell her the truth now? It had been hard before, now it was impossible. He'd lost her. That one word – boyfriend – was the final nail in the coffin. He'd lost her.

'As I said,' he stated through a very forced smile, 'I want my staff to have a good work life balance. Good for you.'

'Thank you, Mr Bird.' Beth then must have misunderstood the look in Simon's eye, as she quickly corrected, 'I mean, Simon.'

He needed to hide this pain, this hurt, this disappointment. Let her be scared of him, what did it matter anymore?

'Will that be all?' he asked.

Beth looked thoroughly confused. 'You said you needed to see me.'

Simon tried to find clarity through the fog in his head. 'Of course. I wanted to talk to you about...' Think quick, think quick. He was her boss. Nothing more, just her boss. 'Your appraisal.'

'Appraisal?'

'Yes. I insist that everyone has a six month appraisal.'

Again, this seemed to surprise Beth. 'But I haven't been here six months.'

'No.' He realised that he hadn't actually got a clue as to how long she'd been working for the company. He knew it was at least more than three months, but that was all. 'We always do them at the same time of year. June. It's the sixth month of the year,' he said, relieved that his brain worked quickly.

'Oh, right.'

'We need to book in a time. We'll need an hour. Two hours.' If he was going to get time alone with her, then he might as well make it last. That, he couldn't resist. 'No, make it half a day.'

'Half a day?' she asked, stunned.

'Yes.'

'Am I in trouble?'

'Why would you be in trouble?'

'It's just... that's a long appraisal.'

He looked at her sternly. 'No, I think that's quite standard. Standard for Bird Consultants anyway. Best to be thorough.'

'Oh,' she replied. 'Will I need to do them with my team too?' He admired this. Her first consideration was for her team.

'Of course.'

'Oh. Okay. How do I do that?'

Simon wanted to smile. He wanted to wrap his arms around her and kiss her. God, he was in love with her. 'I tell you what, let's do your appraisal next week, and as part of it I'll show you how to complete the form for your team as well. Is that okay?'

Beth once again didn't respond straight away, almost like she was lost for words. Then she said, 'That would be very kind of you.'

'Nonsense. It's my job.'

'When do you want to do it?'

'As soon as possible. Check your diary and send me a calendar request.'

'But...' Beth didn't continue with whatever she was going to say. Instead she simply finished, 'I'll do it as soon as I get back to my desk.'

'Anything else?' Simon asked, now feeling mixed up again. He wanted her to stay so they could get to know each other better. He wanted to curl up on the sofa with her and then maybe kiss her. But he also wanted her to leave so he could wallow in his own self-pity. He'd lost her. She was with another man and there was nothing he could do about it.

'No. Thank you. See you next week.'

Simon looked straight back at his laptop, pretending to not be interested anymore. He heard her leave, he heard her carefully close the door behind her, and then he glanced up ever so slightly so he could watch her walk across the Executive Floor. He watched her until she disappeared.

Then a very strange thing hit him. His eyes started to sting. He felt a hard punch deep in his stomach. He quickly snapped his fingers so all the windows went black and he flicked the door so it locked. What was happening to him?

He couldn't fight it. He took a deep breath as a single tear escaped from the corner of his eye. He'd never been in such a state in all his life. He wanted to run away so badly, to flee back to America and take comfort in the distance from all this pain. What was he going to do?

He'd lost her. He knew now, without any shadow of a doubt, that he was madly in love with her. And he'd lost her.

TWENTY-ONE

For the first time in just over a week, Paul felt quietly confident during that Friday. Simon was a fighter, and he'd seen determination in his boy's eyes that morning.

Knowing there was nothing more they could do at that moment, Paul and Jane had chosen to have a day together. They'd been given the gift of time, albeit in the most awful of circumstances. No matter what, though, they had to make sure that they properly optimised on the short time that they had together. Jane had to go home soon. It was inevitable.

They'd gone for a picnic, as it was a beautifully sunny day, followed by a long, romantic walk together.

However, all the happiness of the day was starting to rock when, by seven o'clock that evening, Simon still hadn't come home and no one had heard from him since he'd left that morning.

Jane and Paul were now sitting at the breakfast bar in Simon's kitchen chatting to Jim as he checked on the curry in the slow cooker.

'He could be in Beth's flat right now, a new love blossoming,' Jane reasoned.

'It's time to call,' Paul said. He'd texted Simon twice

but hadn't had a reply. He didn't want to push Simon, he knew this was a delicate situation, but everything inside of him told him that something wasn't right.

'Do you want me to do it? Find out if he'll be home for dinner?' Jim suggested.

'No. He won't be honest with you. He'll just give you an unhelpful one word answer or something. I'll do it.'

Paul dialled Simon's number and took a deep breath. He was so nervous that something else had gone wrong.

'Hello.'

Paul's body relaxed ever so slightly with the relief that at least Simon had answered. 'Hi mate, where are you? Jim's got dinner on.'

'I'm still at the office,' Simon replied.

'What are you doing there?'

'I've got work to do. I am CEO, you know. I'm busy.'

'Oh, Simon.' The relief was short-lived as Paul felt a sickening dread grow in his stomach. It was never a good sign when Simon was throwing himself into his work.

'This place doesn't run itself, you know.'

'What happened with Beth?'

'What?'

'What happened with Beth?' Paul pushed.

'Nothing.'

'Simon!' Paul hated it when Simon wouldn't talk to him. And he'd been doing it far too often of late.

'Nothing happened. She politely told me about her boyfriend and then the conversation ended. Anything else you'd like to know?'

Paul froze. Boyfriend? Where had this come from? She'd only been on one date with Brian. What on earth was she playing at?

It didn't matter, though. How could it matter? Boyfriend or no boyfriend, she still loved Simon. She had to.

'So you didn't tell her?' Paul asked.

'How could I tell her that I love her right after she'd

told me about her boyfriend?'

'She's your wife, Simon! Get some perspective!' Paul was getting riled now. 'You need to fight for her. As Jane said, she's going through far more at this moment than you, so you need to be the strong one and make her see.'

Simon didn't respond for a minute. Then he said, 'How?'

'Go and find her. Look, I'll deal with this ridiculous boyfriend situation, you just need to make sure that you're never far from her mind. The more she's around you, the more she'll remember how she feels.'

'How are you going to deal with her boyfriend?'

'Never you mind that. You just need to focus on getting Beth to remember how much she loves you.'

'Do you think that's possible?'

'I think it will be easy if you put your mind to it and stop letting every small obstacle get in your way.'

There was another short pause before Simon asked, 'So you don't think it's the end?'

'A boyfriend never has a chance against a husband!' Paul's bright start to that statement quickly vanished as he looked at Jane. It was true. He didn't stand a chance against her husband.

'I suppose when you put it like that,' Simon sighed. 'First thing Monday-'

'No, now Simon,' Paul interrupted. 'Go and see her now.'

'How am I supposed to do that? What reason have I got? I don't even know where she is.'

'Give me two minutes, I'll find her for you.' Paul turned to Jim and whispered, 'Get Toby on the phone.' Jim nodded his understanding, then grabbed his mobile and left the room to make the call.

'You're going to do a location spell?' Simon asked, curiously.

'Of course not. There are other ways, you know.'

'Like what?'

'You need to trust your uncle more. I'm always looking out for you. I'll never let you down, Si.'

'I know. You've always been there for me. I am grateful.'

Jim came back in the room. 'Hang on, Si,' Paul said, covering the receiver so he could speak to Jim.

'She's at The Rose, the pub right by the office,' Jim said.

'Oh shit. Please don't say she's there with Brian.'

'Actually no. Toby said there's no one else with her.'

'She's on her own?'

'Apparently so. But she did used to work there. I suppose she could be catching up with her old work friends.'

Paul nodded and put his phone back to his ear. 'You're in luck, Simon.'

'There's a first,' he replied sarcastically.

'She's at The Rose.'

'Where?'

'It's the pub just down the road from the office. She used to work there, so she's all on her own chatting with old work friends. It's perfect. Just go and casually have a drink and bump into her.'

'How do you know this?'

'Like I said, I have my resources. Do you want to go and see her or not?'

There was a short pause before Simon said, 'I want to go and see her. I suppose I can just go and have a casual drink.'

'It's just a drink. Nothing more. Don't overthink it.'

'I'm sure it's as easy as that.'

'Go on. Get down there. And good luck. Keep us posted.'

'Will do.'

Paul hung up and sighed. 'What a mess!'

'What was that about a boyfriend?' Jane asked.

'She's only bloody dating Brian. She told Simon that he

was her boyfriend.'

'What? Look, let's not worry too much about that,' Jane said. 'More likely than anything, she's just trying to make sense of all the things that have been happening to her. She feels all this emotion but is too scared to admit that it's aimed at Simon, so she's pushing her attention on to someone else. It'll never last. It's hollow and she doesn't really feel this way.'

'It'll never last, all right!' Paul said. 'What does he think he's doing? I know he's new, but Beth is Mrs Bird in the office. She's Simon's wife. What sort of bloke cracks on to the boss's wife? Even if Brian believes they've broken up, he's wasted no time. What a slimy little git. He's getting what's coming to him.'

'What are you going to do?' Jim asked.

'Send him off to the States for starters.'

'What?'

'Book him a plane on Monday, Jim. I think it's time our new Sales Director spent some time with his counterparts overseas. It's all part of the job. Two weeks ought to do it. Then we'll see where he's at.' Paul looked at the clock on the wall. 'Right, it's just after lunch over there, so I'm going to call them now to warn them of their guest next week. Then I'll let Brian know he needs to pack. Little git.'

* * *

Simon had seen this pub numerous times but he'd never been in. Or at least not that he could remember. He drove into the little car park at the back and then made his way around to the entrance at the front.

Walking past, he straight away clocked Beth and her so-called boyfriend cuddling up on the sofa by the window. So much for her being alone.

He reached the doors and stopped. Did he really want to go in? What was he going to do now that she was with her boyfriend? As much as everything in his head told him his journey had been wasted and nothing could come from this chance meeting, he suddenly found himself pulling open the door and entering the busy pub.

Although he was totally out of his comfort zone and he was hating the thought of seeing Beth with another man, a part of him just couldn't resist having one quick drink to find out who the competition was. His logical, calm side didn't want to know a thing about the man who was now curled up with his wife. Yet at the same time his heart was screaming out to find out everything he could about the bastard who had stolen away the love of his life. He had such a burning desire to bring him down once and for all.

Everything about that moment was strange new territory for Simon and it left him feeling even more wretched than he had done earlier that day. He hadn't been able to glance over yet at the loved up couple by the window. He just made his way to the bar and was waiting to be served. He was focussing hard at the drinks on offer so as to not be tempted to look Beth's way.

'What can I get for you?' the girl behind the bar asked.

Simon most definitely needed alcohol if he was going to survive this. 'I'll have a whiskey, please,' he said.

'Any one in particular?'

Simon scanned the small array of whiskies on offer. This was quite a long way from the sophisticated places he normally drank at and there was only about one choice that he'd even consider. 'Chivas Regal, please.'

His drink was poured and cash exchanged, and then he took a deep breath. This was it. He stood back from the bar, away from as many people as he could, and then he looked down towards the window; down towards Beth.

He was in the perfect place. He could clearly seem them whispering sweet nothings to each other, but he knew they wouldn't be able to see him in return. Not that they seemed to be noticing anyone else around them anyway.

He couldn't take his eyes off them. Then the jealousy

started to ache inside. His whole body tensed as he witnessed the boyfriend's hands touch Beth. He was touching Beth far too much. This really wasn't suitable for a public place.

Then Simon stopped breathing. A realisation hit him that he hadn't yet considered. Boyfriend meant more than just a quick kiss. Boyfriend meant more than a fumble at the pub. Boyfriend meant sex. Oh God, what if they'd had sex?

He felt that hard punch deep inside again at the prospect of Beth having sex with another man; any other man. He took a deep breath as the upset and jealousy shook him. He had to keep a hold of himself, this was getting ridiculous. He couldn't take it, though. What if this man had gone back to hers last night?

Simon was the only man who should be seeing her naked; who should be waking up next to her. This man should be keeping his hands off! Simon suddenly felt the urge to go over there and throw the so-called boyfriend through the window. He imagined punching his face over and over.

Then he saw Beth stand up. She was heading to the toilets. It was now or never. He had to know.

He darted through the crowd of people and within seconds he was standing over the "boyfriend" who was sipping his pint on the sofa.

'Evening,' Simon said menacingly.

'Y'alright?' the man asked. Simon noted his northern accent.

'Was that Beth Lance I saw you with?' Simon asked. He wanted to sound casual, but his adrenaline was pumping far too fiercely for him to have any hope of remaining calm.

'Yeah. You know her?'

'I'm her boss.'

'Oh, right. That's all right then.'

'You're her boyfriend?' Simon demanded to know.

The man hesitated. He went to say something, then stopped. He just glared at Simon as if he was unsure what the right answer should be.

Simon sat down next to him. He knew he didn't have long and he didn't care what this horrid, despicable man thought. He had to know.

'Have you had sex with her?'

'Have I what?' the man replied, quite taken aback by the sudden question.

This so-called boyfriend was far from small, but Simon was always the greater man, no matter who he was with, so powerful was his stature. It's the strength his magic gave him, and he knew it. 'Have you had sex with her?' Simon repeated, using his intimidating nature to his advantage for a change.

'What's that got to do with you?'

'I'll ask you again,' Simon stated in a deeply fierce tone. 'Have you had sex with her?'

'This is a bit-'

'Tell me,' Simon demanded. He was glaring with such intensity, his eyes were like green fireballs.

'No!' the man replied, edging away with a touch of fear. 'I ain't touched her.'

Simon backed away, just in time to notice Beth walking over towards them. She ground to a halt just to the side of the sofa when she saw Simon.

'Good evening, Beth,' Simon greeted.

'Hello.'

'I was just saying hello to your new man. How are you?'

Beth stood tall, although Simon could see the wariness in her eyes. 'I'm good. I'm very good, thank you.'

Just then a flash of Beth being naked with this man shot through Simon's head. They may not have had sex yet, but it wouldn't be long. They were in a new relationship, it was sure to happen soon. Simon couldn't let that happen. He had to stop them.

Then a flicker of genius sparked in his head. He

grabbed the man's arm. 'Let me apologise,' Simon said. But as he spoke he was conjuring up his power. 'I didn't mean to scare you earlier, if I did.' He built up the power in his chest then flushed it through his arm into the man's body. 'I like to look out for my employees. I just wanted to make sure that Beth was in good hands.' He concentrated for a second as he made sure that his power had properly been received. He watched the man shudder, ever so slightly, and Simon felt relieved.

He took his arm away and the man looked horrified.

'Have a lovely weekend, Beth,' Simon said, standing up. He then knocked back his whiskey and left. He couldn't take another second of seeing his wife like this. But at least he'd guaranteed that they wouldn't be consummating their relationship.

He walked out into the warm evening and headed straight for his car. He sat in the driver's seat, slammed the door behind him, took a weak breath, and then everything fell apart.

His powerful stature dissolved, like melting ice cream, and he flopped his head against the steering wheel. His whole life was slipping through his fingers and he'd never felt so low.

TWENTY-TWO

'What did he want?' Beth asked as she watched Mr Bird walk away.

'Don't know,' Toby shrugged.

She looked back down at Toby sitting on the sofa. He looked far less relaxed than he had done five minutes before. Then something occurred to her. She glanced quickly across at Mr Bird through the window as he headed towards the car park. She'd never realised it before, but they actually looked quite alike. They both had very similar builds and were roughly the same height, and their faces weren't too dissimilar either.

However, there was one main difference. Despite the fact that their measurements were physically alike, Mr Bird seemed to drown Toby with his presence. Mr Bird had such an incredible aura. Before she knew it, Beth found herself admiring him. In fact, she couldn't help but feel a little bit in awe of him.

Suddenly realising the warmth she was developing towards the man, Beth immediately tried to shake it off. It wasn't good to think such things. He was getting under her skin again. She was on a date with Toby. Why was Mr Bird even there?

171

'Was he warning you off me?' Beth asked, piecing together Mr Bird's motive. She imagined that he'd followed them out so he could spy on them, always trying to control the situation. He clearly wanted her back to finish off his sick game. It really was best that she stay away from him.

Toby just shrugged again. 'I don't know what he wanted. He's a bit of a freak.'

'You can say that again. You're not the first person that's got close to me that he's warned off.' Beth thought of Damien. She'd not heard from him since the very bad end to their "date".

'He said he was your boss. Is that right?' Toby asked.

'Sadly.'

'Well I pity you having to work with that weirdo.'

As Toby criticised Mr Bird, Beth was aware of a very slight tinge of anger that flared in her stomach. She actually felt defensive towards him. How did that make any sense? Mr Bird was a weirdo and a freak. But she also suddenly couldn't stop thinking about how breathtakingly handsome he'd looked that day. He was so sexy.

He was clearly getting into her head again and she mustn't let him. It was dangerous to get sucked in. She should have learnt her lesson.

'Another drink?' Toby asked.

'Definitely,' Beth smiled. 'Isn't it my round?' Beth searched in her bag for her purse, but Toby grasped her hand to stop her.

'When I take a girl out, I take a girl out. Don't offend me by offering to pay. It'll only end in an argument. And I'll win.'

Beth smiled. She liked being treated like a lady. Although she did make a vow to herself that she would buy at least one round that night. 'That's very kind of you. I'll have the same again.'

Toby headed off to the bar. Beth definitely found him attractive. He was a nice, good looking man. So why could she not stop thinking about Mr Bird?

Mr Bird had surprised her more than once earlier that day. An appraisal? Why would a blood sucking, crazy man who wanted to control everyone and everything care what his staff thought and what progress they were making?

She decided to reserve judgement until next week when the appraisal actually happened. Maybe it was all part of his elaborate scheme to win her back. She'd have to stay strong. This time, at least, she had people looking out for her.

It also deeply surprised her that he was so willing to work around her. She'd heard that he was a busy man who never had time for anyone, yet he had an open calendar for Beth. More elaborate deception? None of it added up.

How she wished she could remember those three months. How did she end up marrying him in the first place? What tricks had he used?

If they were married, had they kissed? At the moment where the vicar says 'you may now kiss the bride', had he kissed her? She got lost for a second thinking about his lips.

She snapped herself out of it. It was like she was drugged again, falling for his evil ways. It probably wasn't a vicar that married them. They'd probably gone to some backstreet place that Mr Bird knew of, away from everyone, where no one would notice how Beth was being forced into a marriage that would ultimately be her undoing.

Was it really her undoing, though? She'd lived in a mansion and had been promoted with a very generous salary. There are worse people to marry. A lot worse.

Before she knew it, a small smile had crept onto her lips as she once again thought to how sexy Mr Bird had looked that day. She hadn't been close enough to smell him, but she imagined his heavenly, manly musk.

She had to stop it! This was far too dangerous. Yes, he was an incredibly gorgeous man who always brought the room to a halt when he walked in. Then Beth thought about the vacuum that she'd always noticed whenever he left. It was as if every time he stepped away, the room itself became sad that he was gone, no matter how many people may still be there.

But despite all of that, he was still a murderous, controlling madman who had taken away three months of Beth's life. And now he was trying to end her date with a lovely man.

Much to Beth's relief, bringing an end to her cycle of torment, Toby returned and placed two pints of lager on the table in front of them. As he sat down next to her, he kissed her firmly on the lips and then once again wrapped his arm around her. Beth felt herself calming down and she knew it was time to get back to her date.

They enjoyed the next hour or so, getting to know each other better and sharing lots of stories. There was also a lot of kissing, and with every sip of their drinks, their lust for each other increased.

They were just finishing their third pint when Toby looked deep into Beth's eyes. 'What's your flat like?' he said, quite out of the blue.

Beth laughed. 'Tiny.'

'You got a studio flat?'

'The smallest little place in the whole world!'

'Can I see it?'

Beth sat up straight. This really was out of the blue. She knew what he was after, but she couldn't decide how she felt about it.

'I thought we were going into town?' Beth asked. She knew that she liked Toby, and it had been a long time since she'd been with a man, but she couldn't help but feel a tinge of disappointment that their plans to visit Piccadilly Circus might no longer happen.

'We can do that anytime.'

'You can come back to my flat anytime.'

'Is that a promise?' Toby smirked, kissing Beth on the

lips.

'No, I didn't mean that,' Beth giggled. 'Are we going into Central London or not? I can afford a taxi.'

'It's so late now, though.' Toby pulled a sad face.

'It's only just after nine. The night's still young, and so are we!'

'We can party back at your flat,' he said.

Beth looked at him. She felt utterly confused as to what she wanted more. She wanted to see London at night so much, but she also couldn't deny how turned on she felt. Would it be such a bad thing to invite him back to her flat? She was young, free and living a new life, why shouldn't she just enjoy herself? London would still be there tomorrow, right?

She needed to clarify that first. 'So, say you come back to my flat?' she started.

'Liking it already.'

'When are you taking me to Piccadilly Circus?'

'You keep going on about Piccadilly Circus. Who cares? Manchester's where you want to go. I'll take you to Manchester.'

'Manchester?' This didn't have the same appeal to Beth. As much as she was sure that Manchester was a lovely city, London was where she'd always seen herself. It was the home of her ambition. She didn't just want to see any city, she wanted to see London. She was destined to be a high flying Londoner, living the dream, earning the mega-bucks and spending her days in her million pound apartment overlooking the Thames.

'Yep. We'll have a whole weekend in Manchester.'

Deciding that it was best to temporarily say goodbye to her London sightseeing adventure, and not at all excited by the prospect of their potential weekend in Manchester, Beth stood up. 'Come on then.'

Toby's face lit up. 'Yeah?'

'Yes,' Beth nodded.

They walked out hand in hand and made the small

journey to Beth's flat. She pressed her key in the lock and opened the door, before noticing the cheeky smile on Toby's face. It made her giggle and it helped to extinguish any disappointment from their sudden change of plans. She suddenly felt very desired and it felt very good.

She stepped in and held the door open for him to follow. He picked his leg up to move but he just stopped. He stayed there, not moving forward.

'Stop messing around,' she smiled. He looked confused and then he sighed with frustration, as if he'd forgotten something really important.

'Fucking hell!'

'What?' Beth couldn't help but feel very worried. Had she done something wrong? Had he noticed her hairy legs? No, she was properly up to date with all her hair management. Did she have bad breath? They'd been kissing all night! What could it be? Why did she suddenly have the sinking feeling that she was about to get dumped?

'This isn't right.'

'Don't you want to come up?' she asked meekly.

Toby looked at her with sincerity. 'Yeah I do. I really do. But it's not right.' He looked around awkwardly. 'I mean, you're a lady. I shouldn't be coming up to your flat, you should be coming back to mine.'

'What?' This made no sense to Beth.

'That's what a gentleman does. He invites the girl round to his.'

'But we're here now.'

'And that's not a problem. It happens that I live just across the road.' Toby pointed to his flat as if revealing a magic trick.

'You live there? You never said.'

'You never asked.'

'So you want to go to yours?'

'Yeah.'

Beth tried to find the logic. Then more paranoia set in and she started to sniff in case there was a funny smell that was putting him off. None of it made any sense, but, she figured, it didn't really matter.

She closed the door and followed Toby over the road. His flat was on the ground floor, but just before entering, he stopped her.

'Shit, I better tidy up. Stay here.' He left her outside in the corridor while he dashed inside.

On her own again, she couldn't help but let her mind wander. What was she doing? Did she even want to be there? She didn't think it felt wrong. A flash of Mr Bird suddenly appeared in her head again. It was as if she missed him. He really had messed with her mind. He was a bad mad and Beth needed to get him out of her system. She needed a new man to think about, and she was about to put Mr Simon Bird well and truly out of the picture. This was absolutely the best thing that could happen.

'Ready?' Toby asked, opening the door.

Beth stepped in. It was a similar size to her studio flat, but it looked so empty. It was barely furnished and it looked like he was only staying for a couple of days rather than it being his home. Still, she supposed, he had only just moved down. He hadn't even started his new job yet.

'Can I get you a drink?' he asked, going to the fridge.

'What have you got?' she replied.

'Beer.' He handed her a can of Fosters and they both took a seat on the bed.

As they cracked open their cans there was an awkward silence. It lasted for a few minutes until Toby grabbed the can out of Beth's hand, placed it on the floor with his own, and then kissed her.

It was a deeply passionate kiss and Beth knew where it was heading. She didn't fight it, though. This was what she needed.

Toby pushed her back towards the sheets – the scruffy grey sheets – and they kissed again. The kissing got more and more heated, and Toby's hands started to explore. They were on her back, then her arms, then they moved to her hips. Then they started heading slowly northwards. She knew where they were going next. She knew they were heading towards her breasts. It had been a long time since someone had touched her in this way and she was starting to enjoy it.

'Shit!' Toby shouted, sitting up.

'What?' Beth asked stunned.

'Oh God! Nothing. That was mad.'

'What?'

'Nothing. Where were we?' Toby flashed her a cheeky smile and then moved back in to kiss her. His hands started to move again, but just before they explored anything even remotely intimate, Toby sat up again, grasping his stomach.

'What is it?' Beth asked with concern.

'I don't know. I had a kebab earlier, might have been that.'

'Stomach pains?'

'Really sharp, stabbing pains. They kill and then they're just gone.'

'Can I get you anything?'

'No. They're gone now. Here, why don't you go on top? That might help.'

Toby lay on his back and he grabbed Beth's hips to get her to straddle him. If she was honest, all the spark had gone. The talk of kebabs and stomach pains wasn't exactly endearing. She didn't feel in the mood anymore and she was more interested in getting back to her drink. Seeing how excited Toby looked, though, she decided to press on. The spark would come back soon, she was sure.

She got into a comfortable position on top of him and then bent down to kiss him.

'That's better,' he grinned.

They kissed some more and Toby wrapped his hands around her waist. Then slowly, once again, Beth felt them rise. With every touch of their lips, Beth started to feel more relaxed, and she was enjoying the sensation of his gentle fingertips.

Suddenly, just like before, just before he reached her breasts, he snapped up in pain again, knocking Beth backwards. 'Fucking hell!' he shouted. 'I'm so sorry.'

'I don't think you're well at all,' Beth said. 'Maybe I should go.'

'No! I feel better again now.'

'Look, it's been a great night, don't worry about it. You should get some rest.'

Toby sighed. 'I don't want you to go. But it was quite painful.'

'Let's do it again soon.'

'You want to?'

'Absolutely! We'll speak this weekend?'

'Definitely. Shall I walk you home?'

Beth stood up and smiled. 'I think I can cross the road all right.'

'Well, I tell you what, I'll watch you from the window.'

Beth looked out. There was the perfect view of her flat. She suddenly felt quite safe.

'See you soon,' she said, kissing Toby goodbye. Then she left.

She walked home overwhelmed with emotion. The day had turned out so differently from what she'd expected. But it had been very good.

It wasn't even ten o'clock, but Beth let herself in, put her pyjamas straight on, brushed her teeth and wrapped herself up in bed.

What a week she'd had. She was learning the ropes of a very difficult new job, she'd had a disastrous date, and then she'd been saved by a very lovely man only to go on a date with him. A very special man, she thought, as she closed her eyes.

She might have been overwhelmed by the amount that had happened to her recently, but she was feeling very happy. She felt desired and cared for and proud of herself.

Within minutes she fell to sleep, the broad smile still

stretched across her face. But it wasn't her job, her family nor Toby that she was thinking about. That night, all she dreamt about was Simon.

TWENTY-THREE

Early Saturday morning, Damien was at Malancy HQ, having being summoned by George for another meeting.

'Morning!' Damien grinned. He was last to arrive again, and George, Brian and Mr Taylor all stared at him as he grabbed a chair and joined them around George's desk. 'What's the latest, then?'

'I'm being sent to New York,' Brian stated, clearly displeased.

'What? Why?' Damien asked.

'Paul Bird phoned me up last night and said it made sense that I forge a relationship with the New York operation and find out how they do things. It's a great opportunity, I suppose-'

'What?!' Damien interrupted, anger flaring inside of him. 'Paul Bird is sending you to New York?'

'Yes, I'm supposed to be flying out on Monday.'

'I've never been to New York.'

'So?'

'You're doing my bloody job. Why did I never get to go to New York?'

'I don't know.'

'I don't think this is relevant at the minute, Damien,'

George said.

'He's doing the same job I was. Only I worked there for years, fought my way up to director level. Why do you get to go to New York when I didn't? Did you tell them you wanted to go?'

'I don't want to go!' Brian stated.

'Damien, shut up,' George demanded. 'The only thing we need to be concerned about is that our in-house spy is going to be out of action for a couple of weeks.'

'They must know you're a spy. That's why,' Damien concluded. 'They're trying to get rid of you.'

'How can they know that? The only people who knew can't remember,' Brian said.

'Precisely,' Damien replied. 'Simon figured it out, so who's to say other people couldn't?'

'Because Mr Bird's a genius,' Mr Taylor answered. His words were like venom, burning Damien inside.

'Look, Damien, I don't think anyone knows anything,' George said, trying to calm the tension. 'And if even they did, wouldn't they just sack Brian? Why would they send him to their New York office?'

Damien took a deep breath. There was something going on, this didn't add up at all. Why was Brian getting such special treatment? Maybe Brian's really crap at his job, Damien justified. So they're sending him overseas to learn more and improve. That could make sense.

'With Brian out of action, we're asking you, Damien, to step up into the surveillance role,' George continued. 'Simon still believes that you're a Bird Consultants employee and Brian has vouched for you with that ridiculous bodyguard that's watching Beth, so we need to use that to our advantage.'

Damien sighed. 'You can count on me.' He then turned to Brian and said, 'I want a full report from you as to what the New York office is like. I want photos and profiles on everyone.'

'What does it matter?' Brian asked.

'You never know. It could matter a lot.'

'Maybe you never went over there as they wanted to keep away from you,' Mr Taylor said, quite to the point. 'Maybe that's why Mr Bird spent so much time in New York, so he didn't have to see you every day. I can believe that.'

'Piss off!'

'Gentleman!' George snapped. 'We're supposed to be working together, not bickering about things that aren't even relevant to our mission. Brian, I don't see any harm in you making some notes on New York and reporting back. In the meantime, though, Damien I need you to find a way of keeping Beth away from Simon.'

Damien considered this and a small smile crept up on his lips. 'That would be my pleasure.'

'And can you please do it this time without leching all over her,' George added.

'What do you mean, leching?'

'You asked her out on a date,' Brian replied.

'It was part of the plan.'

'Yes, and we all know full well what plan that was,' George said. 'We all saw you up in Scotland. You don't just want Beth to be kept away from Simon, you want her all to yourself.'

'She's an attractive girl.'

'You want one up on Mr Bird,' Mr Taylor argued.

'What?'

'Damien, cut the bullshit,' George said. 'No matter what Beth looked like, the idea of you getting Simon's wife for yourself is more appealing than anything. To be honest, I don't really give a damn about who she ends up with. What I do care about is ending the Malancy, and you're putting that at risk.'

'How can you say that? You'd have lost everything if I hadn't got Beth to sign that contract,' Damien countered.

'That's true,' George said. 'But you're going to put all that hard work to waste if you don't stop perving over her all the time. She doesn't like you, and I doubt she ever will.'

'Let's face it, if Mr Bird's her type, you're never going to get a look in,' Mr Taylor jabbed.

'I got her to kiss me!'

'Just stop it, Damien!' George's temper was clearly starting to flare. 'The more you push, the more she'll resist, and then we'll end up with her running straight back into the arms of her husband. We need to be winning her over right now not making her sick.'

'Thanks a lot,' Damien huffed, folding his arms defensively. He couldn't believe how much they were all ganging up on him. After all he'd done for them!

'Can we count on you to put the future of the Malancy before your personal vendetta against Simon?' George asked.

'Especially now with their upcoming meeting,' Brian added.

'What meeting?' Damien said.

'On Tuesday afternoon Simon's booked in time with Beth to do her appraisal. But it's a very long meeting. Three hours or something like that. There's no way that's going to end well for us.'

'You need to keep them apart, Damien. And do it properly,' George ordered.

'You know I will. Nothing is more important to me.'

'I mean it, Damien. If you ruin this mission just to get one over Simon, then Simon will be the least of your worries. You'll be thinking fondly of the days when you were on his bad side, believe me. Do I make myself clear?'

Damien felt the hairs on his neck stand on end. He was learning fast that George wasn't a man to be messed with.

'Well?' George pushed.

'Whatever you need doing, I'll get it done. Trust me, you don't need to worry about a thing.'

* * *

Monday morning soon came around. It was just after eleven and Toby was sitting in the sandwich shop, just down the road from the Bird Consultants office, tucking into his toasted sandwich and cup of coffee.

He'd not officially seen Beth since his very strange stomach aches on Friday night. In all honestly, he was a little embarrassed. He could only put it down to a dodgy kebab, and, typically, the pain vanished the minute that Beth had left. But it wasn't pleasant at the time.

He'd texted Beth a few times, and although they hadn't made plans yet for a third date, she'd barely been out of his sight all weekend. He'd been mainly following her on her solo jaunt around London. It was a bit random. She just sat on the Piccadilly Line for ages, then got off at a stop, walked around a bit, and then got back on at another stop. Then she did the same thing all over again. It all seemed a bit boring to Toby, but she looked happy enough.

Just as he was finishing off the last bite of his sandwich, he heard a strange 'Hello Toby' behind him. Before he even had chance to look up, Damien was taking the seat opposite.

'What do you want?' Toby asked, knocking back his coffee.

'To apologise.'

This, Toby hadn't expected. 'You should be apologising to Beth, not me.'

'I'm going to. I wanted to see you first, though. You did the right thing. I was getting carried away. I behaved very badly and I'm just glad you were there to put me right.'

'Yeah, me too.'

'She's a beautiful woman. She has this way of getting under your skin.'

Toby couldn't help but nod. Then he shrugged. 'No hard feelings. What's done is done.'

'Surely you can appreciate Beth's beauty too?'

'She's a good looking bird. Who couldn't see that?'

'I bet you've thought about her, haven't you? I reckon you'd be good together.'

'Me and Beth?'

'Why not? You're about the same age. You're both free and single.'

'I'm her bodyguard.'

'Even better! No one is going to have her best interests at heart like you. She'd be a very lucky girl.'

Toby shrugged his shoulders.

'You'd be crazy not to at least try!'

Toby smiled. It made him happy that Damien agreed with his line of thinking. He had been feeling a little bit guilty about the possibility of abusing his position.

'Unless... Have you already?' Damien asked, studying Toby's face.

'What?'

'I know that look.'

'We went for a drink.'

'And the rest.'

'What do you mean?'

'You went back to hers, didn't you?'

Toby couldn't believe how forward everyone in the south seemed to be. 'What is it with you people?'

'What?' Damien asked.

'Why is everyone obsessed with whether I've had sex with Beth or not?'

'I was just...' Damien stopped himself. He stared hard at Toby for a minute. 'What do you mean, everyone?'

'That boss of hers. He cornered me in the pub the other night and asked me point blank if we'd had sex or not.'

'Boss? You mean Simon?'

'I never caught his name.'

'What was he like? A tall man?'

'He was shit scary, and I don't mind admitting it.'

'Simon! He wanted to know if you'd had sex?'

'Just like that. Just came out with it.'

Damien stopped for a second, processing something. 'What did you tell him?' he then asked.

'Oh, you can all fuck off! It's nothing to do with any of you.'

'You're not understanding me. You need to listen. Simon isn't just Beth's boss, he's obsessed with her.'

'No shit.'

'She can't stand him, she must have told you. But he wants her all to himself.'

'Paul or Jim never said anything about him. Is he the one that's put her in danger?'

Damien thought for a second. 'No. He's not a threat to her. He's a threat to you. He's a very jealous man. So you definitely told him that you hadn't had sex?'

'We hadn't.'

'Hadn't?' Damien challenged.

Toby sighed. He wasn't used to telling the world so much about his sex life. 'She came back to mine later that night but I wasn't very well.'

'You weren't well?'

'Are you deaf?'

'What were your symptoms?'

Toby shook his head. Who the hell was this bloke to want to know so much? 'I had a dodgy kebab, it made me sick. It happens.'

'Sick how?'

'What are you on? Can you stop grilling me?'

'No, you must tell me. You really don't understand. Simon is the most powerful Malant on the planet. Just tell me this: you tried to have sex with the woman that Simon is obsessed with but suddenly you couldn't because you fell ill. Is that right?'

Toby processed this. He didn't like where this was heading. 'Yeah.'

'He's cast a spell on you.'

'That's ridiculous.'

'Did he touch you while he was with you?'

Toby thought back to Friday night. 'I don't know. Yeah, he grabbed my arm. Yeah, he did, it was really weird.'

'That's when he did it.'

'What are you talking about? What, he just walks around with elements in his pocket so he can cast random spells on blokes that chat up his girlfriend?'

'He doesn't need elements. As I said, he's the most powerful Malant that has ever existed. He can do any spell he wants with just his mind. He's very gifted and now he's very angry with you.'

Toby took a second to think through all that he was being told. He hated to admit it, but it made far too much sense. 'He made me sick?' Toby thought back to when he was with Beth. 'He did, didn't he! It was only when me and Beth were getting... you know... that's when I had the pains. After she'd gone, I didn't get any pain at all.'

'See!'

'That fucking bastard!' Toby felt a sudden burst of anger.

'Calm down, it's all right.'

'It's bloody not.'

'You're a Malant too, aren't you?'

'Yes.'

'Do you know how to self-heal?'

'Of course I do.'

'Then self-heal. It will counteract the spell. Just don't tell anyone. As long as Simon thinks you get sick every time you're near Beth, then he'll leave you alone.'

Toby took a deep breath. He let his anger subside as he thought through Damien's simple solution. 'That could work.'

'Of course it will.'

'Cheers pal. I'll do that. You won't say anything to anyone?'

'Of course not. Anyway, he's warned me off her too. I'm in the same boat as you.'

'So we're good?'

'Absolutely. There's just one thing I need to do now. I need to speak with Beth. Would you be okay if I dropped by her flat later?'

'No can do.'

'It would only be for a second.'

'It's not that. Paul and Jim cast a spell on it. No Malant can enter. I couldn't go back to hers the other night, she had to come to mine.'

'Really?'

'But I could ask her to meet you down The Rose?'

'The Rose?'

'The pub down the road from here, near Beth's flat.'

'I know where you mean. That would be great. I'll be there from five o'clock. Get her to meet me. I really want to make peace with her. You understand?'

'No problem. Besides, I owe you one.'

TWENTY-FOUR

At just after five o'clock, Beth left the office and headed on towards The Rose.

She'd had a text from Toby asking if she'd meet him for a quick after work drink. She was so glad to meet up with him again. She'd been worried about him after what had happened on Friday night. Although he had said he was feeling much better.

She opened the door to the pub to be greeted by a virtually empty space. She looked around and saw Toby in the corner. Then she saw that he wasn't alone. She clocked her eyes straight on Damien and hesitated in the middle of the pub. What was he doing there?

Toby saw her and raced over to meet her. He kissed her quickly.

'Why are you with Damien?' she asked.

'Don't be mad. I saw him earlier and he said he wanted to apologise to you but he didn't know how else to do it.'

As much as Beth wasn't impressed with what had happened on their so-called date, she did think it was probably a good thing for them to clear the air. They had, after all, been good friends. And they were also colleagues.

'It's fine,' she nodded. Beth walked over and sat down

next to Damien.

'Hello Beth, thanks for seeing me. How are you?'

'I'm good, thank you.'

'Toby, would you mind?' Damien asked. Toby hadn't even had chance to sit down again. He looked across at Damien in surprise. 'I think Beth and I should talk, just the two of us. Might be a bit awkward... you know.'

'What do you want me to do?' Toby asked, turning to Beth.

Beth looked at Damien. Maybe they did need to talk, just the two of them. It was a bit awkward having both men she'd been on dates with recently sitting next to one another. 'Would you give us a second?' she said.

'If that's what you want. But I'm not leaving. I'll be over by the window.'

'I got you a red wine,' Damien said, the second Toby was out of earshot. He pushed the rather large glass towards Beth. She smiled but it was the last thing that she wanted. It was only Monday night and she hadn't even had her dinner yet. She didn't want to seem ungrateful, though.

'I'm very sorry about last week,' Damien began. 'I treated you badly.'

'It's fine,' Beth said.

'It's not.'

'I get it. Don't worry. It must seem crazy to you. One minute we're going out all the time, planning a holiday, the next I don't seem that interested at all.'

'That's it. I'm so glad you see. Not a couple of weeks ago we were inseparable, and now...'

Inseparable? Beth did have to note to herself how every time Damien spoke, his stories of their time together got a little bit more elaborate. How she wished she knew what the truth was.

'I need to be honest with you, Damien.'

'I know about you and Toby.'

'He told you?'

'We've become friends. It's all fine.'

'I know we were once very close, Damien,' Beth said, grasping her wine tightly. This wasn't easy, but honesty was always best. 'But whatever I was feeling back then, I just don't feel it anymore. I don't see you as any more than a friend. I'm really sorry.'

Damien looked genuinely upset by this and Beth felt immediately guilty. She felt like she'd been leading him on, although she couldn't remember any of it. 'Thank you for your honesty, Beth. I really appreciate it. I'm gutted, obviously. I thought we had something really special. But that's what Simon does. He ruins things.'

Beth's guilt tripled with Damien's words and she took a big gulp of her drink. Something had changed, she just couldn't remember what it was. She hated herself for how she was treating Damien, but she couldn't deny her feelings. When she looked at him, she felt nothing. Any romantic feelings she must have had weren't even a distant memory. It was as if they'd never existed at all.

Then Simon flashed into her head. Despite the fact that she hated him, she couldn't help but admit that he stirred up her senses. She found him beguiling.

There was no doubt that Simon was to blame for all this mess. He'd clearly affected her feelings on a lot of things. She had to be strong, though. Simon was manipulating her somehow and she had to remember that she couldn't trust everything she felt. Whether it was through drugs or hypnosis or some other form of control, he was the bad person here. She had to remember that. She knew she had to stop herself having these warm feelings towards him. They weren't real and they could only lead to bad things.

'Friends?' Damien asked.

'Of course,' Beth smiled. 'Always.'

'Good. Then I have a proposition for you. As a friend.'

'Okay.'

'I've been very worried about you. I heard that Mr Bird warned off Toby the other day. It's happening again. He's trying to get his claws into you again. I can't let that happen. It's already cost me a beautiful relationship, I don't want it to cost you too; nor Toby for that matter.'

Beth just nodded.

'You remember I said I had a potential job opportunity for you?' Damien said.

'Yes.'

'Well, it's a firm offer now. I've already handed in my notice. I won't be back at Bird Consultants. I start my new job next Monday and I want you to come with me.'

'What?' Beth didn't know how to react.

'You'd be working alongside me as the Administration Director. It's a smaller company, but I thought you might find that easier.'

'Smaller company?' Beth had quite liked being a director of a large, international operation.

'It's a six figure salary. What are you on at the minute?'

Beth's mouth dropped open. She wasn't exactly sure what her current salary was. She'd only seen the net amount from one month on her bank statement. Whatever, though, six figures were breathtaking.

'You'll get a relocation package too,' Damien added.

'Relocation?'

'Yes.'

'Relocate where?'

'Sorry, didn't I say? The job's in Manchester.'

'Manchester?' Beth's heart sank. She didn't want to leave London. She was just settling in.

'Oh Beth, I know you love London, but you need to get away from Mr Bird. He's dangerous.'

'Then we should go to the police. I can't move my whole life just because there's a man out there who may or may not drug me again and make me forget my life.'

'No Beth, that's exactly what you should be doing.'

'No!' Beth did have to admit that she was terrified of Mr Bird, and the idea of never seeing him again was... Why was the idea of never seeing him again so painful? The second she processed the idea of living halfway across the country from him, she felt deeply saddened.

He really was getting to her. There was no logical reason why she should feel anything positive towards that horrid man. Maybe she did need to get away.

'It's not a move forever, Beth. In fact, I tell you what. As I said, it's a small start-up for now, but I think we could put in a proposal for a London office. If we did that in the next few months, I bet we could work it so we're both back down here by this time next year. Let's give ourselves a year in Manchester. Then, if it doesn't work out, you'll get to leave with fantastic experience and a boosted CV. Win win.'

Beth knew it made sense. It was an incredible opportunity. But could she really move from London and move from her existing job, just when she was starting to feel comfortable? Then what about Toby? She'd just met a lovely man and was starting the first promising relationship she'd had in years.

'I need to think about this, Damien,' she said.

'I understand you need time, but the problem is we don't have it. I need to know, Beth. We're going on Monday.'

'I'd have to work my notice. I couldn't do that anyway.'

'No you wouldn't. You're still in your probation period. It's six months at Bird Consultants. If you handed in your notice tomorrow, I'm sure he'd let you go by Friday.'

Beth suddenly felt very insecure. 'It seems so ungrateful.'

'What have you got to be grateful for? For the three months that he stole from you?'

'I can't answer this now, Damien. Let me sleep on it.'

'Okay, Beth. Of course. You sleep on it. Call me tomorrow?'

'I promise.'

'I'd better go. I've got another meeting to get to. Take care, Beth.'

Damien walked off and Toby came back over. 'Are you all right?' he asked.

Beth had another massive gulp of her drink. She couldn't tell Toby. She didn't want to lie, but how could she tell a man she'd just started dating that she was contemplating a move across the country? She needed to get her head around it first before she shared it with anyone else.

'Damien and I cleared the air and we're friends,' she said, refusing to say any more.

'You look a bit pale.'

'That's Mondays for you!' Beth was suddenly conscious that she was steering off into the mistruth zone and she wanted to keep out of it. Omitting information was one thing, but she had no reason to lie. 'I'm sorry, Toby. I know I said we'd have a drink, but I think I need to go home. It's been a heavy going day.'

'So it's your turn to feel like crap tonight, then?' he smiled.

'I guess it is. Next time we meet, let's get it right.'

'Dinner Wednesday?' Toby asked.

'Sounds perfect.'

Beth knocked back the rest of her drink, kissed Toby goodbye, and then headed home. She had a lot to think about.

TWENTY-FIVE

By the next morning, Beth still wasn't convinced. Moving across the country was such a major decision. Not one part of her wanted to leave London and she hated that she was only considering it because a single man was driving her away. It was so unfair.

She had her appraisal with Mr Bird that afternoon and she made the decision to see how that went before even considering Damien's proposal for a second more.

Beth was sitting at her desk, typing an email to a prospective new stationery supplier. Now that she was in charge of the budget, she was enjoying being able to explore alternatives to the costly suppliers that they were currently using.

As she typed away, she knew how much she wanted to stay. The job may be a little overwhelming, but with every passing day she was really starting to get to grips with it. On this task alone, she'd learnt how good a negotiator she was. It hadn't been easy at first, but she'd revelled in the thrill that playing one supplier off against another had given her. That was something she'd never thought she'd be able to do.

'Beth!' It wasn't very loud and she wasn't quite sure if

she had just heard her name being called. She turned round to see Diane at the door, waving for her attention.

'What are you doing?' Beth asked.

'Come here!' Diane all but whispered.

'Why?'

'Come here!'

Beth headed over and Diane disappeared into the kitchen. Beth followed her in to find Diane standing nervously in the corner. Beth joined her, eager to know what she wanted. This seemed like very strange behaviour, even for Diane.

'What is it?' Beth asked.

'We have to talk.'

'Why are you whispering?'

'Gayle told me that Mr Bird has started putting microphones around the office as a way of keeping tabs on the staff.'

'He can't do that!' Beth's anger towards the man flared up again.

'He does whatever he likes. Have you not learnt that yet? I've tested the water in the kitchen, though. I think we're safe.'

'Tested the water?'

'Michelle and I made up a conversation about how we'd seen Mr Bird's Aston Martin covered in scratches in the car park. If he was listening... Well you don't have a car like that and not care if it's covered in scratches.'

'I suppose.'

'Survival, Beth. It's all about survival.'

'So what's going on?'

'Things have got bad. Very bad. I don't know how to tell you this.'

'What?'

'You know Brian, the new salesman?'

'Yes.'

'Well I didn't. And now I won't.'

'What do you mean?'

'Did you know that Brian liked you?'

'Brian?'

'Yes. Apparently he sought Mr Bird's permission to ask you out on a date. With the fact that you were married, I suppose he was trying to do the right thing. What a mistake!'

'Brian?' Beth couldn't believe it. She'd never been so desired before.

'It was last Friday night, when everyone had gone home. Mr Bird worked late and Brian took his chance to have a quiet word.'

'Friday night?' Beth thought back to when she'd seen Mr Bird in the pub. He hadn't looked happy.

'No one's seen him since.'

'What?'

'You go upstairs. His desk is empty and no one's mentioning it.'

'That doesn't mean anything.'

'I'm really sorry to say, Beth, but it does. Did you like him too?'

'I'm seeing someone else.'

Diane gasped, as if this was the most astonishing news in the world. 'Does Mr Bird know?'

'Yes.'

'Oh Beth, get rid of him. It's not safe.'

'What?'

'They found a body.'

'What are you talking about?'

'It's all over the office. They say it's Brian's. Mr Bird has killed him. All Brian did was ask if he could take you out on a date and Mr Bird's killed him.'

Beth was horrified. She started to feel faint. 'That can't be true!'

'I have it on very good authority, Beth. It seems if Mr Bird can't have you, then no one can.'

'No, no, no! I know he's a bit jealous. All he did was warn Toby off, though. And he sent Damien to Scotland.

He's not a killer. He can't be a killer!'

'Brian isn't his first victim, Beth. He's done it before. We all know it. It's just never been one of our own before.'

'Well if you all know it, how does he think he's going to get away with it?'

'He gets away with everything! You must know this. He's one of the most powerful men in the country. He's above the law. That's why the salaries are so good here. We're all paid too well to ask any questions and too well to leave. All we have to do is keep our heads down, work hard and ignore the free will of our sadistic boss, and we reap the rewards. I can't afford to leave. Most people can't.'

'So if Brian hadn't have liked me, he'd still be alive?'

'You can't blame yourself.'

'It can't possibly be true.'

'It's all over the news. They found a body dumped in a field just off the M40. In Buckinghamshire.'

'Isn't that where Mr Bird lives?'

'It's where you said you were living when you were married to him.'

Beth's breathing became erratic and she grabbed on to the kitchen side to steady herself. She was trapped in a horrible nightmare.

She needed to see it for herself.

She turned around and headed straight for her desk. She quickly sat down and opened up a new tab on the internet, searching for the latest news. There, at the top of the headlines, were details of a man's body that had been found, just as Diane had described.

'That's interesting work on your computer,' Diane said from behind, a fake lightness to her voice that seemed vastly out of character.

'It's true!'

'Yes, all that documentation you're looking at is very true.'

'But you can't know for sure-'

'Don't forget what I told you!' Diane announced, pressing her finger to her lips. Beth suddenly remembered the microphones. Mr Bird was probably listening to everything right at that moment.

This was all too complicated and far too scary.

Then she thought to Toby. She had to know if he was safe. She felt sick at the idea of Mr Bird hurting Toby. She quickly went to grab her mobile which lay next to her keyboard. Just before her fingers touched it, though, it shot across her desk and hurtled to the floor. She couldn't work out how she'd knocked it, but she was so jittery, it shouldn't have come as a surprise.

Diane bent down and picked it up for her. Beth smiled her thank you and then, with increasingly shaky fingers, she dialled Toby's number.

'Y'alright?' Toby answered.

'Are you?'

'Yeah. What's the matter? You sound weird.'

'Everything's fine. I just wanted to check you were okay. Nothing to worry about. Just checking in.'

'Okay.'

'You have no need to come anywhere near the office, do you?'

'Why, do you need something?'

'No. You have no reason to come anywhere near this building, though, do you? I mean, it's probably best to keep your distance.'

Toby was silent for a second. 'What are you on about? I live just down the road.'

Beth swallowed. Toby was so close. Then she remembered that he was soon to start working at the company. Things could potentially be disastrous. By dating him she could be as good as handing him his death sentence. This was horrendous.

Suddenly tears were filling up in her eyes and she felt all the walls around her close in. She was trapped in a nightmare.

'Toby?' she said.

'Yes.'

'Would you ever move back to Manchester?'

'It's my home. I'd move back any day.'

'Is it nice there?'

'Best city in the world!'

'What are you doing for lunch?' Beth saw her options getting smaller and smaller. This wasn't just about her anymore, this was about the fate of every man that she was ever going to get close to.

'Nothing. I could swing by about one o'clock?'

'No! Meet me at that burger place down the road?'

'If you want.'

'Yes. Definitely. See you there.'

'See you at one.'

Beth hung up and Diane placed a hand on her shoulder. 'Toby's fine,' Beth said, sighing. 'For now.'

'That's good to know,' Diane smiled, keeping up her pretence for the microphones. 'So you're breaking up with him at lunch, then?' Diane's eyes widened, signalling for Beth to play along.

'No. I have a much better idea. I'm just popping out for some air.'

Beth grabbed her mobile firmly in her hand and she headed for the lifts. Once outside in the warm summer air, she walked to the side of the building, out of the view of any colleagues. She took a deep breath, the sickness inside of her throbbing, and she dialled Damien's number.

'Hello Beth,' he answered.

Beth couldn't speak at first. She was so devastated by everything that was happening to her.

'Beth, are you there?'

'Have you seen the news today?' she finally said.

Damien was silent for a second. Then he said, 'You mean the body they've found?'

'Yes.'

'I take it you've heard the truth then? News always did

travel quickly around Bird Consultants.'

'How does anyone know what the truth is?'

'Bird Consultants does a lot of work with the police, Beth. Trust me, I've developed a few contacts over the years. It's been confirmed as Brian's body and it's got Mr Bird written all over it. The problem is, though, Mr Bird knows a lot of secrets that some very important people want to keep secret. They can't afford to put him on the suspect list. I heard it's going down as an unexplained death. But we know the truth. We always know the truth.'

'That's so wrong!' Beth couldn't fight the tears that were now streaming down her face. She felt so guilty. How had she become trapped in such a messy world?

'That's just the way it is with Mr Bird. And it's the way it always will be.'

'I can't believe things like this actually happen.'

'I know it's a big decision, but you need to leave, Beth. It's not safe.'

Beth took another deep breath. She needed to control herself. 'I know.'

'So you'll take the job?'

Beth thought back to her recently acquired skills and she decided it was time to be tough. 'Are you open for negotiation?'

This clearly stunned Damien. 'Is a six figure salary not enough?'

'It's not that. It's just... If I take the job, will you find a new job for Toby too?'

Damien paused again. 'Toby?'

'I can't risk him being next on Mr Bird's target list.'

'But...'

'He already knows I'm dating someone. And with the microphones... I bet he knows loads about Toby.'

'Microphones?'

'Please, Damien. Please help us both.'

There was another short pause before Damien said, 'Okay. Leave it with me. If you hand your notice in today, then I promise I'll make sure Toby is sorted out too. Is that fair enough?'

Beth couldn't help but sigh with relief. Damien's words immediately released the darkness that had been choking her. 'Thanks, Damien.'

'No, thank you Beth. Thank you for giving me peace of mind. Call me when you've done it? I need to make sure you're safe.'

'He won't kill me after I've handed in my notice, will he?' Beth was shaking now, she was so petrified.

'Of course not. Don't worry. Tell everyone the news as soon as you've done it, to cover yourself, and then make sure Toby keeps an eye on you until you leave. Just a few days left, Beth, and then you never have to see Mr Bird again.'

TWENTY-SIX

It was five to two and Simon's heart was pounding. Beth's appraisal was booked in for two o'clock that afternoon and he couldn't wait.

After he'd left her in the pub last Friday night he'd hit a real low. Paul had insisted that Simon keep persevering, turning up wherever she went with the aim of slowly reminding her of how much she loved him, but Simon couldn't do it. He couldn't take the risk of seeing her again with that so-called boyfriend. It made him too angry. And it made him far too unhappy.

Instead he'd pinned all his hopes on the appraisal. He'd convinced Paul, and himself, that if he could have a few hours alone with her, completely undisturbed by anyone else, then they could get to know each other all over again. Maybe that's all she needed to remember her true feelings. It was the perfect plan and Simon felt confident that this was finally going to work.

He heard a soft knock on his office door and his breath extinguished. This was it. Now was his time to get his wife back.

'Come in,' he summoned in his friendliest tone.

Beth opened the door and then shakily closed it behind

her. She looked quite pale, not well at all.

'Are you okay?' Simon asked. Beth just nodded, not saying a word.

'Please, take a seat,' Simon said, as he shifted awkwardly in his own.

Beth glared at the black chair that Simon had placed on the other side of his desk. She didn't move for a minute, but finally she edged forward. She delicately sat down, grasping her notebook in her hand, clearly deeply uncomfortable.

'How have you been today?' he asked, trying to lighten the mood. This was far tenser than he'd anticipated.

'Why?' Beth asked in a meek voice.

Her question totally threw Simon and he couldn't think how to respond. 'Just... I was just... You look a little shaky. I was just checking you were okay.'

'I'm fine.'

Her short, sharp reply killed off any chance of extending that conversation and Simon sat up straight. He shuffled through some paperwork on his desk, trying to think where he needed to start. He prayed to himself that she'd open up a bit more as they went through the motions of this pretend appraisal.

'To your appraisal then,' he said.

'Actually...' Beth started. He watched her as she turned to scan the Executive Floor. Then her pale face turned almost green.

'What is it?'

'Where's Brian?' Her voice was noticeably shaking.

Again, this totally threw Simon. None of this was how he had envisioned the meeting going. 'Who?' he asked. He wasn't sure who she was speaking about nor what the relevance was.

'Brian. The Sales Manager.'

Simon followed Beth's glare out across the Executive Floor where he saw an empty desk. Of course, Brian. Simon recalled Damien's protégé.

'I have no idea,' Simon answered honestly. He'd not seen Brian that day, but he also didn't keep tracks on employees. Brian was Damien's responsibility so he didn't see why he needed to be aware of his whereabouts. As long as the sales came in, Simon wasn't worried.

'Really?' Beth asked in suddenly quite an accusatorially tone.

'No. Why?'

Beth took a deep breath. Simon could see her shaking, far more than on her last visit.

'Why are you asking about Brian?' he queried, totally confused. What did any of this have to do with her appraisal?

A few seconds of very tense silence passed by and then Beth sat up straight in her chair. She took another deep breath and Simon could see her physically psyching herself up for something. 'I don't think we need to do my appraisal today, Mr Bird,' she firmly said.

Simon normally prided himself on reading both situations and people, but none of this meeting was going anywhere near how he'd planned it, and he hadn't got a clue as to why. He didn't even know what to say. All he could do was wait for Beth to elaborate on why she was calling an end to a meeting that hadn't even begun.

Beth ruffled through her notepad and pulled out a folded letter. 'Please accept this as notice of my resignation,' she said as she handed it to Simon.

Simon felt the world around him grind to a halt and then a painful blow hit his stomach. He needed a second to gather his thoughts. Had she really just said she was resigning?

With jittery fingers now himself, he slowly unfurled the letter. It explained that Beth had a new opportunity and, as per the terms of her probation, her last day would be on the sixteenth of June.

Simon placed the letter down. He stared at Beth. The sixteenth of June. That was the coming Friday. She wanted to leave that Friday! He suddenly felt overwhelmed with panic.

'Why do you want to leave?' he asked as calmly as he could, trying to hide his upset.

Beth swallowed. 'As it explains in my letter, I've been offered a huge opportunity that I just can't turn down.'

'A huge opportunity? What does that mean?'

'It's a fantastic new job that I'd be silly not to take.'

'Is it your salary? We can pay you more.'

Beth shook her head. 'It's too good an opportunity to miss.'

'Whatever it is, I'll match it. We don't want to lose you Beth.' Simon could no longer hide the desperation in his voice. He felt a sharp, stabbing pain in his stomach at the very idea of Beth leaving.

'It's totally different. I need a fresh start.'

'A fresh start? You've barely been here. Give us a chance.'

'I need to leave!' The desperation was now apparent in Beth's voice too.

'Where are you going?'

Beth shook her head. 'I'd rather not say.'

'Why?' Simon asked. There was something not adding up about any of this and he wanted to know why. He needed to know why.

'I'd just rather not say.'

'Well I want to know!' Simon insisted. 'I'm losing one of my best members of staff and I'd like to know where you're going. I think I have a right to know who has offered you this "too good to be true" opportunity that you can't turn down.'

'I don't think I'm your best member of staff,' Beth replied. 'I've barely got to grips with any of it. I've hardly been productive over the past few weeks.'

'I know talent when I see it.'

'I just want to leave.'

Simon could see that Beth was getting upset, but he

had to fight for her. He couldn't stand the thought of her not being around anymore. 'Tell me where you're going.'

'I don't think it's appropriate,' Beth firmly stated, although the tears now appearing in her eyes gave away her weak stance.

'You have to tell me,' Simon said, trying to remain calm. He hated the thought of upsetting Beth, but it was better than never seeing her again. 'What if you're going to a competitor? We might have to insist that you take gardening leave.' Simon knew that was complete rubbish. They had no competitors and she was, as she clearly knew, on her probation. He had no right to say such a thing, but he was desperate.

'I'm completely changing industries,' Beth stated, 'so you have nothing to worry about.'

'Tell me where you're going. Please.'

'Why do you want to know?'

He could see how much she was fighting her tears, fighting to stay composed. He felt awful for interrogating her in such a way, but he had no choice. 'So I can find a way to get you to stay.'

Beth just nodded. She looked down at her notebook gripped so tightly in her hands. She nodded again, as if she'd just received the answer to a burning question.

She finally looked up, then she took a deep breath and rose to her feet. 'I think we both know you have to let me go.' She was clearly quivering, but there was a new firmness to her voice that told him she meant business.

Simon could see he was running low on options. It was time to be honest. It was now or never. 'I don't want you to go,' he said, stripping away all of the barriers that he'd held up for such a long time. 'Forget about the business, I want you to stay. I want to get to know you better.' He felt more vulnerable in that moment than he'd ever done before in his life.

Beth glared at him. She paused for a second, her eyes searching every inch of his face. Then she uttered, 'What have I done to deserve this?'

Yet again, her response was far from what Simon had expected. 'What do you mean?'

'You know exactly what I mean. I know, Simon.'

'You know?'

'Of course I know.'

'Do you feel it too?'

'No.' Her answer cut him sharply. No matter how much Simon had tried to ignore his feelings for Beth, he hadn't been able to deny them. There was such a coldness to her answer that he knew she wasn't lying. She meant it. He was wrong. Paul was wrong. The feelings weren't mutual. Beth was never Simon's. The love wasn't reciprocated. It was gone.

'Please let me go, Simon. I need to leave. Please.'

He understood. She didn't want to leave her job, she wanted to leave him. She was terrified, and he could see it evident in every pore of her body. He'd been too obvious, not hiding his feelings well enough, even though he'd had so much practice at it over the years. His hopeless dream of finding love at last had cost him. And it had cost him deeply. He'd pushed her away and now she wanted to completely leave.

He ached inside as he took one last moment to stare at her beautiful face. He had such an urge to curl her soft hair behind her ears so he could see in full how stunning she was. He'd never get the chance to do that now. It was over. He had to accept it was over.

As much as her leaving hurt him, what hurt him more was to see the woman that he loved so afraid. It was the one thing that he knew he could help her with, though. The more he'd want her to stay, the more she'd want to leave. All he could do now was cut her free and at least give her some peace of mind.

He took a deep breath to control the agony that throbbed through his body and he addressed her directly. 'I'm delighted to hear you have a new opportunity. I hope it brings you lots of happiness. You deserve nothing but happiness. Don't worry about working until Friday. Please, take the rest of the week to prepare for your new role. I'll make sure that you're paid in full as per your notice period, but you're free to leave whenever you wish.'

Beth stared at him with uncertainty. 'I can leave now?'

'If that's what you want.'

'You're letting me go? Properly letting me go?'

'I'm sorry Bird Consultants has not worked out for you. We wish you the very best for the future.'

Beth looked a little stunned. Then she slowly straightened herself up. 'Thank you... Simon. I'll go and clear my desk.'

'Best of luck, Beth. You'll never be forgotten.'

Simon watched Beth slowly leave his office and walk confidently to the lifts. Then she was gone. That was it. The woman he loved – the only woman who he'd ever loved and had ever loved him in return – was gone.

TWENTY-SEVEN

In the few minutes that passed after Beth had left, Simon couldn't process anything. He felt numb. He just stared out in front of him, unable to clear through any of this thoughts or gain control of any of his feelings.

She was gone. The woman he loved was gone. Once upon a time she'd loved him too, but now their marriage was over.

Someone had manipulated their relationship and had torn them apart. Someone had messed with them.

Then something snapped inside of Simon and for the first time in days, he grabbed hold of his senses. This wasn't real. This wasn't how it was meant to be. Someone had come between him and Beth and they were messing with them. If he wanted to fix his marriage and get back his wife, he didn't need to win over Beth, he needed to deal with the source of the problem.

What had he been thinking? Why hadn't he just tackled the source straight away?

He knew very little about what had caused their memory loss, but he knew it was the work of a contract. Some horrible, sick person out there had drawn up a contract to deliberately orchestrate the breakdown of his marriage. Paul had insisted that he was looking into the issue, but he'd clearly got nowhere. Now it was time that Simon took over. Things needed to be done properly. He needed to take control of his life.

Two of Simon's key strengths were his ability to control his emotions and his sharp eye when it came to working with contracts. Both of these skills had been wavering in recent times as Simon had tried to deal with an unusually emotional situation, but he needed to focus again and get back in touch with his strengths. If he was going to beat this, he needed to be on top of his game.

How could Paul possibly think that he could beat this without Simon? Breaking down contracts was Simon's forte. He'd been more than willing to let Paul take charge as he'd been so hurt and confused by everything. No wonder things had gone from bad to worse, Simon had been all over the place. But that had to stop, and right now. It was time for him to take control.

With a new determination and fighting spirit, Simon composed himself. Yes, it still very much hurt that his wife had chosen to leave him, but he turned to the logic. The logic gave him hope. The logic helped to calm him.

None of this was what Beth actually felt. It was all down to the contract and what it had manipulated her into feeling. In reality, she had willingly married him and they'd declared, in front of witnesses, that they wanted to spend the rest of their lives together. Anything that had changed was fundamentally the result of magic. Therefore Simon needed to eliminate that magic in order to put his life back on track.

He turned his mind to the problem. If the contract was the issue, the first and only logical thing to do was to get hold of the contract. He'd yet to be fazed by any contract that he'd ever come across. He felt confident that, if he could just get hold of it, then he could probably find a loophole to overcome it. The bigger problem was finding the thing in the first place.

Simon cleared his mind and started to work through the issue rationally. This was what he was really good at and it was time that he started using his strengths for his own gain for a change.

He first considered what he knew. A contract had been written to keep him and Beth apart, and Beth had been tricked into signing it. Who would do that? And why?

Paul had suggested that it was a jealous ex-boyfriend. Jealousy definitely seemed like a worthwhile motive here. Whoever they were, though, they must be skilled. To wield magic through the form of a contract that would otherwise be impossible, they would have to know what they were doing. That was very sophisticated trickery. It was at the high-level end of magic that Bird Consultants dealt with, and Simon knew too well how few people were actually capable of that.

Without his memories, though, it would be very hard for him to even start a list of possible suspects. There would no doubt be gaps in his knowledge that would render the list unreliable. He very much needed to stick to what he absolutely knew.

He toyed with the idea of calling Paul to try and find out where he was in solving this issue, but he quickly decided against it. Although Simon knew that Paul would have his best interests at heart, he knew that he'd also want to protect him. He'd just insist that Simon keep working on Beth, as that would be, to him, the most rational way out of this mess.

Paul hadn't seen the look in Beth's eyes, though. Paul hadn't had to witness how frightened Beth actually was. Simon could quite plainly see that the more he approached Beth, the more he was going to push her away.

So the facts as Simon knew them were that someone had written a contract, they'd got Beth to sign it and then they must have hidden it somewhere. It was a physical contract. It had to exist somewhere in the world.

As he searched his brain for any clues that might have

passed his way, he felt the surge of his newly increased power race through his veins. Then he considered how his magic could help him. Maybe he didn't need to know who or why, maybe just the fact that he knew the contract existed was enough. He'd never heard of anyone locating anything that wasn't sentient before, but maybe, just maybe.

He'd learnt over time that the reason location spells only ever worked on sentient beings was that the magic tapped into their organic nature. So much about the Malancy was connected to the natural world.

Simon was different, though. He rarely needed to harness the power of an element, and he hadn't at all when he'd cast those spells with Paul the week before. What if, just maybe, he could tap into all of his new found strength and override any need for organic matter at all? It might be possible. It definitely could be possible. Maybe it was within his power to locate an inanimate object. As long as he accounted for the extra energy that he'd need to replace the lack of natural elements, then it might just work.

It was worth a try.

Then the next major problem hit him. To locate the contract, he might not need the help of nature, but he'd most definitely need to know something about it. But he'd never seen it. Nor had anyone else that he knew of.

He focussed again. There had to be something about the document that he could use to find it. There had to be a way.

What was the contract about? He could guess roughly what it said, but it could be in Spanish for all he knew. The content was too open, he couldn't utilise that.

Then he thought to the format. If he could imagine what it looked like. Again, though, it could be in any font, in any style, on any coloured paper. That's if it even was on paper. None of it was enough.

There had to be something that he could tap into. He worked with contracts every day. What made each of them stand out? What was guaranteed to be on any contract? What was guaranteed to be on this particular contract?

Like a lightning bolt, he found his answer. The signature. The only thing he absolutely knew for a fact about this document was that Beth had signed it. If he could picture her signature and then search for hidden contracts with her signature on, it could theoretically work.

He looked down at the letter on his desk - the resignation letter from Beth. There, in black ink, was her signature. For a brief moment it made Simon smile.

Beth was so smart in appearance. She always looked flawless, yet her signature was a scrawl. It wasn't even written in a straight line. He loved that she never failed to surprise him. She truly was fascinating.

He had his idea, he had his signature, all he needed to do now was to see if he could get the spell to work. He looked out across the Executive Floor. Even if he blackened his windows, it wouldn't be enough. He needed to be alone. He couldn't risk any disturbances. With so much at stake, he needed to do this right.

He switched off his laptop and placed it, along with Beth's letter, in his bag. Then he grabbed his keys, left his office (locking it as usual behind him), made his way out of the building, and headed straight towards his car.

He wasted no time in pulling away, and he drove straight on towards Buckinghamshire. He knew exactly where he was heading. He wasn't going home, instead he was going to drive deep into the countryside where he knew he could be alone.

Twenty minutes later, he pulled into an opening just off a small country lane not far from his house, and he turned off his engine. His instinct told him to get out and look for a stone, but he stopped himself. He remembered how he'd done his last spell without any support from an external element. Granted, this was a much tougher spell, but he needed to know. He could always repeat it with a stone if it didn't work. He just needed to know how strong he'd suddenly become.

He took out Beth's letter from his laptop bag on the passenger seat and he opened it up. He stared at the signature. His Beth's signature.

He quickly stopped himself feeling anything sentimental about it and he focussed on the task in hand.

He absorbed the image of her signature into his mind, and then he closed his eyes.

He summoned the strength within him, as was normal with a location spell, but this time he gave it far more emphasis. This time he pushed hard, channelling his power with more weight than he'd ever done before.

He sat upright in his Aston Martin and focussed intently on the image of Beth's signature. He then supported this with a backdrop of thoughts about a hidden document that Beth had been forced to sign.

Simon was concentrating so fiercely, his body started to shake. With every muscle clenched tightly, he cleared his mind of all other things except the few items that he knew to be true about this contract.

Suddenly, as the images grew more vibrant in his mind, a bright, golden glow burned on Simon's skin. Within seconds it turned into a scarlet sheen, and Simon could feel the spell working. Not faltering for a second, he continued with his focus. After just a few moments more, the sheen turned into a fiery blaze of red and his whole car was swallowed up.

Then, like a flash, dazzling beams scorched everything in sight and the image hit him.

He quickly dropped the letter from his hand, not losing sight of the location in his mind. The inferno around him vanished in an instant and he placed his hands out before him to start a new spell.

This time he focussed on the location of the contract. He had a crystal clear image of it hidden in a drawer in a rather large, currently unoccupied office. Simon didn't recognise the room, but that didn't matter. All that mattered was retrieving the contract.

He thought to the drawer and once again he channelled his power. This time he didn't need to be quite as fierce about it, and he relaxed a bit more as he let the image of the paperwork come alive in his mind.

As the image became more vibrant, he felt the energy within him surge. Then, literally out of thin air, he felt the touch of paper against his fingertips.

He'd done it. He opened his eyes and looked down. There, in front of him, was the contract. The very document that had set about destroying his marriage. It was now in his possession and no one else in the world knew about it.

He took a second to let the relief settle within him. Where had that power come from? He'd just performed a spell that was virtually impossible, and he'd not only done it all on his own, but he didn't even feel remotely tired. There was no fall out, no hangover, no dizzy spell. He was fine.

Whatever had happened to him recently, he had to acknowledge that he'd somehow received a boost in his power. A rush of excitement hurtled through him as he realised what this could mean. He had a world of power at his fingertips. It was incredible.

Feeling a little overwhelmed by his new found realisation, it took Simon a moment to properly process the document in his hand. But as his eyes started to focus on it, his breath extinguished.

Suddenly a sickness punched him in the stomach as he glared at the document before him. This wasn't just any old contract. He flicked through the pages. There were dozens of them. There was so much detail. It was the biggest contract that he'd ever seen. But that wasn't the thing that alarmed Simon the most. There was something else that angered him, something else that now made his blood boil and his skin pulsate with rage.

He couldn't believe it, but it was there before him.

The very document that he now held in his hand was his own template.

Whoever had created this contract had done so using a Bird Consultants template. It was in every way one of his own documents. That meant only one thing. It meant that whoever had done this to him and Beth was his own employee.

TWENTY-EIGHT

'Paul!' Simon shouted as he charged into his house, his laptop bag firmly gripped in his hand. 'Paul!'

'What is it?' Paul asked with concern, coming down the stairs.

'Did you know?' Simon was alight with fury.

'Know what? Calm down.'

'Did you know that whoever did this to me and Beth - the sick bastard that's messed with our lives - works for us?'

'What are you talking about?' Paul reached the bottom of the stairs looking utterly confused.

'Did you know the person that got Beth to sign the contract - the one that split us up - works for Bird Consultants?'

'What?' Paul looked properly horrified, but Simon couldn't be sure if it was because this was shocking news to him or if it was because he was surprised that Simon had figured it out. At that moment both were reasonable options. It would explain why he hadn't wanted to discuss the contract in any depth.

'Come and sit down, Si,' Paul said, heading towards the living room.

'What is going on?' Jim asked, appearing from the kitchen, but Simon just ignored him.

'Tell me. Did you know?' he asked Paul again.

'Know what?' Jim asked. Jane now appeared on the stairs and Simon felt once again on display.

Paul stared directly at Simon. He was the only person who was never weakened by Simon's forceful nature. He was the only person in the world that Simon couldn't control. 'I'll tell you what I know when you tell me what you know,' Paul firmly replied. 'But I'm not discussing anything until you come into the living room and sit down.'

Simon hesitated. He didn't want to just give in to his uncle, although he could appreciate that sitting down and talking through everything calmly would probably be more productive.

Seeing that he had little choice, Simon barged into the living room and plonked himself down on one of his sofas. Then Paul and his entourage followed.

'What makes you think someone at Bird Consultants has done this?' Paul asked.

'I'll answer your question if you swear that you'll be completely honest with me in return.' Simon had always trusted his uncle, but something about the look on Paul's face unnerved him.

'I think it's time that we laid a few facts out on the table, yes. Let's have a proper discussion about this.'

It didn't go unnoticed to Simon that this was far from a straightforward answer. He decided that it was probably best to tread carefully as the facts, or at least the facts that his uncle was willing to share, unravelled. Paul had always had Simon's best interests at heart, and Simon had no reason to doubt that this was any different, but he couldn't stop the suspicion that niggled at his brain. There was something that he wasn't being told.

'The contract that Beth signed is a Bird Consultants contract,' Simon stated, taking the document out of his bag to show everyone.

'You have the contract?' Jane asked with shock.

'Yes.'

'How did you find it?' Paul asked with equal shock.

'That's irrelevant. But this is it, the one with Beth's signature on.'

'How did you get it?' Jane asked quite forcefully.

'That's not of prime concern at the minute,' Simon replied.

'But...' Jane seemed far more surprised about this than Simon had expected.

'We'll discuss it later,' Paul said to Jane, quite to the point. She nodded her understanding and sat back, but something was definitely churning over in her mind.

Then Paul turned back to Simon. 'Can I take a look?' Simon hesitantly handed over the document and Paul quickly flicked through the pages. 'It's quite a contract, Si. Do you think you can break it?'

'You still haven't answered my question. Did you know?'

Paul turned to Jim. Jim looked horrified but said nothing. Then Paul turned back and addressed Simon directly. 'We very recently found out who tricked Beth into signing it.'

Simon felt the rise of anger again. He hated being treated like this, like he needed protecting. His suspicion had been right after all.

Then he recalled his last conversation with Beth. 'Was it Brian?' he asked.

'No,' Paul replied, although Simon did note how Paul wasn't surprised by the mention of Brian's name. 'It was Damien.'

Simon sat back. Damien? 'What the hell? Why? He's up in Scotland. He's not even here.'

'You remember Scotland?' Jim asked.

'No, but I do keep on top of what's going on in my business. Well, I thought I did.'

'What do you mean by that?' Paul asked.

'I keep in touch with all the directors.'

'Directors? What are you talking about?'

'The directors of the business. Our business. I speak to them all regularly, whether I'm here or in New York.'

'Hang on, when you say directors, are you referring to Damien? Are you saying that you've spoken with Damien?'

'Of course I have. That's what I've been trying to talk to you about. Not that you ever seem to have a minute for me these days.'

'Oh my God!'

'Damien's working on those massive contracts in Scotland. They all seem too good to be true and I wanted your thoughts on the matter.'

'Contracts? No, Simon, no! Damien isn't working on any contracts. You fired him. Weeks ago.'

'I fired him?' Simon was now sitting up straight again.

'Yes. Brian's his replacement.'

'Why did I fire him?' Simon asked. He knew that he'd never really liked Damien, but Simon had never fired anybody. That seemed a bit extreme.

Again, Paul looked to Jim. Jim just shook his head, as if he'd resigned himself to a fate. 'He offered Beth a promotion if she slept with him,' Paul said.

'What?' Simon stood up. How could so much happen in such a short space of time? He was dreading what was going to come next.

This was all getting too much for Simon's nerves. He paced over to his drinks cabinet and poured himself a whiskey. He took a sip and tried to focus his thinking, not able to look at anyone else in the room.

It was so frustrating that he couldn't remember anything, especially when so much seemed to have happened. Anger flared through his soul as he imagined Damien propositioning Beth. Was this before they were married? Afterwards? What had Damien been playing at? Then everything slotted into place.

'So that's why he did this?' Simon said, turning to face the room. 'I fired him so he's seeking revenge. I fired him because he sexually harassed an employee, forget that she's my wife. I had every right to fire him. But this is his revenge. Ruining our lives.'

Paul, Jane and Jim all stared blankly at Simon, not speaking for a moment. Then Paul said, 'Yes. It would appear so.'

'That bastard!'

'Now you know.'

'I can't believe he had the nerve to pretend that he still works for me.'

'He's about as low as a person can get, Simon. At least now we know the truth.'

'Where is he?' Simon said. He knocked back the remainder of his whiskey and slammed the glass down on the top of the cabinet. 'Wait until I get my hands on him!'

'What are you going to do?' Paul asked, standing up.

'I'm going to bloody kill him!' Simon charged towards the door.

'Even if you could find him, what good is that going to do?'

'Killing him will sever the spell. You know that's how it works.'

'It won't,' Paul said, shaking his head.

'Why not?'

'Because this isn't just a spell, it's a contract. And we don't think he was working alone. He's been clever. Really clever. Nothing you can do to Damien will ever sever this spell.'

Simon looked down at the contract in Paul's hand. He was breathing heavily, trying to clear through the web of confusion in his mind. He had to go back to what he knew best. He had to break this contract.

He moved over and took the contract from Paul's hand. 'I'm going to find a loophole, I'm going to get my wife back, and then I'm going to make Damien Rock suffer in ways that he never thought possible. No one does this to me and my family. He doesn't know what's coming to him.'

'Good. That's good. But get Beth back first. Damien can wait. And actually, the more he thinks it's all working without a hiccup, the stronger a position we're in. The last thing we need is him messing with us any more.'

Just then the gate buzzer rang. Jim stood up to do his butler duty, heading to the study to see who it was. Then he came back, a little fidgety.

'It would appear to be a Mr Gardner to see you, Paul.'

'Who's that?' Simon asked.

'Just business,' Paul replied. 'Not Bird Consultants. I mean... about the bar. He wants to discuss me buying the bar. Don't worry about it. You need to focus on the contract. Get yourself upstairs and get that contract cracked!'

Not wanting to waste a second more, Simon headed straight upstairs. He sat immediately down at the desk in his bedroom, took a pencil out from his drawer, and he readied himself to pick the paperwork apart.

Half an hour later, though, and he was exhausted. It was the most complex and intricate contract that he'd ever come across. It wasn't at all clear and concise, like he always insisted Bird Consultants contracts were. Instead it had obviously been devised to plug every hole possible and cause as much confusion in the process as it could. It must have taken some serious man hours to produce. With its intricate layers of detail, it was hard to understand, let alone begin to tackle. This would take ages to pull apart.

Although he acknowledged to himself that this could be his toughest challenge yet, he refused to let it beat him. There was no question that it had been deliberately designed to hinder an attack, but that only fuelled Simon's determination more. This much effort to conceal a weakness meant that someone was very afraid they had one. There was surely something in this madness of words that wasn't sealed tight and Simon knew if anyone could find it, it was him.

Feeling the need for some caffeine to help kick-start this battle, and happy for the short break, Simon headed downstairs. Not even being sure where the coffee was kept in his own house, he opened the living room door to search for Jim.

He was halted in his tracks when he saw, sitting quite casually on his sofa, Beth's boyfriend.

'What the hell are you doing in my house?' Simon shouted as his anger soared again. He was far too overwhelmed with emotion, he couldn't control the rage that pulsated through his body. He charged straight towards the so-called boyfriend and pinned him against the sofa.

'Simon!' Paul shouted, jumping up to try and pull Simon away from his attack.

'What is he doing here?' Simon demanded, backing off so as to not hurt his uncle.

'What are you doing here?' the boyfriend gasped. The six foot tall, well-built man was clearly terrified.

'This is my house!' Simon spat.

'What is going on?' Paul asked.

'This is Beth's boyfriend!' Simon shouted.

'What?' Paul was clearly confused. 'No it's not.'

'Oh yes it is!'

'No, you've got it all wrong, Simon.'

'No I haven't!'

Paul turned to Jim again. 'Why do you keep looking at him?' Simon snapped, feeling very much out of the loop on just about everything.

'Sit down, Simon,' Paul said.

'No, I want to know-'

'Sit down!'

Paul's command was the only voice that Simon ever listened to and Simon obediently did as he was told. Then Paul sat down himself.

'This is not Beth's boyfriend. We hired Toby to look out for Beth. He's been acting as her bodyguard, looking out for her until we could sort out this contract crap.'

'Bodyguard?' Simon snorted. 'Was part of his remit to buy Beth drinks and put his hands all over her?'

'What?' Paul asked, looking to Toby for elaboration.

'Do you want to tell him all about last Friday?' Simon asked Toby.

Toby seemed to physically shrink in his seat. 'I'm not her boyfriend,' he said.

'What have you been doing?' Paul asked Toby.

'It's not quite how it looks. I was trying to help Beth. That Damien, he's the one that kissed her.'

'He what?' Simon shouted.

'She clearly didn't want him in return, though. He was grabbing her, trying to get her to kiss him, so I went over and got him to leave. That's what you wanted me to do, right? She seemed to like that, though. She started flirting with me. I mean I didn't say I was her bodyguard or anything, but we got to know each other. We got to like each other. That's about it, though. I'm not her boyfriend.'

'Toby!' Jim stated with such disappointment. 'How could you?'

'I didn't mean to do anything. I was trying to save her.'

'So where does Brian fit into this?' Paul asked.

'Who's Brian?' Toby asked.

'The Sales Director. You said he asked Beth out.'

'No, Damien asked Beth out. He's the Sales Director.'

'Damien asked Beth out?' Simon's anger was reaching peak levels.

'Yeah, when they had that meeting.'

'Don't tell me she said yes?'

'Yeah, they went out to Ealing. That's when he tried to kiss her.'

'What the hell is Beth doing going out on a date with Damien?' Simon was rubbing his head with confusion. 'How could she after everything he's done?'

'She doesn't remember, Si,' Paul reasoned. 'Just like you don't. And clearly Damien has been using that to his advantage.'

'But Damien. I mean...'

'Weren't they old friends?' Toby asked. 'Hadn't they already been out on dates?'

'That fucking bastard!' Simon's fists were clenched. He was ready to punch Damien into next week.

'We know the truth now, Si. There's nothing we can do about it. At least he didn't seem to get very far with Beth.'

'No, she pushed him away. That's when I stepped in,' Toby explained.

'You saved the day.' Simon's words were laced with bitterness.

'Okay, so Beth went on a date with Damien, not Brian, and you got rid of him,' Paul stated, looking straight at Toby. 'And that's when Beth started flirting with you. Is there anything else you need to tell us? Is there anything else that has happened?'

'No. Nothing. I swear. We've just flirted a bit.'

'Why are you here?' Simon asked. He knew full well why there was nothing else for Toby to mention – Simon had taken care of that himself. Although it wouldn't have surprised him if Toby had at least tried his luck. Simon felt punched with sickness again as he considered the possibility.

'Si, I'm really sorry,' Paul said. 'Toby's here with news of Beth.'

'Is this to do with her new job?'

'How did you know?' Paul asked.

'She handed in her notice this afternoon. She's got some big opportunity, too good to be true. Something like that.'

'So that's why you suddenly managed to get hold of the contract?'

'Did Beth tell you?' Simon asked Toby. He was nauseated by the idea that this virtual stranger knew more about his wife than he did.

Toby just shrugged and Simon felt another kick in the guts.

'There's more,' Paul said.

'Damien paid me a visit today,' Toby explained, the fear still very much present in his tone. 'He found me by your office just before lunch. He told me how he'd heard that Beth was moving up north and-'

'Up north?' Simon interrupted. 'She's moving up north?'

'It seems she has a job in Manchester,' Paul replied.

'No. No! We can't let her.' Simon couldn't hide the panic in his voice. Losing her to another job was one thing, but losing her completely, letting her disappear so far away, he couldn't let that happen.

'Then you need to stop her,' Paul urged.

'I'm trying. Don't you think I'm trying! The contract is so complex. It's going to take me time.'

'There are other ways.'

'Why did Damien tell you this? How do you even know Damien?' Simon was suddenly riddled with unanswered questions.

'He offered Toby a job,' Paul stated.

'He wants me to be a double agent,' Toby mumbled. 'I thought he worked for Bird Consultants. He told me you'd all filled him in on who I was. Then today he said he wants me to pretend to work for you, but actually report stuff back to him.'

'That fucking bastard!' Simon hissed.

'This could work for us, Si,' Paul said. 'Damien's clearly been one step ahead of us for quite some time, but this could be our chance to gain the edge. Toby could be a double, double agent. Or triple agent. Whatever! He could agree to work for Damien, but still actually work for us. That way we'd get to know everything that's going on with Damien for a change, instead of it being the other way around.'

'This is all such bullshit,' Simon stated. 'We can't trust this idiot.'

'Hey!' Toby objected.

'We can,' Paul said.

'Of course we can't.'

'Damien is clearly very much in control here, Si. We need something. We need leverage of our own.'

'Yes we do, but not through him. Not through the man that's too busy feeling up Beth instead of doing what he's being paid to do.'

'Nothing's happened between us!' Toby argued.

Simon knew his spell was the only thing that was stopping Toby. He wanted this man to be far away from his wife.

'Si, he's all we've got,' Paul practically pleaded.

Simon felt stumped. As much as he hated it, having someone out there who Beth felt comfortable with and who was reporting back was an asset. As his current presence demonstrated, he was willing to report things back to the Bird base. He also wasn't going to be sleeping with Beth anytime soon thanks to Simon's spell. So where was the harm for now? Simon had so little ammunition at that moment, he was in no position to argue.

'Fine. Be the double agent. Go with Beth. But the second this contract has been rendered null and void, I want you out of her life for good. Do you understand?' Simon said to Toby.

'What contract?' he asked.

'It's a long story, you don't need to know the details,' Paul answered.

'As soon as she's out of danger, she's never to see you again.'

'Whatever,' Toby shrugged.

'I'll be watching.'

TWENTY-NINE

The week had sailed by and it was Saturday before Beth knew it.

She'd spent her last few days in Heaningford doing little else but packing and preparing for her move up north. She'd had goodbye drinks with Gayle, Diane and Michelle in The Rose on Thursday night, and all that was left was to actually move.

If only it was that easy, though. Beth felt depressed. It had broken her heart to tell her landlord that she was moving out of her flat, and she felt real grief at the thought of leaving London.

It was mid-morning and Beth was just waiting for Toby and then she was going to follow him up to Manchester. Damien had done as promised and had offered him a job, although they were both being very cagey about exactly what it was. But, Beth supposed, it didn't really matter as long as they were away from Mr Bird and were safe.

Beth stared out of her window. She watched the life of Heaningford below her and she felt mournful. It just seemed so grossly unfair that she'd been driven out of her job like that. She felt that she'd had little choice but to jump all over this new opportunity, but she didn't want to leave. She'd started to feel settled, she'd started to actually feel at home.

She also felt completely mixed up about Simon. Yes, what he'd done was utterly unforgivable, and when she thought about it she was terrified, but she couldn't deny how calm and warm she actually felt in his presence. It was like her mind and her heart were fighting against each other. It made no sense.

Logic had to take precedence, though. He was a murderer. He was a dangerous man with far too much power. He'd found a way to live above the law and Beth wasn't safe around him.

Beth saw Toby appear across the road. He'd been acting very strangely all week, and it had got even weirder that day. His interest in her had definitely dwindled, and earlier that day he'd flatly refused to help her finish packing. Instead, he'd just waited outside where the only thing he was willing to do was take boxes to her car. She'd had to do all the lifting up and down the stairs herself. It was so chivalrous of him!

Maybe them moving together was putting a bit too much pressure on him. They still barely knew each other and now they were starting a new life at the same time. Beth hoped it wouldn't make him back away completely. She needed a friend right now. She wanted his companionship.

Beth suddenly noticed Toby waving, as planned, and she signalled back that she understood. He was ready to go. They were ready to go. This was it.

Beth took one last look at her now very empty flat. It was so sad, she almost felt like crying. With her mind missing three months, it only felt as if she'd been living there a few weeks, but she'd become very attached to her little home.

She had no choice but to leave, though. She had to. No matter what, life was taking her down this unexpected route and she had no choice but to follow it.

She walked to the door, taking one last look around, and then she left. They were due to drop the keys off at her landlord's house on the way, and then all her connections to London were cut.

The journey to Manchester seemed to take forever. It had been traffic jam after traffic jam. It was just over six hours later when Beth finally followed Toby into the car park of her new block of flats.

Fortunately, the sight of it quickly softened the negative thoughts that had been weighing down Beth's mind during the long drive. It was such a fancy, brand new block of flats, right in the city centre.

Damien was waiting for them outside, as planned, and Beth walked up to the door in awe.

'Can I afford this?' she asked, taking the keys from Damien's fingers.

'On your new salary?' he smiled. 'I think you'll be all right. Besides, as part of the relocation programme offered by the new company, we'll cover the first three months' rent.'

Beth, gobsmacked, pushed the key into the lock of the main door and headed inside. She walked up the clean, fresh staircase to the third floor where Damien had directed that she'd find her new home.

She stepped inside and her mouth dropped open. It was worlds away from her little studio flat in London. It had two bedrooms and was so stylishly decorated. The kitchen was massive, with all the mod cons, and it had two separate bathrooms as well. Beth was overwhelmed.

'This is all mine?' she asked.

'For as long as you want it,' Damien nodded.

'It's big,' Toby said, following Beth around as she explored.

'Right, I'll leave you two to it,' Damien said, heading for the door. 'See you in the office on Monday?'

'A new exciting start!' Beth grinned.

'You'll never look back.'

Toby showed more chivalry that afternoon and he helped Beth carry all of her boxes into her new home. After that they took a quick walk around the local area, where Toby pointed out all the relevant sites, including Beth's new workplace. Then they readied themselves for the evening ahead.

All dressed up for a Saturday night in the city, Toby took them for dinner and a few drinks in a very busy place somewhere near a river. Beth wasn't been able to get her bearings at all but she quite happily followed the very knowledgeable Toby around. She was grateful to have such a willing guide.

By midnight they were both exhausted and they hopped in a taxi back to Beth's new flat. Beth hadn't really drunk that much, she was far too overwhelmed by the sudden and drastic change in her life. She hadn't even eaten that much either.

Manchester so far had proven to be lovely, just as Toby had promised. There seemed to be plenty going on and she'd met some really friendly people, but Beth couldn't ignore the hole inside of her that was steadily growing. As nice a city as it was, it just wasn't where she wanted to be. She missed London. She missed Bird Consultants. And as much as she didn't want to acknowledge it at all, as crazy as it seemed, she felt undeniably sad that she would never see Simon again. She'd told herself over and over that it was just the manipulative effect that he'd cast over her, but she couldn't shake the inexplicable misery that hurt from being away from him.

'Lunch tomorrow then?' Toby said as soon as Beth opened the door to her flat.

'You're leaving?'

Toby hesitated. 'Yeah.'

'Have I done something?'

'No.'

'Ever since we got these new jobs, you've been quite

distant. Do you not want to be with me anymore?'

Toby looked at her awkwardly. 'It's just been a big week.'

Beth suddenly felt quite miffed. She'd gone out of her way to ensure that Toby, as her boyfriend, was safe, and now he didn't seem that interested anymore. If he was going to dump her couldn't he have done it before they moved halfway across the country?

She went to the fridge to find shelves full of food and drink that Damien had kindly gifted to them. She pulled out two bottles of Peroni and handed one to Toby. 'Stay and have a drink.'

He seemed unsure for a second.

'Stay the night,' she then added.

A little smile suddenly crept up onto Toby's lips. 'Yeah?'

'You can't leave me on my own in a new city like this.'

'So you just want company?' he asked hesitantly.

'I want you,' Beth replied, as seductively as she could.

Toby's smile expanded. 'I'll drink to that!' Then he popped off the lid of his beer with his teeth.

Beth had never seen anyone do that before and she hastily looked in the cutlery drawer for a bottle opener, not so keen on trying it for herself.

'You know, a Peroni is best drunk in the bedroom,' Toby smirked.

'I've heard that. I think that's definitely true.'

Toby reached out and grabbed Beth's hand. 'We'd better go straight there then.'

They headed into the master bedroom and Toby slipped Beth's drink out of her hand. He placed it on the bedside table with his own and then he turned back to her. He stood right before her, so close their skin was almost touching. Then, without any warning at all, he threw his arms around her and kissed her.

He edged her over towards the bed and slowly pushed her down onto the duvet. He softly climbed on top of her as their kissing increased in passion.

He yanked off her cardigan, throwing it to the floor, and then he placed his hands on her breasts. Beth had half expected him to yelp in pain, like last time, but this time there was no hesitation at all.

Their desire for one another developed and Toby pulled off Beth's top, revealing her black, satin bra underneath. He fondled her some more, but his touch was getting rougher as his lust increased, and Beth immediately knew that she didn't like it. It just didn't feel right at all.

'I'm a lady, you know. I need to be handled gently,' she said, trying to calm him down.

'No can do, I'm afraid,' he smirked. 'You drive me far too wild for that.'

Beth didn't know what to say as he moved around to undo her bra. It wasn't that she wasn't enjoying it... well actually, she wasn't.

As he took a long, drooling look at her half naked body, a flash of Simon suddenly appeared in Beth's mind.

Toby leaned down to kiss her breasts, tugging hard in a way that was actually more torturous than tantalising. As she screwed up her face in discomfort, another flash of Simon popped into her head. Why was she thinking about him? And why was it that she didn't want the image of him to go?

Toby yanked off his shirt, revealing a toned and rather hairy chest below. He then came back in for more kissing, pushing hard against her lips.

'I'm going to make you scream,' he whispered in her ear and Beth's heart sank. Scream with pain, maybe, but not pleasure. She didn't want any of this.

The image of Simon grew more vibrant in her mind and she tried to push it aside. It was too difficult to think about him right now. But the only other thing she could think about was how she didn't want to be with Toby like this. She wanted to make love, not have raw, lusty sex. It was clear, though, that he wanted the complete opposite.

'Need the loo!' she said, pushing Toby away. She jumped off the bed and raced to the bathroom. She glared at herself in the mirror, not needing the toilet at all.

It dawned on her that she felt guilty. But it wasn't about Toby. She didn't know what it was about, but it tugged at her inside quite hard.

Nothing in that moment felt right, and Beth knew that she wanted Toby to leave.

Suddenly, making her jump out of her skin, the door buzzer rang. Feeling utterly exposed, Beth grabbed a towel from the rail. She wrapped it around the top half of her body and then she raced out of the bathroom to see who was at her front door.

Toby joined her in the hallway and they both looked to one another with confusion. It buzzed again.

'Let me get it,' Toby said. This was what Beth liked; someone who was bothered about her. He picked up the receiver. 'Hello.'

Beth couldn't hear who was at the other end, but whoever it was they'd clearly made an impact. Toby's face quickly changed from surprised to frightened.

'What's this about?' Toby asked.

'Who is it?' Beth said.

Toby glared at her, a little pale. 'It's Simon Bird. Your old boss.'

'What?' Beth felt goose bumps prickle her skin as she thought of Simon being just a few metres down below her.

'She's not available right now. I'm sorry,' Toby said, although his voice was far from confident.

Beth grabbed the intercom receiver out of Toby's hands. She was shaking, but at that moment she knew it wasn't fear. It actually felt more like excitement. She couldn't help it but she was buzzing with adrenaline.

'What do you want?' she asked.

'I want to see you.'

Beth didn't know what to say. As scared as she knew she should be, she couldn't help but feel happy that he'd come all this way to see her.

'We have unfinished business,' Simon continued.

Logic then kicked in. Unfinished business meant that Simon hadn't finished manipulating her. He wanted her back and he was using his bewitching ways again to do it. She didn't know how he was managing it, but it was like he'd cast some sort of spell over her.

'There's nothing else we need to say,' she replied.

'There is. Believe me, there's something you need to know.'

'I'm not interested, Simon. You need to leave.'

'Beth, this is important.'

'I can't let you do this. I need to stay strong. If you don't go then I'm calling the police.' As soon as she'd said the words, she knew they wouldn't be much of a deterrent to a man who had literally got away with murder, but it was all she had.

Simon remained silent for a few moments. 'Okay, I realise it's late, I'll leave. But I need you to keep in mind that there's something very important you don't know. Something that you need to know. Please remember that. Don't do anything rash until you've at least heard me out. We'll do it in a public place, I don't care. Just hear me out.'

'I'm going to get my mobile,' Beth warned, keeping up the pretence that the police would in any way care that Mr Above-The-Law was bothering her.

'I'm leaving. Look after yourself, Beth. Goodnight.'

Beth placed down the receiver and she let out a huge sigh. She looked to Toby who seemed half the man that he had been before.

'I'm really tired now, Toby. I'm just going to go straight to bed.' Toby just nodded and Beth added, 'I'll call you a taxi.'

'I thought you wanted me to stay?'

'You know what, you were right. It's been a big week. I just need some sleep now. But let's definitely have lunch tomorrow.'

'I can stay in the spare room.'

'Please, Toby. Please understand. This isn't about you. This has been a lot for me to deal with. You do understand, don't you?'

'All right,' he shrugged. 'I'll come and collect you tomorrow. Is noon okay? I know a great carvery we could go to.'

'Great,' Beth nodded, kissing Toby on the cheek. Then she went to her bedroom, threw her top back on and called Toby a taxi.

THIRTY

Simon walked down the road from Beth's flat and returned to his Jaguar. He felt enraged with jealousy. He hated the idea of that man being in his wife's flat. What was he doing there at this hour? And why hadn't Toby let him in? He should have insisted. He needed to talk to Beth. He'd had enough of the games, it was time to properly talk.

Simon had spent the last few days battling with the contract, the one that had torn him and his wife apart. But despite days of doing nothing but pouring through every line and questioning every word, he'd got nowhere.

It was like nothing he'd ever come across and he was facing a challenge that he'd never had to face before. Not only was the contract so intensely complicated and deliberately designed to confuse and distract, it was also deeply personal. It was so difficult to read about the supposed wishes of his wife, where she was apparently stating that she no longer wanted to know him. It had been painful to read how she also wanted all of his memories of her to be compromised as well. He'd never been emotionally connected to a contract before, and this had been extremely testing.

He'd been over the reams of paper multiple times. Every time he'd thought he'd found a loophole, another more complicated stitch in the tapestry would pop up that opened up five more confusing issues. Then, before he could get his head around them, he found himself being emotionally kicked in the guts as his understanding of the cruelty of the contract deepened. It was like a vicious cycle of torment that had lasted for days.

It was early Saturday afternoon when the final kick gave its ravaging blow and Simon was snapped into action. After days of torture to no avail and having read the manipulation and the falseness that was his and Beth's situation one too many times, Simon could take it no longer. A new determination sparked up in his soul.

He hadn't lost Beth. It wasn't over. None of this was real. It was time to stop meandering around and fight. He could dabble with the contract forever and just get more confused, so what he actually needed was to finally stop the madness and just be honest.

Simon had found out from Paul (who had found out from Toby) the address of Beth's new home, and he'd wasted not a second more. He'd jumped straight in his car and had driven north.

He'd waited for hours for Beth to return home. Then, when she finally had, it took him a while to find the courage to press her buzzer. But all the courage in the world wasn't going to help him. Forget about getting Beth to believe him, he had to get her to listen to him first. That was a major hurdle.

Simon started the engine of his car. He knew of a hotel about half a mile away, somewhere that he'd stayed before when he'd been to Manchester for work. Not halted too much by the late night traffic, he soon found the hotel. He parked his car in the off site car park, made his way to the reception, and sighed with relief that they had a room available.

He let himself into the room, immediately noting how

small it was, but he hadn't been blessed with a choice. All of his adult life he'd only stayed in suites or upgraded rooms and he hadn't seen the inside of a standard room in quite a while. Still, it was clean, convenient and close to Beth. That's all that mattered.

He unpacked his small bag, ordered a whiskey from room service, and relaxed on the bed. The next few days were going to be crucial and he knew he needed to clear his head if he was going to have any chance of success. He had no clue what the next day was going to bring, but he had to focus on his mission. Their future happiness was at stake and he was the only one who could fix it.

The next day, Simon followed Toby and Beth to a pub for lunch and then they went straight back to Beth's flat. Simon was relieved to see that after just a few minutes of them returning home, Toby left. He walked over to his car and sat there, doing his job for a change and keeping an eye on her.

Simon desperately wanted to ring her doorbell again, but he was afraid that it would just alienate her even more. If he was going to have any chance of her listening to him, he needed to bump into her on neutral ground, so she at least felt safe.

Hours went by and Beth didn't leave her flat again. He imagined her unpacking, watching rubbish on the television and cooking... he didn't even know what she liked to eat. It was so sad. He knew so little about her.

It was just after seven o'clock when Simon finally gave up. Confident that she wouldn't be leaving her flat again that night, he drove back to his hotel. Sunday hadn't been successful, but he knew that she'd most definitely be leaving the confines of her home the next day. She had a new job to go to and that might just give him his chance. He was also very curious as to who had stolen her away from Bird Consultants with such a so-called amazing opportunity.

Monday had the potential to be a pivotal day for Simon Bird.

He returned to his spot just down the road from Beth's flat at six o'clock the next morning. It was probably far too early for Beth to be leaving for her job, but he needed to make sure he was there when she did leave. Toby was nowhere to be seen. So much for keeping an eye on her!

It wasn't until just before eight thirty that Beth finally made an appearance. She looked stunning. She was smartly dressed in a black pencil skirt and white blouse, and she marched on towards her destination with such confidence.

She was heading in the opposite direction to where Simon was facing and he quickly negotiated the traffic to make sure he could follow her.

He drove on and pulled in as much as he could. He knew he was probably a hazard to other drivers, but he didn't care. Beth was all that mattered.

Finally, after only about ten minutes, Beth headed into a large office block. It looked like a generic building that housed multiple companies. Simon quickly darted around to the car park at the back, thanked his good fortune that there was a space, and then virtually sprinted around to the front door.

He headed into the reception. There were at least twelve companies listed on the wall that resided in the building and his heart sank. This wouldn't be easy. He stood back for a second to contemplate his next move when Toby suddenly walked in.

Before a single thought could enter Simon's head, acting in a way that was so very rare for him, Simon let his emotions completely take charge. He grabbed Toby by his collar and dragged him outside onto the fairly busy street.

'Where's Beth?' he demanded to know, his heart thumping at how angry he was towards the man before him.

'Get off me!'

Simon pushed Toby against the wall of the building. He knew people were watching, but it didn't matter. 'Which company is Beth working for?'

'Rock Consultants. Now get off me!'

Simon flashed his mind to the companies that he'd just seen displayed in reception. He couldn't recall seeing Rock Consultants in the list. Then a sickening dread pulled in his stomach and he stepped back. 'Rock?'

'Yes,' Toby replied, straightening himself up.

'You don't mean as in Damien Rock?'

Toby looked fearfully back at Simon. 'Yes.'

Simon felt the anger explode through him. Wearing just a T Shirt and jeans, his skin was visibly throbbing on his arms, and the sight of it only fuelled his anger more. 'Where are they?'

'The sixth floor, I think.'

'You stay away from my wife,' Simon ordered.

'Your wife?' Toby was clearly surprised by this.

'Beth is my wife. You stay away from her. I don't care what Paul says, from this moment on you back away or you'll have me to answer to. Do you understand?'

'But-'

'Do you understand?'

'I didn't know. She never said.'

'She can't remember! But she's my wife and I'm trying to get her back.'

'So that's why you cast the spell on me?'

Simon was taken aback by this. 'Spell?'

'So I couldn't sleep with her.'

'How did you know about that?'

Toby just shrugged.

Then a realisation horrified Simon. He hadn't cast a complicated spell, there was no dark magic involved. He'd never factored in that Toby would find out. Self-healing would counteract it immediately. 'You haven't...' but Simon couldn't finish.

'No.' Toby shook his head, but Simon could see the

vulnerability in his eyes.

Simon's breathing quickened as he started to imagine Beth and Toby together. 'Did you?' Simon asked, but he wasn't able to find the words to complete the question.

Toby stared back at him terrified. 'No.'

'Did you fuck my wife?' Simon hissed as the fear of Toby placing his hands on Beth stormed his mind. How could he believe anything the weasel before him said?

'No.'

'Tell me the truth!' Simon's eyes were like green lava as his anger and jealousy peaked.

'No! We started to mess around but we didn't get very far.'

'What does that mean?' Simon was fuming.

'Nothing!'

'You bastard.' Simon punched Toby right across the face and he fell to the ground. 'If I find out that you've laid one finger on my wife, I'll be coming for you. You were supposed to be looking out for her not pursuing her. You should be ashamed of yourself.'

Toby scrambled to his feet. He grabbed his cheek in pain, took one last look at Simon and then ran off.

Simon took a deep breath. He needed to control his anger. It was useless, though. He'd just fought off one man who had his sights on Beth, now he had to go and see another one. And he knew Damien Rock was going to be a whole new issue.

He walked into the reception, his skin flaring against his rage, and he headed into the lift.

THIRTY-ONE

Beth entered the tiny office and her heart sank. She knew it was a start-up, but she at least thought there would be other members of staff.

In the bare space, with just two desks and two laptops, sat Damien, alone.

'Morning!' he chimed, looking up from his mobile that he'd been fiddling with.

'It's just us?' Beth asked, not at all trying to hide the surprise in her voice.

'For now. We have to start somewhere.'

'How can it be just us?'

'What did you expect?'

Beth thought back to what Damien had told her. In truth, he'd said very little. She couldn't think that he'd actually lied to her, but he'd clearly misled her, which was the same thing in her book. 'A proper job,' she stated.

'That's exactly what you've got. Come on, sit at your desk, get your laptop on. Then we can start to make some money.'

'Doing what?'

'Consulting, of course. I'll do the consulting, you do the paperwork.'

'That's just admin. You could have hired anyone to do that. Why me?'

'Because you're the best!' Damien jumped up from his seat and pulled out the only other chair in the room. He gestured for Beth to sit down and she felt immediately weighted with disappointment.

She headed over, with her heavy heart, and made herself comfortable in her chair.

Just then, the door burst open. As if out of nowhere, Simon charged straight in and made a beeline for Damien. 'You bastard!' he said before punching Damien sharply across the face and flooring him in seconds.

Beth stood up in shock. She immediately feared that he was going to kill Damien, and she knew they were in serious danger. Not sure what else to do, she bent down to check on Damien who was curled up on the carpet in pain. His face had already vastly swollen but he wasn't knocked out.

Shuddering with anger and fear, Beth turned to look up at Simon. He was now standing over her, glaring down at her, appearing bigger than ever. His eyes were violently green and his skin seemed to eerily pulsate.

She slowly stood up straight, fearing for her life. He didn't take his eyes off her.

'Beth, we need to talk,' he said.

'You said you'd let me go,' she replied, shakily.

'You need to hear what I have to say.'

'No I don't.' Beth glanced quickly at the door, but her only way out was blocked by Simon. She was trapped.

'There's something you don't know. We've both been tricked.'

Beth wasn't interested. This was more manipulation. This was probably what got her mixed up with him in the first place and she wasn't going to fall for it twice.

'Please let me go.'

'Just listen to what I have to say, that's all I ask. You need to know the truth.'

246

Beth thought through the situation in her mind. There had to be a way out of this. She needed to get outside. She was in grave danger being trapped in that room with him, and Damien wasn't being much use, still curled up on the floor in self-pity. She looked around the room for inspiration, then an idea hit her.

'Okay. You have my attention, I'll listen. But can I please sit down?'

'Of course,' Simon said, acknowledging that he was standing in the way of her chair. He stood aside, allowing her to take her seat. She moved towards it, pulling it out slowly, making out that she was going to sit down, and then she ran. She ran away from him, out of the door and straight down the stairs, too fearful to wait for the lift. She virtually flew down the six flights of stairs, feeling a power within her that she'd never noticed before help her on her way.

She was too scared to look behind her, but she knew that Simon wouldn't be far. She got to the reception and bolted straight outside, out into public, out into the safety of the street.

Without considering any other option, she ran in the direction of her flat. But her feet suddenly ground to a halt when she realised that she didn't have her bag with her, which meant she didn't have her keys. Nor her phone. She gasped for breath as it hit her that she was completely stuck and completely alone.

She looked up ahead, and suddenly Simon was standing in front of her. How the hell had he managed that? She hadn't seen him pass her. The terror inside of her froze her to the spot.

'I'm not going to hurt you, Beth, you just need to listen to me. The least you can do is hear what I have to say.'

'I don't have to listen to anything!' She was trying to be confident. She had to fight his manipulation.

'You're my wife!'

'No I'm not. Not anymore.'

'We're still married. And we wanted to be married.'

'Because you tricked me.'

'I did nothing of the sort. I love you.'

'Don't make me sick!'

'You love me. You just don't remember.'

'Because you drugged me.'

'What? How can you say that? You know you love me. I couldn't remember either, but I couldn't stop thinking about you. You can't just switch it off. Tell me you don't feel the same way.'

'I don't feel the same way.' As the words left Beth's mouth she knew they were a lie. Everything in her gut told her that those words were a lie. But how could that be the case? How can she love him?

'That's not true. We love each other.'

Beth turned to walk away in the opposite direction, now far too confused to speak to him. But, like an impossible flash, Simon appeared in front of her again.

'How did you do that?'

'I love you, Beth.'

Simon grabbed Beth firmly by the arms, so quickly she barely had time to fight it. Then he kissed her. It all happened so fast, she didn't get a chance to resist. And then she didn't want to.

As she felt the touch of his lips, despite their tense desperation, waves of passion crashed through her. It all felt so familiar and all of her senses became electrified.

Then her head started to spin. As Simon's lips softened and the kiss between them deepened, it was as if a plug in her mind was yanked free and memories start to spill out all over the place.

She'd made Simon a cup of tea in the kitchen.

They'd met in The Rose and had spent so much time getting to know one another.

They'd had their first date at that party. The bouncers. The healing. They'd made love.

The Malancy!

The feathers.

Paul. Jane. Malancy HQ.

Her near marriage to Damien. Then her actual marriage to Simon.

The pen flying across the room. She's a Malant!

Being kidnapped. Being chosen ones. The end of the Malancy. Saving the Malancy.

Her parents. Her real parents.

Waking up and not knowing who her husband was. Not knowing the only man she'd ever truly loved. Not knowing her soulmate.

Bloody hell! How could she forget all that!

She fell backwards but Simon caught her in his arms.

For a moment she felt nothing. The sudden flood of memories overwhelmed her and she couldn't process anything. She took a few deep breaths before looking up at Simon.

He was still holding her tightly in his arms. His strong, safe arms. She enjoyed the sensation. It had been far too long since she'd felt it.

Beth took another deep breath and then she straightened herself up, not looking away from Simon once. She studied his chocolate eyes, his troubled face, his soft lips and pale skin. Her Simon.

Simon moved his hands gently and curled Beth's hair behind her ears. Then he smiled warmly. How she'd missed him. Without thinking about it, she threw her arms around him and they hugged.

The two of them stood in a close embrace for what seemed like an age. In fact, Beth considered never letting go.

People walked by, people stared, but they both just held each other tightly, making up for the weeks that they'd been cruelly torn apart.

But as the relief settled between them, questions suddenly started appearing in Beth's head. She had so many questions. She didn't want to leave Simon's arms, but the niggling unanswered issues were now taking precedence in her mind.

She stepped back, grabbing on to his hands, making sure she wasn't letting go completely. 'What happened to us?' she asked.

'Yet again, we fell victim to a cruel and self-serving spell. You were tricked into signing a contract that insisted that we forgot all about each other.'

'What?'

'But we're a pretty unbeatable team.'

'I'm a Malant,' she whispered, more to herself.

'We're the most powerful Malants in the world. As good as that contract was, I guess nothing can stop us when we're together.'

'That was one hell of a kiss,' Beth said, enjoying the tingle that raced through her as she recalled the sensation of Simon's touch.

'I didn't expect it to have quite that effect. I thought it might just jolt some feelings, not completely restore our memories. That really was one hell of a kiss.'

'I love you, Simon Bird.'

'Oh Beth, I love you too.'

Beth hugged him again. Then she felt agonising guilt as the memories of the last few weeks scattered through her mind. 'I'm so sorry,' she said, looking him directly in the eyes.

'For what,' Simon asked, curling her hair behind her ears again.

'I've not been faithful to our marriage. I'm a horrible person.'

'You mean Toby?'

'I didn't know what I was doing. I thought I was single. It was all so messed up.'

'Please don't be sorry, Beth. You couldn't remember. You were just living your life.' Simon looked back into her eyes with hesitation. 'I need to know, though. Just so we can put it properly behind us. I won't be mad, I just need to know the truth. I can deal with the truth.'

'What truth?' Beth asked.

'Did you sleep with him?'

'No,' Beth immediately answered. She saw the relief physically drain through Simon's face and she wanted to leave it at that, but she knew she couldn't lie. She had to tell him everything. It was only right. 'We got close, though. The first time he got ill so nothing happened, then on Saturday night we tried again. It was horrible, though. I hated it. Before we really got anywhere, I sent him home. He barely touched me. But still, I'm really sorry.' Beth felt sick with herself for what she'd done.

'Please don't be sorry. I hate the thought of anyone else touching you. You're my wife, I don't want to share you with anyone, but you're not to blame.'

Then something else jumped into Beth's head. 'Damien!'

'What about him?'

'That lying git!'

'At least he's consistent.'

'He told me that we'd spent the night together. He told me that we'd dated. I went on a date with him, believing that we'd done it before. Then he kissed me. God, it was disgusting.'

This time Simon's eyes blackened and Beth felt his whole body throb. 'Damien is the one that forced you to sign the contract.'

'Contract?' Beth flicked through her memories. 'I did sign something. He said the anti-Malants were going to kill me and the contract was the only thing that could save my life. Was that the contract that split us up? I'm so sorry.'

'Right,' Simon declared with more conviction than Beth had ever seen before. 'I think it's time we bring down Damien Rock once and for all, don't you?'

THIRTY-TWO

When Beth and Simon re-entered the office of Rock Consultants, Damien was sitting in his chair, still clearly feeling very sorry for himself.

'Having trouble self-healing?' Simon asked. Damien bolted to his feet, the shock and fear visibly tensing him.

Beth was standing confidently next to Simon but she didn't speak. She was too eager to see what he was going to do. He was fuelled with such a fiery determination.

'That's what happens when an all-powerful Malant takes away your magical ability,' Simon added. 'And didn't you deserve it.'

'What?' Damien asked cautiously.

'I will admit, it was a very clever contract. I could almost admire its intricacy, layered with confused lines and a great deal of equivocation. It made it impossible for me to get a handle on any of it. You knew exactly what you were doing.'

'Contract?'

'I think you'd factored in pretty much everything. I can honestly say that I was struggling to find any way around it, and that's unheard of for me. Isn't it just lucky that you forgot one very important detail. You totally overlooked the most vital thing of all. You never seemed to consider the united strength of the two most powerful Malants in the world.'

'Simon's just kissed me and it all came flooding back!' Beth beamed, too much adrenaline racing through her to stay quiet for long.

Damien was silent. He looked absolutely terrified.

'You should be scared, Damien,' Simon warned.

'What are we going to do?' Beth asked Simon, her body jittery with the thrill of revenge and excited by her new found memories. 'Are you going to punch him again?'

'No.'

'What are you going to do to him?'

'I should never have punched him in the first place. Although I was under the impression that he could self-heal. I guess he's only got himself to blame for that.'

'What are we going to do then?'

'Do you remember the last time we went to confront Damien and you said you wanted to pin him down?' Simon asked Beth.

'Yes,' she answered with enthusiasm.

'Do you think you could pin him against the wall?'

'Oh yes!' Then Beth stopped. She hadn't used, or even known about her magic in a long time. 'How do I do that?'

'Just summon up your magic like normal. Remember how you moved the pen?' Beth nodded her reply. 'It's exactly the same, but this time move Damien. Then hold him in place against the wall.'

They both turned to look at Damien who now seemed frozen with fear. He was just a normal human being against two of the most powerful people in the world, and everyone in the room knew it.

Beth recalled how she needed to focus all of her emotion to get her magic to work, and she had plenty to tap into at that moment. She concentrated all of her anger, love, excitement and fear into one massive ball in her chest. As she sensed the power build up inside of her, she let it intensify. Then she threw it all towards Damien, just like she had towards the pen. He made it so easy as he fearfully stuck to the spot.

Damien immediately lifted into the air and then he hurtled back towards the wall, smacking against it about a metre off the ground. Beth giggled with joy. It felt so good.

He let out a fearful groan as he looked down at his trapped torso, with just his arms and legs dangling freely.

'Now what?' she asked.

'Are you all right to hold him in place?' Simon queried. Beth nodded her reply and Simon smiled. 'Good.' Then Simon turned his attention to the trapped man.

Simon's eyes fixated on Damien and his face darkened. 'Do you remember, Damien, when we came to your house?'

'What?' Damien gasped, the terror shaking him.

'I told you that if you ever so much as thought about my wife again, let alone touch her, I would burn you. I think it's fair to say that in every way you've gone against my wishes.'

'What?' Damien breathed.

'Telling her you were dating? Kissing her? Getting her to resign from her job and then moving her to Manchester? Is there anything you've done that I would approve of?'

'None of it was my idea.'

'And what about Brian?' Beth suddenly asked, recalling the horror of the week before. 'Did you kill Brian?'

'Kill Brian?' Simon asked with surprise.

'Brian's not dead, you stupid girl,' Damien virtually spat.

'Where is he then?'

'Your husband sent him to New York.'

'I didn't send him anywhere,' Simon replied.

'Well he's in New York, courtesy of Bird Consultants. Why did I never go to New York?'

'Why has he gone to New York?' Simon asked.

'So he's not dead?' It was all Beth wanted to know.

'Of course not,' Damien replied.

'But what about that body they found?'

'We're Malants, Beth,' Damien said. 'We can make anything happen if we want to. And we needed you to believe...' Damien stopped and glared at Simon with fear.

'You wanted people to believe that I'd killed Brian?' Simon finished.

Damien didn't say a word.

'So it's you who's been spreading all those rumours about me?'

'No, it's all George Malant. It's nothing to do with me. George is behind all of it.' Damien was practically pleading.

Beth thought through the logic in her head. 'Is Diane working with George, then?'

Damien shook his head. 'Don't be ridiculous. Don't you know how powerful George is? He's the true leader of the Malancy and he's been doing it for years. He's got people everywhere and they'll spread whatever word he wants. Diane has been an especially useful asset. She'll believe anything, that one.'

'Believe from whom, though?'

'I think you'll find she's very good friends with George's wife.'

'So she's working with Mrs Malant?'

'They've been using her, Beth,' Simon explained. 'Her and many others at the office by the sounds of it. They've been feeding people lies and then getting them to spread them as fact around the office.'

Beth's initial thought was to feel sorry for Diane. She'd been used in a very cruel way. Then her sorrow quickly turned to irritation as she questioned how easy it had been for Diane to spread such gossip, truth or not.

Then it dawned on Beth that she didn't work there anymore. A flush of panic rattled her. 'I can have my job back, can't I?'

'Of course,' Simon replied, his eyes softening as he looked at her. 'I'd be devastated if you didn't come back. I want you to come home, to your home with me, and I want you back in our joint office, right where you belong. Is that okay?'

Beth felt her heart sink for a second as she recalled that she'd move out of Simon's lovely mansion. She couldn't believe how quickly she'd wanted to get away from him. Then she remembered hating the idea of sharing an office with him. How could she have ever felt that way?

'I'm as much a victim here as you,' Damien suddenly blurted out.

'Victim?' Simon almost laughed, turning his attention back to Damien. 'You're the most self-serving person I've ever met. Nobody could ever make you do anything that you didn't want to. You had a choice, Damien, you always have a choice, and you chose siding with George over listening to me.'

'It wasn't like that!'

'And you know I'm a man of my word. Last time I promised to kill you, and I did just that stopping your heart. And this time I swore I'd burn you.'

'What!' Damien shrieked.

The terror of Simon's stark words and Damien's harsh reaction momentarily shuddered Beth. For a split second she lost her hold on Damien and he slipped down the wall a few centimetres.

'You're going to what?' she asked Simon. She thought he might knock Damien about a bit, nothing as dark as burning him.

'I've always been a man of my word, Beth. You know that. If I don't burn him now then no one will ever take me seriously again.'

'Simon that's horrific,' Beth gasped.

Simon came in closer to Beth and he looked at her with sincere eyes. 'Do you trust me?'

'Yes,' she responded without thinking about it.

'Then play along.'

Beth nodded. She refocussed on Damien. It was hard to witness the utter horror across his face. She most definitely trusted Simon, but it didn't stop her heart pounding at the thought of what he was going to do.

Simon flicked out his hand in front of him and he concentrated hard. Beth could hear her heartbeat echoing in her ears as she anticipated what was to happen. She wanted to close her eyes, but she needed to keep Damien in place. After everything they'd been through, she had to stand by her husband.

Suddenly Damien's hair caught fire, and in a rapid flash all of his hair burnt off his head. Then just as quickly as they appeared, the flames vanished. That was it.

Damien screamed, but it couldn't have hurt him. There was no sign of any damage. All that was left was a clear, unmarked, bald head.

Beth couldn't help but laugh. It was a laugh both of humour and of sheer relief.

'See, I'm a man of my word,' Simon smirked.

'What have you done?' Damien asked.

'Burnt your hair off!' Beth giggled.

'What?' Damien touched his head and then shouted out with anger. 'No! What have you done?'

'I think you've got off lightly!' Beth shouted back. 'After the torture you've put us through, being bald is a blessing.'

'You took my powers!' Damien argued back.

'You abused your power,' Simon countered. 'You broke the law. We're now in charge of the Malancy so we had every right to strip you of your powers. You only have yourself to blame.'

'No one has the right to do that!'

'You couldn't be more wrong,' Simon firmly replied.

'What now?' Beth asked, enjoying the sense of relief that they were finally in control.

'We need to pin him there permanently. Do you know how to do that?' Beth just shook her head. 'Okay, just focus everything you've got and give it one enormous push. Throw everything you've got at him and imagine it's like glue, sticking him there.'

Beth did just that, once again channelling all of her emotion, but this time she imagined it more as a sticky, adhesive ball. Then she threw it with all her strength towards Damien's torso. As she felt the power peak, she slowly relaxed her body, letting go bit by bit. Much to her surprise, Damien stayed exactly where he was.

'Yay! Look at that!' Beth grinned.

'Like a duck to water,' Simon smiled back.

'This is fun!'

Simon touched her cheek and kissed her gently. Then he whispered in her ear, 'I have other much more fun things in mind for us now.'

'Oh yeah?' Beth grinned, although she wasn't quite sure what he meant.

'I think it's time to leave Damien to it.'

'Leave him? Like that?'

'Yes.'

'We can't. Can we?'

'What else are we going to do?'

'Shouldn't he be arrested or something?'

'Yes, but by the Malancy police. The Malancy needs to deal with him now. So he'll have to wait here until we can notify the right authority.'

'How long will that take?'

'I don't know. A few days?'

Beth didn't know what to say. Then a cheeky smile spread across Simon's face and she could see how much he was enjoying himself.

'Do you see a problem with that?' Simon asked.

Beth pretended to search her mind. 'No.'

'You can't leave me here!' Damien shouted. 'That's inhumane.'

'And what's turning someone into a bird?' Beth shouted back. 'What about kidnapping, lying, splitting up married couples? What about rape?'

'I never raped you!'

'You have no defence, Damien,' Simon replied. 'You're evil. That's all there is to it. And now you're going to pay.'

'You can't leave me here. Even in prison you get food and water.'

'You're right,' Simon nodded. 'We can't leave you without nourishment. That would be wrong.'

'What do we do?' Beth asked.

'Is your head cold now?' Simon asked, and Beth could sense that he was cooking up something mischievous again.

'You know it is!' Damien threw back at him. 'You burnt off my bloody hair!'

'Then I have an idea that will kill two birds with one stone. And I know how much you'd like to do that.'

Damien looked horrified again as Simon lifted his hand in the air and clicked his fingers. All of a sudden a beer hat, in pink no less, appeared on Damien's head. But rather than beer, the two sides of it held bottles of water. The bottles then had two large straws flowing from them that hung down for Damien to drink from.

Beth burst out laughing. 'You look ridiculous!'

'Now you're warmer and you're watered,' Simon concluded.

'What are you playing at?' Damien asked, feeling the hat on his head.

'I know what you're thinking, and don't worry. I'll add in a bit of magic so every few hours the bottles will replenish themselves. You won't go thirsty, I promise.'

'You are so funny!' Beth chuckled, hugging Simon. How could she ever forget loving this man?

'You bastard! You'll regret this.'

'What are you going to do?' Beth snarled, angered by the nerve of Damien's threat. 'We're ultra-powerful and you're a pathetic little man who's now pinned against the wall with a stupid hat on his head. A hat that hides his now bald state. And if you don't stop moaning, then I'll make sure your hair never grows back. How would you like that?'

Damien stopped talking.

'Remind me never to mess with you,' Simon sniggered, kissing Beth on the head.

'It's fine. I like your hair too much,' Beth grinned back.

'Can I have food?' Damien then whimpered. 'You can't let me starve.'

'Of course. We're not animals.' Simon then flashed his mischievous grin again and Beth couldn't wait to see what he had in mind. 'Hold out your hands.'

Damien did as requested and held out both of his hands in front of him. Simon once again clicked his fingers and something popped into Damien's palms. Beth couldn't quite see what it was at first.

'What the fuck is this?' Damien asked, holding up two bags for Beth to see.

She instantly cracked up laughing again when she saw Damien holding two bags of bird seed.

'Like I said,' Simon replied. 'We're not animals-'

'We're Birds!' Beth finished with a satisfied chuckle. 'I love it! That'll teach you! Never mess with us Birds.'

Beth turned to Simon and hugged him again. Then they kissed, a warm, loving kiss. 'Now can we get to the better fun?' Simon asked.

'The sort of fun we haven't had in a very long time?' she asked, realising that they'd not spent a night together since Florence. And even then she hadn't believed that he loved her.

'I've missed you.'

'Then what are we waiting for?'

Beth and Simon didn't even look back at Damien. They left the room, hand in hand, magically locked the door behind them, and then they made their way out of the building as quickly as they could.

THIRTY-THREE

Beth and Simon sat in his Jaguar at the back of the office block not able to take their eyes off each other.

'Are you ready to go home?' Simon asked, curling Beth's hair behind her ear.

'Home?' Beth thought to the many places that she'd called home over the past few months and her head started to spin. So much had happened, she didn't even know how to start processing it. 'Where's that again?'

'With me,' Simon said, squeezing her hand.

'All my stuff's in Manchester. Everything I own. Even my car.'

Simon looked at her with concern. 'Do you want to stay here?'

'No! Definitely not. I want to go back to London. I want to be back in our bedroom, just twenty minutes from our London office, and then just a tube ride from that wonderful city centre. I want my life back. I was finally happy, finally at home. It all just got so messed up.'

'It's not messed up anymore.'

'No...' Beth recalled her London life and she reminded herself that it wasn't as rosy as she'd perhaps like to believe.

'Is there something wrong?'

'No, no, of course not. It's just... Work stuff.'

'Do you not want your job back?' There was a hint of panic in Simon's voice.

'Of course I do! It's just... What do I say to people now?'

'What do you mean?'

'My team. Maybe not so much Gayle, but definitely the others. They barely spoke to me when I was Mrs Bird the Admin Director. But when they found out that... well, when they thought that... oh, it was so horrible what they said about you.'

'It was all manipulation. Idle gossip that they foolishly fell for.'

'But what am I going to tell them now? How am I going to explain that I hadn't been drugged-'

'Drugged? You said that before. Is that what they were saying?'

'It's probably better you don't know.'

'So let me get this straight: these people, that you claim to be your friends, stopped talking to you when you got married and you got your promotion. Then, when they thought we'd split up and I'd treated you in whatever awful way they were willing to believe, they spoke to you again. But now, when you tell them the truth that you actually want to be married to me, you're worried that they'll once again stop talking to you?'

'Yes,' Beth meekly answered.

'How can you call these people your friends, Beth?'

'But they-'

'They're not true friends if they only treat you well when circumstances meet their approval. They don't sound like nice people at all. I think it's a blessing if they don't speak to you.'

'I know you're right, but-'

'But what?'

'It was so lonely before. When I got my promotion,

you were the only person that was nice to me. Don't get me wrong, I wouldn't change our marriage and my new job for the world, but it was nice for a while to have friends at work. Friends other than my husband.'

'Lonely?' Simon seemed very surprised by Beth's admission.

'Gayle was all right if I'm honest, but it was so hard for her as Gus made my life such a misery.'

'Gus?' Beth could see that Simon was now processing something. 'How long has it been since you got your promotion?'

'I don't know, time has lost all meaning of late.' It took Beth a second to align everything that had happened in her head. 'Well, we got married on the twelfth of May and what's today?'

'The nineteenth of June.'

'So what's that, five or six weeks? Why?'

'Just thinking things through in my head. Look, don't worry about the office. I'll help you. We'll think of the right back story together and we'll make sure that people have the right approach moving on. The last thing I want is for you to feel lonely at work. I've been there, I don't want that for you.'

'I suppose it is lonely at the top,' Beth shrugged.

'That's utter nonsense. Trust me, Beth, we'll figure it out together. But I don't want you worrying about that for now. One step at a time. Let's just get home first.'

'Okay. I suppose we could pack up quickly if we go now. Then I'll just follow you and we could be back home, at our home, before dinner.'

'You're not leaving my side for one minute, Bethany. Get that idea right out of your head. We've been apart for far too long as it is.'

'But-'

'You're really not used to it yet, are you?'

'Used to what?'

'Although, I suppose you've not had a lot of time to get

used to it.'

'Used to what?' Beth pushed.

'You're a Malant. You have powers. More powers than anyone else; well except me. You can do anything you want. Why on earth would you go back to that flat, physically pack up all your stuff, put it all in your car and then drive behind me back down south? Instead we could simply summon all your belongings down to the house when we get there. Isn't that easier?'

'We can do that?'

'Piece of cake. Don't you remember summoning our passports in Florence?'

'Yeah, but they're like bits of paper. It must be different summoning a flat full of items and a car?'

'Of course not. You won't even break a sweat.'

Beth couldn't help the smile that touched her lips. 'So I never have to go back to that flat again?'

'Not if you don't want to.'

'I don't. I mean, don't get me wrong, it was luxurious. Okay, perhaps not as luxurious as your mansion, but for a simple girl from Staffordshire, it was very nice.'

'No one could call you simple,' Simon smirked, giving her hand another squeeze.

Beth's face suddenly dropped again as another loose end flared in her mind.

'What is it?' Simon asked.

'Toby. Oh God, Toby. I'll have to-'

'I wouldn't worry about him,' Simon interrupted.

'Why not?'

'Let's just say, that matter's been taken care of.'

'What have you done?'

'A husband is allowed to get jealous when another man is trying to have sex with his wife.'

'Is that right?' Beth smirked, enjoying the idea that she could make Simon jealous. 'What did you do?'

Simon looked straight ahead, out of the windscreen, not able to meet Beth's eyes. 'Well, firstly, I suppose I should tell you that Toby wasn't strictly ill the first time... you know.'

'What do you mean?'

'Do you remember when I saw you in The Rose that Friday night?'

Beth thought back. 'You looked gorgeous that night. Why was it that I could find you ridiculously attractive yet be utterly terrified of you at the same time? It was so confusing.'

'That was another part of Damien's evil scheme. Not only did you forget about me, but all the terrible things that you'd heard about me were escalated in your mind. It rendered you absolutely petrified.'

A chill prickled Beth's skin as she thought to how much their lives had been played with. 'Why the hell did he do all that?'

'Jealousy. Control. To try and stop us taking our rightful place in charge of Malancy HQ. There are probably numerous reasons.'

'I'm glad you burned his hair off.'

'That took some control, believe me. I could have done a lot worse.'

'He would have deserved it.'

'You looked horrified when I said I was going to burn him.'

'I hadn't thought it through then.'

'No, you were right. We have to rise above it. Be the better people.'

'Like rise above making my boyfriend ill so that he can't have his wicked way with me?' Beth knew it was time to lighten the mood again. She didn't want to think about Damien anymore.

Simon smirked. 'That was different. You needed protecting. I couldn't take the thought of you and him... so I put a spell on him that meant if he tried to touch you then he'd be overcome with excruciating pain.'

'Oh Simon! I'm so relieved!'

'You're not mad?'

'Of course not! I never wanted him, not really. But how come that only happened the first time?'

'Somehow he figured it out and self-healed. It was a simple enough spell. I didn't want to harm the bloke. Well, I did I suppose...'

'But you're a good man.'

'I try to be.'

'So Toby's a Malant? I suppose that figures, what with him coming to Bird Consultants.'

'He wasn't working for Bird Consultants.'

'Well he never started. Although, that doesn't make any sense. How could Damien have hired him? Was it Brian?'

'Paul hired him. Paul and Jim. He was supposed to be your bodyguard, keeping the likes of Damien away from you. Overall I'd say it's not a great career path for him.'

'My bodyguard? He was supposed to be looking out for me?' Beth felt utterly bewildered. 'So how come...'

'I wouldn't worry about it. He failed you in so many ways.'

Beth had to acknowledge how true Simon's statement was. She couldn't be more relieved that she'd not got any closer to Toby.

'So I take it I don't need to send him a bugger off text then and he's already up to speed?' she said.

Simon shrugged. 'I might have told him to back off, keep away from my wife and if he ever touched you again I'd come for him.'

'You didn't?

'Oh, and I might have punched him.'

'Simon!' Beth shook her head and tutted in mock disapproval. 'You've had quite a punchy day, haven't you?' Although not normally one to applaud violence, on this occasion Beth was willing to forgive it completely. In all honesty, she'd never felt so loved.

'It's that anger of mine, I shouldn't let it get the better of me. But you drive me wild. I can't help but feel protective of you.'

'I love that. Don't ever change.' Beth kissed Simon gently on the cheek.

'I love you. So much. I've really missed you.'

'Oh, me too.'

Simon shook his head. 'How I wish things could be simple. We're supposed to be newlyweds but we've barely seen each other.'

'I know.' Beth felt deeply saddened as the truth of Simon's words sunk in.

'And it's not over yet. As soon as we get home, we're going to have to explain everything to everyone. Then we'll have to sort out the Malancy, arrange all those arrests. There's so much work to do.'

'We don't have to go home straight away, do we?'

Simon considered this and Beth could see his face lighten. 'No. I don't suppose we do. Of course we don't. You know I'm liking the idea of us just getting lost.' Beth looked at him with confusion. 'I know a lovely hotel in the middle of nowhere that's about halfway home. Let's go there. We can spend the rest of the day tucked away, ordering room service and just forgetting that the rest of the world exists. How does that sound?'

Beth sighed. 'I've never heard a better idea in all my life.'

Simon and Beth strapped themselves in and Simon started the engine.

Their journey took them back down the M6, virtually all the way to the end, finally getting off at junction two. Then they headed into the countryside, far away from the motorway, far away from the traffic and far away from civilisation.

Passing field after field, they finally arrived in a tiny little village with just one pub and one post office, and then they only had a couple of miles to go. They'd been travelling for three hours but they'd spent the time quite happily discussing all the things that they wanted to do together. This included their proper wedding, still very much going ahead in September.

Eventually, heading down a tree lined driveway, a beautiful, modern hotel appeared in front of them. They parked in the car park that overlooked nothing but miles of countryside and they breathed in the glorious fresh air. Then they made their way into the reception.

'Can I help you?' the young, friendly receptionist asked.

'We haven't booked. Do you have a room for the night? A suite if possible?' Simon asked.

'No problem, let me check for you.' The lady typed something into her computer. 'You're in luck. We have one suite left for tonight. The rate is two hundred and fifty pounds.'

Beth couldn't help but smirk. That seemed far more reasonable than that hotel in Florence. Although that hotel had been quite spectacular.

'Great, we'll take it please.'

'It really is your lucky day, it's also already available. Check in normally isn't until three, but I can check you in now.'

Beth looked to the clock at the back of reception and saw it was approaching two o'clock. They had all afternoon and all night. She felt a rush of excitement.

Simon dealt with all the paperwork and payment, and then they headed up two floors to their suite.

It was a delightful room, with a hallway, separate living area and two bathrooms. There was also a complimentary bottle of wine waiting for them.

'I was going to say let's order champagne,' Simon said, 'but it can wait.' He then grabbed Beth's hand and led her into the bedroom.

They kissed gently at first, and then lust took over. Wasting no time in stripping off each other's clothes, before they knew it they were lost in an orgasmic state. They had missed each other so deeply and coming together after such a long time gave them both a renewed sense of love. They barely considered anything else other than being together, other than pleasuring each other, and other than enjoying one another as man and wife. In fact, they got so caught up in the intense craving that they had for one another, they completely forgot about contraception.

After an afternoon and evening of lovemaking, eating delicious food that was delivered to their door, and indulging in mounds of champagne and strawberries, Beth awoke the next morning on top of the world. Their incredible time alone together had wiped away all of the horror of late, and she felt renewed in every sense. At that moment, life could not be any better.

They enjoyed breakfast in bed and then got ready to face the day ahead. After a smooth check-out, they got back in their car and headed on towards Buckinghamshire. Their escape had been the perfect stop gap, but it was now time for them to get on with their lives and to sort out George Malant and his Malancy once and for all.

THIRTY-FOUR

The journey back to Buckinghamshire was short, not much over an hour. It was nowhere near long enough for the smiles to even start to fade from either Beth or Simon's faces. They both felt utterly content.

It was late morning when they finally arrived at the gates of their mansion, and for the first time in what seemed like forever, Mr and Mrs Bird arrived home together. Properly together.

Simon parked the car in front of the house and Beth waited for him to open the front door.

'We'll have to get you your key back,' he said.

'I can't remember now what I did with it.' Then Beth looked down at her hand. 'Does Paul still have our rings?'

'I have no doubt.'

They entered the house to be greeted immediately by Paul, Jane and Jim all pouring out of the living room.

'Where the hell have you been?' Paul blurted out. Then suddenly he seemed to clock Beth and he stopped.

'Putting everything back together,' Simon smiled, pulling Beth in next to him for a hug.

'You remember?' Jane asked.

'Simon can be very persuasive,' Beth grinned.

'Together, we managed to get all our memories back.'

Paul sighed, his body noticeably relaxing as he did, like mounds of worry were instantly released.

'Did you find a loophole in the contract?' Jim asked.

'We didn't need to,' Simon explained. 'Turns out our united power can overcome anything.'

'Simon kissed me and everything just fell into place.'

'Wow. You two really are special,' Jane said.

'It seems Damien was behind pretty much everything. He was the one that got Beth to move.'

'There wasn't even a job,' Beth added. 'It was just him and me in an office. It was so creepy.'

'We've taken care of him, though.'

'What have you done?' Jane asked.

Simon turned to Beth with a sly smile. 'Let's just say he'll be hanging around in his office until we're ready to arrest him. No rush.'

'What have you done?' Paul nudged.

'Nothing he doesn't deserve,' Beth shrugged.

'Next step is to arrest George and all of his associates,' Simon said.

'All of the anti-Malants,' Beth corrected.

'I guess it's time for me to get back to work,' Jane said, turning to look at Paul with slight sadness.

'The Malancy is about to be saved once and for all,' Simon said.

Jim turned to Paul and they shared a look of concern.

'What is it? You keep doing that.' Suddenly Simon's calm, happy demeanour instantly changed.

'It's nothing,' Jim said.

'We'll tell you later, Si. Now's not the time,' Paul added.

'I want to know.'

'We've got enough on our plate at the minute. Let's deal with one thing at a time.'

'You're absolutely right. One thing at a time. You tell us what we don't know and then we'll sort out the rest of the Malancy. I am sick to death of the secrets and the furtive looks. Tell us or we're not going anywhere.'

Paul sighed and Jim nodded. 'Perhaps we should sit down.'

'No!' Simon was so riled, Beth felt herself inch away.

'If we just sit down,' Paul suggested.

'Stop it. I'm fed up with everyone else in the world deciding what's best for me and Beth. We're in charge now and we've been purposefully chosen to be in charge. So maybe everyone else doesn't know what's best and you should start trusting us. How about you tell us what you think we shouldn't know and we'll decide for ourselves how to deal with it.'

Jim and Paul once again shared a look and then Paul nodded for Jim to continue.

'You haven't saved the Malancy yet,' Jim stated. Beth felt her heart pound. That had to be a mistake. There had to be some sort of confusion.

'Of course we have,' Simon replied. 'We can feel the magic coursing through us.'

'No. I don't know why you don't know about this, I haven't been allowed all the information, but there is one final step you need to take. And you have one year from the date you cast the spell to do it.'

'What it is?' Beth pushed. She felt dizzy at the thought of having to face more challenges. She was reaching her limit as to how much she could cope with.

'To ensure the future of the Malancy, the two chosen ones, that is you two-'

'Will you just tell us!' Beth demanded.

'You need to start a new line.'

'What does that mean?' Beth was becoming a little breathless as her concern took charge.

'Of course,' Simon said, clearly realising what Jim was talking about.

'What new line? What does he mean?' Beth turned to Simon, desperate for clarification.

'It makes perfect sense,' Simon said, addressing Beth

directly. 'We've saved the Malancy from Mr Malant and his associates, but in doing so we've changed things. We're in a state of transformation. Don't you see?'

'No I don't. Not at all.'

'To ensure the future of the Malancy, you need to...' Jim was now visibly uncomfortable.

'We need to have a child and start the next generation of Malants,' Simon finished.

'What?' Beth gasped. 'We can't have a baby! Not just like that!' Beth felt her head cloud up with panic. Then a realisation hit her. 'Oh my God! We've just... What were we thinking? How could we be so stupid?'

'Beth, calm down,' Simon said, pulling her in towards him so he could hold her, but she resisted. She needed to think. She had to get hold of her thoughts.

'What have we just done?' she muttered.

'What have you just done?' Paul asked.

'Beth, it's fine,' Simon insisted.

'What's going on?' Paul asked.

'We've just been so stupid. This is too much. What were we thinking?'

'Beth, what is it?' Paul asked again.

'This is between me and my wife now,' Simon stated quite to the point. 'Thank you for the information. I understand everything now. But this is our lives, our family and our future. We need to discuss this between us.'

'But-' Paul went to argue.

'You're absolutely right,' Jane interrupted. She glanced at Paul as if to silence him, but Beth barely noticed. Her head was spinning.

'Beth, let's go upstairs.'

Beth was finding it hard to breathe. Everything in their lives went at such a ridiculous pace, and it was finally taking its toll. She nodded, but she didn't move.

'Beth, come on,' Simon soothed, taking her hand. He led her up the stairs and into their bedroom. Beth sat on the bed and Simon headed into the en suite. He came back out with a glass of water and she sipped at it gently.

'We just had sex,' Beth stated, but much calmer. 'God knows how many times. Why did we not think about contraception? How could we just forget something so basic? We need our heads looking at.'

'I would guess that it's not us losing our minds, more that our destiny is taking charge again. Subconsciously, we must know that we need to conceive a child to keep the Malancy alive. We didn't consider contraception because everything in us is telling us to have a baby. You have to admit, that was the most incredible sex we've ever had. I don't think any of it was a coincidence.'

Beth felt like crying as Simon curled her hair behind her ears. She was just starting out in her life, it was all too much. She'd gone from single to girlfriend to wife in the blink of an eye, and now she was being given no time to get used to that before she had to add mother to the list. At this rate, she'd be a grandmother by the time she was thirty.

'So, I'm already pregnant?' she asked, her heart sinking.

'Is that so bad?' Simon asked. 'I mean, forget about the future of the Malancy, let's put that aside. Is having my children such a bad thing?'

'Of course not!' Beth declared. 'But I'm only twenty-six. I've only lived away from home for a few months. We're not even properly married yet. We wanted to do it right. I don't want to look back at my wedding pictures sipping orange juice in a maternity dress because I'm carrying our first born. That's not how I want any of this. We've already had so much of our lives sacrificed, is there nothing we can have just for us?'

'Is that the problem? That you want us to be properly married before we think about children?'

'For starters. It know it probably seems silly to you.'

A grin spread across Simon's face. 'That's not silly at all. And you're right, that's how it should be. Marriage then children. But after we're married, you do want to start a family, don't you?'

Beth took a deep breath. 'Shall I just be completely honest?'

'I thought we were always honest with each other?'

'I don't think I can remember what honesty is anymore,' Beth mumbled. She'd been so caught up in her new world of secrets and lies, that old Beth, the girl who always believed in nothing but honesty, seemed like a ghost from a past life.

Beth turned to Simon and she noticed how physically sad he seemed. His eyes had lost some of their depth. 'I do want a family with you,' she said, not wanting to be the cause of any of his sadness. 'You'll make a great dad. But it's just so soon. We have less than a year to have a child now, like a ticking clock. I wanted us to travel the world, build up the business, learn about each other and do a million other things together. Instead, though, I'll finally just be getting to grips with my job when I'll have to go on maternity leave. Then there's all the worry of childcare. Gone are the days of eating out and nightclubbing. We've barely done anything together and we'll never have the chance to now. Well not until we're in our fifties or something.'

Simon's eyebrows furrowed. He was focussing on Beth intently. She could see that he was processing something. 'This is what's worrying you?' he finally asked.

'Children change lives. We don't even know what our life is yet and we're already looking to change it.'

'Beth, have you forgotten that we're millionaires?'

This silenced Beth. That hadn't really occurred to her during her recent worrying session.

'Money opens up so many possibilities that other people just don't have. If you want to go out clubbing and go on exotic holidays and visit Piccadilly Circus every other Saturday night, then we'll just hire a full time nanny. If, when the times comes, you want to have minimal maternity leave, we'll pay for childcare. We don't know how we're going to feel when our baby comes along, but we can pay for as much help and support along the way as we need. The impact on our lives is as much as we want it to be. And we can decide as and when we want to.'

'I suppose. I never thought about it like that.'

'I can't see us wanting to go out all the time without our child, especially on holiday, but you have to realise that we have the option. Life isn't over. We're in a very fortunate situation.'

'I guess. But it still doesn't change the fact I could now be, in fact probably already am, pregnant. Thanks to our careless antics yesterday, and this morning, I'm still going to be pregnant on our wedding day.'

'Well let's just see, shall we?' He gently pushed Beth backwards. 'Lie down.'

She hesitantly did as requested and lay flat on the bed. Simon carefully placed his hand on her stomach and took a second to concentrate. 'You're not pregnant, not at the minute,' he said, then he squeezed his fingers and closed his eyes. Beth could see a very slight red tinge to his hand and she felt a small pressure on her stomach. She trusted him completely, but she was very curious about what he was doing.

'Now there's nothing to worry about,' he said.

'What did you do?' she asked sitting up.

'I removed any part of me inside of you. It's not caused you any damage, don't worry. I've just made sure that any potential chance of you becoming pregnant in the immediate future has been eradicated. Better?'

Beth didn't know what to say. Their power really was incredible. She was starting to believe that there really wasn't anything that they couldn't do.

'Are you okay with that?' she finally asked.

'Of course. Marriage first, then children. I want exactly the same as you.'

Beth screwed up her face. 'That being the case, and I hate to say this, but maybe we shouldn't have sex again until after we're married. I mean properly married. I can see that we're going to find it hard to resist trying to get pregnant.'

'No sex before we're married?' Simon clearly wasn't happy about her suggestion.

'I don't think we have a lot of choice. You can't keep doing spells to stop me getting pregnant. That's far too crazy. It can't be good.'

'If that's what you want.' Beth could see the disappointment in Simon's whole body.

'I don't want it to be like that,' she said defensively. 'We just don't have much choice. I mean, I know we've only just got back together and we've barely been together at all. But...' Beth felt herself getting riled again. 'I know it's shit. I know it's another way in which we're being cruelly manipulated and once again our own free choice is being taken away from us. But hopefully, it really has to be now, let's hope so much that it's now the last time. This has to be the last step in our destiny to save the Malancy. If we have to have children before we're ready, or at least I'm ready, then so be it, but the least we can do is make sure that we have a proper wedding day. And if that means holding out for-'

'Let's get married next week,' Simon suddenly cut in, breaking Beth's manic rant.

Beth glared at him with shock. 'Next week?'

'I know it's soon - sooner than we thought about - but what are we really waiting for? We're already married, so we know we want it. I know you wanted to spend time planning it, but how much does that really matter? We're Malants, we'd just magic most of it up anyway.'

Beth considered his proposal. She'd always imagined spending about eighteen months planning her wedding. She wanted to do dress try-ons and make-up trials and to visit wedding fairs... didn't she? The more she thought about it, though, the more she realised that she just wanted the day to arrive. She wanted to be married. With their power, there was, in reality, nothing they couldn't have.

She hated to admit it but time was against them, in so many ways. Having their official wedding so soon would solve a great number of issues and it would mean that they could officially become Mr and Mrs Bird so much faster. She liked the idea of that.

'What about next Saturday?' Beth counted the days in her head. 'That'll be the first of July. How about then? Giving me time to at least do some planning.'

Simon took Beth's hands and he pulled her to her feet. He curled her hair behind her ears and kissed her lovingly on the lips. 'If that's what you want, then that's exactly what we're doing. Next Saturday, the first of July, we'll get properly married.'

Beth felt a flutter of excitement race through her.

They ran downstairs to break the news to the rest of the family. They burst into the living room, full of adrenaline, but were halted to the spot when they saw Jane sobbing on the sofa.

Beth's heart stopped as she could see something was very wrong.

THIRTY-FIVE

'What is it?' Beth asked, running to Jane's side.

'It's nothing. I'm just being silly.'

'But something must have happened.'

'Nothing. Honestly,' Jane said, wiping away her tears with a tissue.

'She's all right,' Paul said, but there was quite a sour tone to his voice.

'It's time for Jane to go back to her husband,' Simon stated.

'Oh,' Beth said, not at all ready for something that wasn't dramatic for a change. 'Isn't that a good thing?'

'They're having an affair,' Simon said, quite coldly. This totally threw Beth. Not just the fact that Paul and Jane were having an affair, but Simon's asperity.

'It's not as simple as that,' Paul explained, pacing the room.

'You're messing with a marriage, Paul,' Simon warned. Although Beth was pleased to hear that Simon approached adultery with such disapproval, his disdain was causing a lot of uncomfortable tension.

'It's really not that simple, Si.'

'If Jane doesn't want to be with her husband-'

'I don't!' Jane cried.

'You love Paul?' Beth asked her.

'We've always loved each other,' Paul replied.

'Then...' Beth went to ask for clarification, but the look of fear in Jane's eyes made her stop.

'So yet again there's something you're not telling us,' Simon said directly to Paul.

'It's a very long story,' Jane said.

'Jane's husband blackmailed her into marrying him,' Jim stated from the back of the room.

'What?' Beth asked with shock.

Paul sat down next to Jane and held her hand. 'We were engaged. Virtually married.'

'My sister got into trouble with the law. She didn't mean to, she's genuinely a good person, but she made a mistake. She got away with it and no harm was done, but then Darren – that's my husband – he found out. He told me if I married him then he'd make sure that no one else found out and Lily would be free. However, he said if I ever leave him then he'll do everything in his power to prosecute her. What was I supposed to do?'

'That's awful! When did this happen?' Beth gasped.

'A lifetime ago. Before Simon came into my life. Before Bird Consultants,' Paul answered.

'What does he have on her?' Simon asked.

'He has a file hidden somewhere,' Jane explained. 'He's got CCTV footage and a few other bits of evidence, I'm not really sure. I just know it would be enough to prosecute her. He's made that abundantly clear.'

'So instead of ruining your sister's life, he's ruining yours,' Beth said. Then she looked at Paul. 'Both of your lives.'

'Yeah,' Paul nodded.

'And you have absolutely no idea where this file could be?' Simon asked.

'Not a clue. Believe me, we've tried,' Jane replied.

'Do you know anything about what's in it?'

'Like I said, I think it's just bits of evidence that he's scraped together.'

'But could you tell me anything specific?'

'Leave off, Si,' Paul said. 'We've been through this a hundred times ourselves. Don't make it any worse.'

'But, as usual, you never thought to consult your incredibly powerful nephew.'

Jane's head flicked up to look at Simon. 'You located the contract,' she said.

'I did.'

'You can locate material things?' she asked.

'If I can pinpoint something about them. I can't do it completely randomly, but if you can give me something that's in the file that I can tap into, then I should be able to locate it.'

'Bloody hell!' Paul said. 'Why didn't you say so?'

'Why did you never ask?'

Paul shrugged. 'I didn't want to talk about. It's not easy admitting that another man has stolen away the only woman you've ever loved.'

'You men and your stupid pride!' Beth said.

'So what's in the folder?' Simon asked Jane.

'CCTV footage, but I don't know in what form. Other than that, I really don't know. Darren's kept it vague to keep me in line.'

'We need something concrete,' Simon pushed. Beth could tell that his brain was working in overdrive again.

'I don't know.'

'You used a picture of Jane to hide her. What about a picture of Lily?' Paul suggested.

'It has to be in the folder,' Simon replied.

'There has to be a picture of her in there! If he's got CCTV footage of her, then there has to be an image of her at least,' Jane said.

'That's worth a shot. Do you have a picture of her on you now?' Simon asked.

'On my phone.' Jane picked up her iPhone from the

coffee table.

'That'll do.'

Jane flicked through the images on her phone and then handed it to Simon. Simon took a seat on the sofa opposite, staring intently at the picture. After a few moments he looked around the room. 'You're welcome to stay,' he said, 'but be warned, it might get bright.'

'That's an understatement,' Paul said. He then grabbed Beth and Jane's hands and led them to the back of the room where Jim was already standing.

Beth watched Simon with fascination. He sat silently and once again studied the image on the phone in his hand. He was concentrating so hard. Then he closed his eyes.

Beth suddenly recalled how Simon had taught her the location spell when she'd tracked down Damien. She assumed that he'd be doing something very similar right at that moment. He made it look so easy, as if it was the most natural thing in the world to him.

Then she realised that he was doing it without an element. He hadn't gone into the garden to choose a stone or a leaf or anything else. Beth looked within herself and she sensed the power inside. She'd felt it for weeks, although at first she'd put it down to being unnerved at losing her memories. Now she recognised it as her new strength, and it was incredible.

They really were the most powerful people alive. Beth couldn't help but gasp a little as her brain suddenly contemplated the opportunities that were now available to her. Unimaginable power was now at her fingertips.

Telling herself that it probably wasn't the best time to be cogitating this massive new development in her life, she focussed back on Simon. Just thinking about how powerful she was left her overwhelmed and she tried to stop her head spinning. She had millions of questions. She'd definitely need to discuss it all with Simon. At least he'd have plenty of answers.

Thankfully, Beth was helped away from her thoughts when a stark red beam suddenly shone across the living room. She snapped her eyes shut, so bright were the rays of scarlet. Then, within a few seconds, it disappeared. She slowly opened her eyes again to find Simon taking a deep breath.

No one said a word and Simon just stared straight out, lost in concentration. Then he placed his hands out before him and he closed his eyes once more.

Beth recognised this to be a summoning spell. He must have located the document and now he was summoning it up. It was brilliant to watch. And then she felt a small buzz of excitement as she told herself that she had equal his power. She had, no doubt, quite a learning curve to reach his standard, but it was all within her. And it always had been. It was her destiny and her right. It was what her parents had given up their lives for. It utterly was mind-blowing.

Once again Beth was pulled from her thoughts as a box file suddenly appeared in Simon's hand. It was A4 in size and looked a little tattered around the edges, but it was real.

Jane and Paul ran over to him. 'Is this it?' Paul asked.

Jane grabbed it from Simon and opened it up. She flicked through the paperwork inside. 'This is it,' she whispered, then tears started to stream down her face. She flopped down on the sofa. 'You've done it. You've set us free.'

'Where was it?' Paul asked.

'In a safety deposit box somewhere. He wasn't messing around, you really never would have found it.'

Paul grabbed Simon's shoulder. 'Thanks mate.' Simon stood up and they hugged each other. It was so beautiful to watch, Beth felt teary herself.

'I'd do anything for you, you know that. You should have told me,' Simon said.

'I know.'

'No more secrets. They have to stop.'

'How can I ever thank you?' Jane said to Simon.

'You never need to. You're as good as family, and us Birds look out for each other.'

Paul turned his attention to Jane. 'Actually... I don't want you to be just as good as family.' Paul got down on one knee and Beth gasped.

'Jane,' he said. He placed the box file aside and took her hand. 'I know you're married already, but would you consider leaving him and marrying me instead?'

Jane's face lit up. She then threw her arms around him. 'Are you kidding? Of course!' Her eyes filled up with tears again, only this time they ran down her face to a beaming smile.

Beth turned to Simon who was already looking right back at her. She fought hard to halt tears of her own. This was such a magical moment.

Simon moved over to Beth, not taking his eyes off her once. Then he placed his hands on her cheeks and he kissed her.

'Let's tell them later about our wedding plans, shall we?' he whispered.

Beth gazed across at Paul and Jane who were still wrapped up in each other's arms. This was their moment. 'Good idea.'

'I think there's only one thing now that can make this day truly outstanding,' Simon suddenly stated, looking across the room. Everyone turned their attention to him.

'Well, Beth and I are back together and Paul and Jane have finally beaten her husband. All that's left now is to help Jim finish his battle once and for all.'

'What?' Jim asked. He'd been keeping a low profile at the back of the room, but all eyes were now on him.

'We owe so much to you,' Simon said. 'Not just because you've been an exceptional butler, but because you've supported us all through so much. I don't think we'd be here today if it wasn't for you.'

'I did it for the Malancy.'

'You did it because you're a good man,' Beth corrected. 'I think you've waited long enough,' Simon said. 'I think it's time we paid George Malant that special visit, don't you?'

THIRTY-SIX

Early that Tuesday afternoon, Simon, Beth, Paul, Jane and Jim all made their way to Malancy HQ. Jim drove Paul and Jane, and Simon insisted on taking his Aston Martin behind with Beth.

They parked right outside the front of the building and Simon brushed his hand over the cars, making them disappear from view. The five of them then entered the front door.

They had no issue passing through reception. In fact the young receptionist seemed delighted to see Jane and Jim. They smiled in return and then headed straight up to George Malant's office.

Jim had waited so long for this, everyone insisted that he be the first to open the door and break the news to his brother. As he turned the handle, a smile stretched right across his face.

'Good afternoon, George. For a change, it really is a pleasure to see you.'

'James?' George said, utterly shocked. Mr Taylor sat before him and the shock on his fact was just as apparent.

'The odds might have been against me, but I think it's fair to say, I won.' Jim stepped aside so that Jane, as the law enforcement official, could make her arrest.

'George Malant, I'm arresting you on charges of abusing your power, kidnapping, using dark magic and attempting to bring an end to the Malancy. I'd ask if you were guilty, but I don't think there's ever been such a certainty before.'

Jane stood before him, waiting for him to stand up. He just looked at all five of them as if they were crazy.

'Security!' he shouted. Within seconds, about twenty black clad men came pouring into the room. 'Remove these trespassers.'

Simon raised his hand and with just a small movement of his fingers, he brought all of George's army to a halt. They were frozen still.

'Bring a hundred, bring a thousand, it won't matter,' Simon said. 'Your biggest army is defenceless against me and Beth. We're more powerful than you could ever imagine. But you know all that, don't you. Give in George. You fought a pointless battle and you lost. End it now with your head held high and let the new era of the Malancy begin. It's what they wanted. It's what your own family wanted.'

'It's what most people want,' Jane added. 'Your followers are very few in number.' She turned to Beth. 'What did you call them? The anti-Malants?'

'Yep,' Beth nodded.

'I think you'll find most people are pro-Malant and are ready for this new start.' Jane grabbed her mobile from her pocket and dialled a number. 'Hi, Jane Parker here. Could you get some troops together, we need to make some arrests. Great.'

'You have no right,' George hissed. 'It's the Malancy. It's our birth right. It's got nothing to do with you.'

'It has everything to do with them!' Jim snapped back. 'As per the written wishes of the original Malants, our very own flesh and blood. Ultimately they put Simon and Beth in charge. It's their destiny and there's nothing you can do about it.'

Beth looked across at Simon. She'd accepted that it was their destiny and she knew that they were now in charge, but she couldn't help her deep concern about what that meant. She didn't want to sit in that office and run a magical community. She wanted, more than anything, just to go back to being the plain, normal Admin Director at Bird Consultants. That was where her heart lay; that was all she'd ever wanted.

Simon looked back at her as if he could read her thoughts. He mouthed 'I know,' and then turned back to address the room. She had no clue if he really did know, but she was willing to put her faith in him. Remembering how much she'd doubted him not so long ago, she now wanted to give him her complete trust.

'Beth and I have no experience within Malancy HQ. I think we're far from the best candidates to replace Mr Malant and his team.'

'But it's your birth right,' Jim argued.

Simon looked at Beth, making it seem as if it was their mutual decision. She nodded along, at least liking it so far. 'Instead, I think we'll just take up more of a consultancy role. We are more experienced in a consultancy environment, after all, so that makes far more sense.'

'What are you saying?' Jim asked, desperately.

Simon turned to Beth and smiled. 'You tell them,' she said, continuing with their show that she was on board with the plan.

'Beth and I think it's best to make only necessary changes to Malancy HQ. There's no need for any dramatic overhauls.'

'But it's time for a fresh start.' Jim appeared devastated.

'Fresh starts don't always mean massive changes. I mean, there is so much experience already here, we'd be crazy if we didn't promote from within.'

Everyone fell silent as they waited for Simon to continue, but Beth could see the slight glint in his eye and she was starting to understand.

'As of this moment,' he continued, 'James Malant and Jane Parker are the new Joint Presidents of Malancy HQ. If they accept?'

Jane gasped with joy and Jim remained stock still. 'Do you mean that?' Jane asked.

'What?' George boomed.

Simon gave Beth a small glance, just to check that she was okay with it all. She kissed him firmly on the cheek and whispered, 'The perfect idea,' in his ear. Then a large, satisfied smile spread across his face.

They'd barely noticed Jim walking over towards them. He grabbed Simon's hand and shook it. 'Thank you, Mr Bird,' he muttered, clearly trying to keep his emotions under control.

'There is nobody else in the world that I'd trust the new Malancy with more than you.'

Jane had handcuffed George and was leading him to the door and Jim wasted no time in dashing over to George's chair. He sat down and a huge grin overwhelmed his face. 'I think I'm going to like it here.'

'Simon, what are we going to do about these men?' Jane asked as she passed him, still with George in her grasp. They glanced at the frozen bodies around them.

Simon raised his palm in the air and he let a spell encircle the room. 'All sorted,' he said. 'As soon as they're handcuffed, they'll come back to life. You can deal with them one at a time, then.'

'Thank you. That was easy. I can see you're going to be a great asset,' Jane said.

'We're always here to help.'

Beth was slightly in awe at how easily Simon had commanded the room. 'I have exactly the same power as you?' she asked, not quite believing how much potential she really had.

'You must have. And I have every intention of getting you fully up to speed as quickly as possible.'

Beth hugged Simon tightly. As intimidating as it was to know she had practically unlimited power, she couldn't wait to start using it.

They looked around them. It was mayhem. More good Malants arrived to help out Jane and Jim, and slowly they started to make their arrests.

'Where did you say Damien was again?' Jane asked as she came back into the room.

'Oh, do you know, I don't remember,' Simon said with a smirk. 'How about I text you in a day or two, when it's come back to me?'

Jane was hesitant in her reply. Then she grinned and nodded. 'You have had memory issues of late, I suppose. Oh well, whenever you do remember, be sure to let me know. That's one man I'll most certainly be arresting in person.'

'Take pictures!' Beth said, giggling to herself as she thought to Damien pinned up against the wall in that stupid hat.

'I think we should leave them to it. We've done all we can,' Simon whispered in Beth's ear.

'Yeah, good thinking.'

'Are you okay if we pop to the office?'

'What?' That was the last place Beth wanted to go to.

'I've just got a few bits I need to do.'

'But you said-'

'We'll be in and out.'

'Fine,' Beth sighed.

They weren't in and out. Beth was flopped on the sofa in Simon's office downloading Wedding Apps and browsing dresses as he typed emails, made calls and, well, worked.

'How long are you going to be?' Beth said after an hour had gone by. It had crossed her mind to do work herself, but she didn't want to go anywhere near her team. As far as they were concerned she'd left, and she hadn't thought of how she was going to explain to them everything that had happened. She'd have to come up with some sort of convincing story, and as much as Beth was now becoming more comfortable with dishonesty, she was far from well-practised in it.

'One more thing to do,' Simon said. Then he picked up his landline. 'It's Mr Bird. Please bring all your team – and I mean all of them – up to my office now. I mean now.'

'Do you want me to leave?' Beth said. Simon had that "not to be messed with" look on his face and she started to pity whoever it was that had crossed him.

'No. Please stay. Just come and sit next to me.' Simon clicked his fingers and a black chair appeared next to him. Then he clicked his fingers again and four black chairs appeared on the other side of his desk.

'What's going on?' Beth moved, as requested, but he didn't respond. He just carried on typing and she thought better than to push the subject. He clearly wasn't happy about something.

Not minutes later, Gus appeared, followed by Gayle, Diane and Michelle. They all looked terrified as they took the seats in front of Simon. Beth's heart stopped as she feared what Simon was about to do.

'Thank you for coming,' Simon began. 'It would appear there's been quite a lot of nonsense going on in this department and it's time for it to end. Do I make myself clear?'

Beth wanted the world to swallow her up. This was unbearable. What was he doing?

'I'm going to lay out a few facts for you all. Please listen carefully. I have never killed anyone. I have only ever sacked one person and that was because they sexually harassed another member of staff. I would wager that all the other rumours that sweep through the office here are also completely fabricated. In addition, Brian, our Sales Director, is not dead. He is in New York visiting our office over there. However, he won't be returning to Bird

Consultants as the moment he returns he will be arrested as an accomplice to a string of crimes. But, be sure, although you won't see him again, he is still very much alive. I'm sure you could visit him in prison if you desired further evidence.'

Beth watched as the faces of her colleagues grew paler. He had their attention, though.

'I am only a scary man in that I don't like being messed with. All I've ever wanted is the best for my business and my employees. I won't tolerate any more ridiculous behaviour, and you can count this as your first verbal warning. Do you understand?'

All four of the people in front of him nodded their understanding.

'Now, to me and my wife. Mrs Bird has been through an incredibly distressing time of late. She wouldn't want me to tell you this, but I think you need to know.'

Beth's breathing completely halted, but Simon just carried on.

'In the last few weeks, my wife has been attacked, kidnapped and abused in ways that you could never imagine. She's been through some immensely life changing events and it resulted in her temporarily losing her short-term memory. She now has all of her memories back and we are once again very happily married. I did not nor will ever drug my wife. She has not been manipulated into marrying me and I have not been the one to cause her this harm. Although I am deeply sorry that this has happened to her and I wish I could have prevented it.' For the first time Simon glanced towards Beth.

'Whether she shares her ordeal with you or not is her business, but I think she deserves nothing but utter respect from everyone in her team. Whatever your opinion is on who she's married, she deserves to be treated as the friend she's been to all of you in return. Do I make myself clear?'

There was a muttering scatter of 'Yes, Mr Bird' from the admin team.

'Now, more specifically. Diane.' Beth was surprised to see that Simon stared straight in Diane's direction as he said this. She couldn't think how he knew who she was.

Diane just nodded nervously.

'Stop believing every horror story that you're told. Mrs Malant is not a friend. She's been manipulating you for her husband's gain for years.' Diane's jaw dropped open.

'Michelle,' Simon said, quickly moving on. 'You are young and naïve but that's not an excuse. From now on I suggest that you start questioning things you're told.' Michelle nodded, but she didn't say a word.

'Gayle,' Simon then said, his face softening ever so slightly as he turned his attention to her. 'All I can say to you is that I'm sorry for the way you've been treated. You haven't been treated fairly since your promotion and that will be rectified. Your support to Beth has been noted and your hard work recognised. No verbal warning will get reported against your name.'

'Erm... Thank you, Mr Bird.'

'Which leaves Gus.' Simon glared far more fiercely towards Gus. 'I take it the issue is more to do with Trisha than anything else?'

'What?' Gus asked, a look of guilt slapped across his face.

'You covered well for her, but I don't like that sort of loyalty. When at work, you should show your loyalty to the people that pay your wages, not the people you're sleeping with.'

'But...' Gus went to argue, but he didn't finish. Beth couldn't believe it. No wonder Trisha got away with never doing anything. She really was the world's worst manager.

'It was deeply disappointing for me to learn that Paul Bird had to escalate Gayle's knowledge. You had more than sufficient time to do it. You let us down, so now you can make up for it.'

Simon raised his hands up and his laptop flew into the air. He sent it soaring around the room and Beth watched the faces of her colleagues. Gus and Gayle seemed quite accepting, but Diane and Michelle were horrified.

After a few moments, Simon gently brought the laptop down towards his desk and he looked back at the differing faces before him.

'I'm fed up with the secrets,' he said, 'and I'm fed up with the lies. From now on, this department is going to be completely open and honest and you're all going to work as a team, headed up by my very talented and very dedicated wife. She hates dishonesty and so this department will now be running with nothing but openness. Does anyone have a problem with that?' For just the second time, Simon turned to look at Beth.

She didn't know what to say. Everything suddenly felt different and a huge weight lifted off her shoulders. 'Erm... From now on,' Beth said, addressing her team, 'we're going to be the best admin team ever!'

Diane and Michelle were still open mouthed at the laptop flying incident and Simon quickly picked up on it. 'Gus, it's over to you. I'm guessing Mrs Bird will be expecting that all of her team are, not only up to speed, but are also fully comfortable with their new found knowledge by the time we return from our trip.'

'You're going away?' Gus asked.

'Yes. You'll be in charge in the meantime, reporting straight to Mrs Bird as soon as we get back. Whenever that will be.'

'What level of escalation do you want me to go to?' he asked.

'Did I not make that clear?' Simon replied. 'No more secrets and lies. This team is to go straight to the top. I want them to know everything.'

'Are you sure?' Beth whispered, trying to work out how Diane was going to react.

'All or nothing now.'

Beth reached over and squeezed Simon's thigh.

'Gus, it's all over to you.' Simon clicked his fingers and

his door pinged open. Diane and Michelle gasped as they all stood up.

'Thank you,' Beth whispered in his ear.

THIRTY-SEVEN

With work now at the back of their minds, the Malancy left in the safe hands of Jim and Jane, and with only ten days to plan their wedding, the very next morning Beth and Simon got straight into organising mode.

Simon wanted Beth to have the wedding of her dreams, so he let her take charge of the planning whilst he took sole responsibility for the honeymoon. Her parents joined them for the week to help with the plans, leaving their coffee shop in the safe hands of Beth's brother. He was due to travel down just the day before the wedding.

The first priority for Beth was to try on lots of dresses, and she felt completely spoilt by the fact that price was no issue. With the help of a Malant dressmaker, she opted to have a unique gown that was made within just a couple of days.

Her next priority was location and they chose to have a marquee in the garden. It didn't need to be massive, between them their families were only small, but it was enough. Then from there, cakes were tested, meals were sorted, the Malant registrar was booked, decorations were ordered, other outfits were bought and the honeymoon was set. Everything was completed in a matter of days and

Beth had never felt so enthralled.

Both Bride and Groom had agreed to take a sabbatical from work until after the month long honeymoon. Then Bird Consultants – the family business - would take its dominant place in their lives again, as they both wanted it to.

The fact that they could do that was a major perk of being in charge, and Beth loved the power she had; in every sense.

Despite all of the turmoil, everything that had happened to her over the last few months had given Beth the sense of belonging that she'd always searched for. Even if it had come in the most unexpected way.

Life had turned out so far from what she'd expected, it was almost unreal, but she couldn't deny how happy she felt. She really had met her soulmate and she truly believed that everything had finally fallen into place.

The wedding day soon arrived and Beth glittered in a stunning, satin strapless gown. It was simple and elegant, yet glimmered beautifully.

They'd opted for a red colour theme, the colour of their destiny, and the day sailed by perfectly.

It ended with fireworks and music, and so much laughter, but Beth and Simon barely noticed. They couldn't take their hands off each other.

That night, for the first time as far as they were concerned, they properly made love as man and wife, and nothing had ever felt so good.

The next day, late on in the Sunday afternoon, they flew off on their honeymoon. Simon took Beth for a few days to New York, so she could truly understand his other life before she met him, and then they spent the next two weeks touring through America. They finally then relaxed in Hawaii where they finished their month away in the warm sunshine.

It was the first week of August when they opened the front door to their mansion and they arrived home. Tanned and refreshed, the newlyweds found Paul, Jane and Jim waiting for them in the kitchen with champagne, all ready to celebrate their return.

'Welcome back!' Paul beamed. 'We haven't half missed you!'

'Did you have a good time?' Jane asked.

'Off the scale,' Beth grinned, taking a glass of champagne from Jane.

'I'm so glad, but it's good to have you home,' Jim nodded.

'What's been going on here?' Simon asked, sipping at his drink.

'Oh, the usual,' Jim shrugged. 'We've arrested quite a few more anti-Malants. We've been working really hard to get the Malancy back on track. Damien's been sentenced to twenty years in our Malant prison. Oh, and I've finally moved out into my own place.'

'We haven't missed too much then?' Beth smirked.

'We've set a date for our wedding!' Jane added.

'Oh wow, congratulations!' Beth beamed.

'I told you the divorce would be no issue,' Simon said.

'I think I'm going to look forward to being a Bird,' Jane smiled. 'You really do find a way of getting things done.'

'Don't we just,' Paul said, clinking his glass with Simon's.

There it was again. Ever since they'd landed back in Heathrow, Beth had been sure that Simon had been watching her, like there was a giant pimple on her head that he couldn't take his eyes off. She'd ignored it at first, putting it down to jet lag or something, but she could tell that there was something on his mind and it was now starting to niggle at her. Something was wrong. She could feel it.

'We're getting married in October,' Jane announced.

'That's so soon,' Beth said, still with half a mind on her

husband.

'We didn't want to wait long, much like yourselves, but we haven't quite got your power to summon things up.'

'We can help,' Simon said.

'We may need your help. But this is the only wedding that's ever going to matter to me, so we'd like to do as much of it on our own as we can,' Jane replied.

'Of course,' Beth said. Then she felt Simon's eyes burning into her again. 'Is there something wrong?' she mouthed so that only he could see. He just shook his head.

'I feel the need to unpack,' Beth suddenly said. 'Come on Simon, please help me.'

'Now?' Simon asked. 'Can't we just wait for the cleaning lady to come tomorrow?'

'No. It won't take long.' She turned to everyone else. 'We've just got a couple of bottles in our suitcase that I'm worried about. We'll be back in a mo.'

Beth yanked Simon's arm and led him upstairs, grabbing their suitcases from the hallway as they passed.

'Since when do you get the urge to tidy stuff up?' he gibed as Beth shut the door to their bedroom.

'Since you won't stop looking at me like I've grown a second head. What's going on?'

'Right,' Simon said. Then he stood up tall.

'What is it? Do I have something stuck to my face?'

'No, don't be silly.'

'What then?'

'I just noticed something about you. I noticed it as soon as we got off the plane.'

'Is it bad?'

'No,' he whispered. Then he moved over so he was standing as closely to her as he could. He curled her hair behind her ears and kissed her gently. 'You're glowing,' he muttered.

'That's what two weeks on the beach will do for you,' Beth muttered back.

'No,' he replied. Then he placed his hand gently on her

stomach. He concentrated for a moment and then a huge grin spread across his face.

'What?' Beth asked, but she knew the answer.

'We're pregnant,' he said, kissing her again.

'Pregnant?' she asked.

'We've finally had something go our way. We've had a month absolutely all to ourselves with no interference, but the second we touched back down in England, I noticed something light up inside of you. I could sense it. I don't know how.'

'It went our way?' Beth smiled, feeling strangely thrilled by the news.

'It's over Beth. All the manipulation, all the secrets, all the not knowing and being twisted and abused. It's all over. From this moment on, we're in charge of our own destiny.'

'We've won?' Beth asked, virtually touching Simon's lips with her own.

'We've finally won.'

Simon placed his lips firmly on to hers and they enjoyed a passionate embrace. Knowing she was carrying Simon's baby sent waves of pleasure through Beth. She couldn't believe it. She had literally never felt happier, and she didn't think she could get much happier after the past few weeks.

'I love you, Beth Bird,' Simon uttered, breaking away for just a moment.

'I love you too, Simon Bird,' Beth replied. Then they kissed again and Beth felt the last piece of the jigsaw slot into place. Her life was finally complete.

The End

ABOUT THE AUTHOR

Lindsay is a British author who lives in Warwickshire with her husband and cat. She's had a lifelong passion for writing, starting off as a child when she used to write stories about the Fraggles of Fraggle Rock.

Knowing there was nothing else she'd rather study, she did her degree in writing and has now turned her favourite hobby into a career.

This is Lindsay's third novel. You can follow her blog at lindsaythewriter.blogspot.co.uk.

Printed in Poland
by Amazon Fulfillment
Poland Sp. z o.o., Wrocław